AFTER LIFE

A *Blue Bloods* NOVEL

AFTER LIFE

A *BLUE BLOODS* NOVEL

MELISSA DE LA CRUZ

HYPERION
Los Angeles   New York

First Edition, July 2022
10 9 8 7 6 5 4 3 2 1
FAC-004510-22147
Printed in the United States of America

This book is set in Baskerville MT Pro/Monotype
Designed by Marci Senders

Library of Congress Cataloging-in-Publication Data
Names: De la Cruz, Melissa, 1971– author.
Title: Blue bloods : after life / Melissa de la Cruz. Other titles: After life
Description: First edition. • Los Angeles : Hyperion, 2022. • Series: Blue bloods • Audience:
Ages 14–18 • Audience: Grades 10–12 • Summary: After defeating Lucifer and sacrificing the
love of her life, Schuyler wakes up back in New York but soon discovers she is in an alternate
reality where Lucifer is alive and well and she is the only person who can defeat him.
Identifiers: LCCN 2021037384 • ISBN 9781368066945 (hardcover) •
ISBN 9781368067317 (ebook)
Subjects: CYAC: Vampires—fiction. • New York (N.Y.)—fiction. • LCGFT: Vampire fiction.
Classification: LCC PZ7.D36967 Blc 2022 • DDC [Fic]—dc23
LC record available at https://lccn.loc.gov/2021037384
Reinforced binding

Visit www.HyperionTeens.com

For my Blue Bloods family
The Mimi cosplayers
The Jack vs. Oliver arguers
The Kingsley diehards
The army of Schuylers
Thank you
Thank you
Thank you
This is for you

PART ONE
NEW WORLD, WHO DIS?

THE PAST IS NEVER DEAD. IT'S NOT EVEN PAST.
—WILLIAM FAULKNER

ONE

SCHUYLER

*S*chuyler Van Alen jolted awake at the first clap of thunder. From flat on her back, she saw the roiling purple clouds churning like a witch's brew. Cold concrete under her back and raindrops on her face. Once, years ago, she'd fallen asleep on the M106 bus coming home from school, and it had taken her a startling moment to realize she'd missed her stop. Now a similar but more desperate panic gripped her heart.

She felt strange, disoriented, like everything had turned upside down. Where was she? What was happening? Why was she lying on the street?

Another raindrop splattered on her cheek, and she wiped it away. She pulled herself up. Her head hurt, but her heart hurt more.

Her memories were hazy, but through the blur she felt an excruciating grief. Then it all came rushing back: the wet, bloody frenzy of the fight, the demons attacking as she rallied the Blue Blood vampires to her cause, the wolves arriving at the last moment, the Battle for Heaven at the Gates of Paradise, holding her sword aloft as the Dark Prince loomed before her . . . and . . . She caught her breath.

She remembered what happened like a punch in the gut.

What happened to Jack.

Jack.

She'd been holding the archangel Michael's flaming sword, and she'd been faced with a choice: save Jack Force, the love of her life—or kill Lucifer and save everyone else, ending the angelic war forever. Defeat the Morningstar and lead her people back where they belonged.

How beautiful Jack had looked, even then, at the end, his teeth clenched, his platinum hair plastered to his face. He had caught her gaze and nodded. He knew what she would choose, and he loved her for it. He'd reached out to her with his heart, assuring her that everything was going to be okay. He knew what was coming, and yet—it would all be fine. *Always. Always and forever.* And then the demon Danel drove his sword into Jack's back, striking him dead before he even hit the ground.

Schuyler gasped at the memory, at the shock of it. She remembered the look of surprise on Lucifer's face when she plunged Michael's sword through his chest in the next moment, the rattle of his final breath leaving his lungs, and the resounding explosion as the very fibers of the universe quaked with his death, the cacophony rivaling the scream that escaped her throat.

Lucifer's words had torn into her soul: *You loved him and you let him die.*

She had chosen.

The last thing she remembered was collapsing near Jack's body. All she had wanted was to be close to him. She looked into Jack's lovely but unseeing emerald eyes one last time, and then came darkness. But now she was awake.

Where was she?

Thunder rolled overhead, followed by a crack of lightning. Something was wrong.

What had happened? How did she get here? Where was *here*?

It was as if she was waking up to her immortal memories again. Blue Blood vampires believed themselves to be mortal until their teenage years, when they started to remember their past lives and started to come into their powers.

Headlights washed over her as she sat up to the sound of screeching brakes. A yellow cab rocked to a stop just inches away. The driver leaned out the window, silhouetted against the streetlights. He shook his fist and yelled, "Get out of the damn street!" before peeling off.

On unsteady feet, Schuyler stood up and looked around. The tops of high-rises disappeared into the storm clouds, but she'd have recognized the skyline anywhere. She'd grown up here, after all. New York City. Manhattan.

How was it possible?

She had just been in London. At the Gates of Hell.

One minute she was halfway across the world, the next she was in front of the Brooklyn Bridge. Her head ached with confusion, but she needed to find at least something that could explain what was going on.

A copy of the Sunday *Times* sat discarded on top of a trash can near an apartment building's front door. The headline stated DUNCAN DOMINATES DISSIDENTS above a black-and-white photo of a striking man with a strong chin and a charming smile standing behind a podium, waving to the camera. She didn't recognize him at all.

More raindrops splattered and darkened the front page; then the storm opened up.

She didn't have any money to take the subway, so she used the newspaper as a makeshift umbrella and began walking toward the only place she knew to go: home. Even though she hadn't been there in so long, it was one place where she knew she belonged.

Schuyler had grown up with Cordelia Van Alen, her maternal grandmother and guardian, in a town house on the Upper West Side.

A stern, severe Blue Blood, Cordelia had never been particularly warm or grandmotherly, but she had been there for Schuyler when the first signs of Schuyler's vampire form began to manifest: the blue veins on her forearms, the fangs, the craving for human blood—all of it. Cordelia had been a model of guidance.

It was she and her estranged husband, Lawrence, who had first warned of the return of the Silver Bloods. In the end, the demons had killed Cordelia and Lawrence both. Silver Bloods were former Blue Bloods under Lucifer's command who entirely drained other vampires, consuming their blood and immortal lives in order to acquire more power, which ultimately transformed them into deranged creatures unable to distinguish between thousands of years' worth of memories.

Returning home, however empty it would be now that Cordelia had been dead for years, was all Schuyler wanted to do. To collapse into her own bed would be enough.

Usually, Schuyler didn't mind walking in the city, but tonight, the storm seemed determined to slow her down. The duct tape covering the hole on the right toe of her Jack Purcells did nothing to stop the puddles from immediately soaking her socks as she went. In minutes, the newspaper had disintegrated into mush and Schuyler threw it away. It wasn't doing much good anyway. Her black cardigan and long skirt had gotten drenched almost instantly.

The storm raged. The rain was brutally cold, and the wind whipped her long dark hair, stinging her skin. As she walked past the former tenement buildings of the Lower East Side and the East Village's Federal-style town houses, Schuyler began to notice that Manhattan was not what she remembered. Streetlights remained off despite the raging storm, and shadows dominated the landscape.

New York City had gone dark.

The city she'd always known was usually packed to the brim with people. Everywhere she went there would be signs of life, from the cars stuck in traffic on Third Avenue to parents pushing their babies in strollers, from brass-band musicians performing on the sidewalk for change to bike messengers careening through red lights.

However, the longer Schuyler walked, the more everything looked wrong. In one of the most populous cities in the world, there were few cars on the street, and most parking spots were empty. Residences and bodegas alike were boarded up with plywood and smeared with graffiti. Garbage, piled as high as snow mounds, gathered on street corners.

Dozens of identical posters covered a row of boarded-up windows. Upon closer inspection, they revealed themselves as campaign posters saying VOTE FOR ALDRICH BELPHEGOR DUNCAN, the words framing Duncan's head like a halo. It was the same man from the newspaper photo. With his chin raised and his visage depicted against a red, white, and blue background, he looked like a conqueror.

Popular places on her route, like the Strand Bookstore and the Flatiron Building, were closed.

Even Times Square was a ghost town.

The neon billboards, blank and unlit.

The café chairs and tables, gone.

Restaurants and theaters, chained shut.

No swarms of people lined up at the TKTS booth, no panhandlers jangling coins in cartons asking for spare change, no costumed characters having a smoke break by the Cohan statue in Duffy Square. It was as if everyone had simply vanished.

Manhattan was so empty that Schuyler was able to walk safely up the middle of Broadway. Everything was eerily still in the torrential downpour.

"What happened here?" she whispered.

New York City wasn't entirely abandoned, however. Every so often a cab or car went speeding down the street, as if wherever they were going, they needed to get there fast. And a handful of times, Schuyler spotted people, small clusters of two or three, who stuck to the edges of buildings, watching her warily. If she got close enough, they would disappear into the shadows.

One thing was clear: Something terrible had happened.

Schuyler quickened her pace. She passed Columbus Circle, skirted Central Park—at least the stinky gingko trees in autumnal bloom hadn't changed—and had broken into a flat-out run by the time she reached Riverside Drive.

The familiar yet imposing shape of home sent a wave of relief through Schuyler's body. The Van Alen domain looked unchanged, just as she remembered it, peeling paint and crumbling roof tiles and all. She climbed the stairs and rang the bell next to the front door. Hattie, the housekeeper, was always scolding her for forgetting her keys, and finally this time Schuyler had a good reason. But the bell wasn't working. She knocked on the giant double doors and waited, shivering uncontrollably by that point and so cold she couldn't feel her fingers anymore.

The latch on the lock clicked and one door creaked open just a crack. A man's eyes peered out at her. Schuyler didn't recognize him, especially since he wore a surgical mask over his mouth and nose.

"Hello?" she said reflexively, despite her confusion.

"You forget my lo mein?" he asked as he glanced at her empty hands.

Schuyler frowned. "What? I live here. . . . This is my house."

The man's eyes widened, startled, and he moved to close the door, barricading himself behind the wrought iron that stood between them.

"If you're not here to deliver my food," he shouted, "get off my property before I call the police!" His voice shook with each word.

"My" property? Schuyler thought, and double-checked the number of the address. She hadn't gotten it wrong; this was her home. And yet she felt that this stranger was telling the truth. There was something in the way his voice cracked and how the whites of his eyes were visible with fear. He wasn't a squatter who had broken in. This was his house.

"I'm warning you," he went on. "I'm giving you to the count of five! . . . Four!"

Before he could get to three, Schuyler stumbled back, tripped on the step down, caught herself as she spun, and took off down the street. The sound of the door slamming echoed behind her. She kept running.

This wasn't home. Cordelia was still dead. And there was no loving housekeeper and loyal driver, no Hattie, no Julius. No Beauty—Schuyler's beloved bloodhound and guardian angel. No one.

Schuyler's home was gone.

This was not her life. This was not her world. She was alone.

Tears mixed with the rain as it pelted her face.

Two

SCHUYLER

*S*chuyler ran until she couldn't run anymore and took shelter in the entryway of an abandoned bodega. The storm was only getting worse the longer it went on. The streets flooded as drains overflowed, clogged with trash and debris. Thunder boomed across the city, rattling windowpanes and making the ground quake with each pass. It was as if God had a score to settle.

From beneath the awning, Schuyler watched the clouds go by. The storm reminded her of a hurricane that had swept through the city when she was a little girl. She had never seen the sky look so angry before.

Lightning flickered and danced between clouds, thunder replied in earnest, and Schuyler's heart ached at all she had lost.

Cordelia and Lawrence; the father she never knew, Stephen Chase, who died before she was born; and the mother whom she only knew in her dreams . . . and Jack. Benjamin "Jack" Force, the Angel of Destruction, Abbadon. *Her* Jack. She could still see his smile. Jack, reborn over thousands of years into thousands of different forms, a being of unknowable power, and yet he had chosen her. Loved her. Died for her. Died for everyone.

The tears fell hot on her cheeks, and a bubble formed in the back of her throat.

She never even got to say good-bye.

Too many people she loved were gone.

But then she remembered the last thing Cordelia had ever said to her, in the Sacred Language: *Facio valiturus fortis. Be strong and brave.*

After allowing herself to cry for a moment, Schuyler wiped her tears, and her eyes landed on an untouched stack of the *Times*, a copy of the newspaper she had seen earlier, with Aldrich Duncan's handsome face smiling at her from the front page. She read the date below the masthead: *September 15, 2020.*

Impossible. That couldn't be right. That was more than a decade in the future. She must be losing her mind. She was also cold and tired, and she was becoming increasingly hungry. Her stomach complained with a low whine. She needed to get out of the storm and find a warm place to rest before she could have any hope of solving this mystery. But it had to be somewhere close, somewhere familiar, somewhere safe. And she knew of only one place left she could try.

"Please," she said, begging the doorman through the glass. "I need to talk to Oliver Hazard-Perry."

"I told ya already, kid," the doorman said, his voice muffled through his surgical mask. "No one by that name lives here."

She had walked all the way from the Upper West Side to Midtown, desperately needing to see her best friend in the world, who also happened to be the one human in her life who knew that she was a vampire.

The whole time, she worried that maybe Oliver's home on Madison Avenue had become a crater in the ground or something equally disastrous. Thinking the worst only made her sick. Everything was already so twisted, all Schuyler wanted was for Oliver to hold her and tell her it was all going to be okay. And, as if her prayers were answered, she found the eighty-story complex looking perfectly normal, brimming with life. Lights glowed in the lobby, warm against the harsh haze of rain. But the doorman saw her coming, furrowed his brow at her, and, after a very quick judgment, made a show of locking the door in her face, effectively living up to his title.

She knew she looked like a mess. Oliver's apartment building was called the Westwell and had been featured in several architectural magazines as the epitome of neoclassical grandeur, with lower-end apartments costing in the hundreds of millions. It had the intended effect of making a person feel underdressed even in a ball gown, and Schuyler's current attire was the polar opposite of the "nines." But she was still a New Yorker, and New Yorkers got their way.

"What do you mean? They've lived here for *years*," she argued. Her temper grew shorter with every degree of lost body heat.

"Did you hit your head?" the doorman snapped. "I told ya, no Hazard-Perrys. The apartment number you gave belongs to the Golding-Chang family. They've lived here since they moved from London a few years back. Either you just woke up from a coma and that other family is long gone, or you got a couple screws loose. I'm inclined toward the latter view."

Hope had started slipping through her fingers when her attention was drawn past the doorman's shoulder. Behind him, the elevator doors opened and a handsome boy emerged, walking while looking down at his phone. He glanced up after hearing the commotion, then cocked his head slightly. He slipped his own mask below his chin. "Schuyler?"

It took her a moment to finally recognize him. "Oliver?"

It was Oliver for sure, but also not Oliver. He was still tall and slim with an elflike face, but his hair was a dark, silky black and his eyes a deep brown. When he smiled, though, she knew it was him for sure. When he smiled, it was like the sun had come out after weeks of rain.

"It's all right, Freddie," Oliver said to the doorman while replacing his mask. "She's a friend."

"You sure, Mr. Golding-Chang?" Freddie, the doorman, asked. "Her?"

"Of course! Now don't be rude; she's turning blue! Let her in!"

Freddie unlocked the door and let Schuyler into the lobby. Oliver wrapped his arm around her as she shivered at nuclear level, and he led her back the way he'd come. "I was just about to call. You never answered my texts. I was freaking out! This explains so much. Did you lose your phone?" he asked. "Sorry about Freddie. . . . He's new."

Schuyler didn't have the strength to answer his rapid-fire questions. Even though she was out of the rain, she felt like she had been carved from an ice block with a chain saw. Oliver took her up in the elevator, which opened right into his penthouse apartment.

While he fetched her a clean towel and a change of clothes, Schuyler waited in the gallery, dripping water on the rug, among paintings by Guy C. Wiggins and Chuck Close.

The familiarity of the penthouse reassured her, made her feel like she hadn't totally lost her grasp on reality. The apartment took up the whole top three floors of the building, including one floor just for Oliver.

Geometric *parquet de Versailles* patterns lined the gallery's wood floor leading to the living room, library, and kitchen; a vase of fresh Queen Anne's lace stood on a mahogany console from Paris, as usual; and the grand floor-to-ceiling windows on all sides of the penthouse revealed the wraparound terrace that allowed her to take in the Manhattan skyline. It was exactly as she remembered.

Just like Schuyler, Oliver's family had a lengthy legacy of wealth and prestige, a foundational element of New York City's growing power through the ages. Even though Oliver was mortal, a Red Blood, he came from a long line of Conduits—secret keepers of Blue Blood history—and had been there for Schuyler even before she learned about her true nature as a vampire. And when he willingly became her Familiar, giving his blood to her in a sacred feeding, their bond had been sealed. Of course, when she chose to love Jack instead of him, it broke his heart. But their friendship was eternal.

She had spent most of her childhood running with Oliver down these halls. Ever since that fateful day in elementary school when he shared his lettuce-and-mayo sandwich with her after she had forgotten her lunch, they had been joined at the hip. She wondered how much of their history was still true. Because—2020? What? Why was she here? How had she gotten here?

When Oliver came back with the towel and fresh clothes in hand, she buried her face in the towel, convinced it was the fluffiest one ever made. It smelled like lavender.

Oliver asked, "Where have you been? You look absolutely knackered."

"S-since when do you have an English accent?" Schuyler stuttered.

Oliver gave her a quizzical smile. "Hurry up, get changed, toss your clothes in the dryer. I'll get the kettle going."

She went to the laundry room and undressed. Oliver had given her one of his softest thermal undershirts, a beige Yosemite National Park hoodie with well-worn holes in the cuffs, and a pair of black joggers lined with fleece. She was tall, but he was taller, and she swam in his clothes. With her own clothes spinning in the dryer, she came back out to the gallery to find Oliver waiting for her with a pair of chunky wool socks and a face mask, which he handed her.

"Did you forget yours?" Oliver asked.

She gladly accepted the socks, but the mask? Schuyler looked at it curiously. First she'd seen the man at the house on Riverside with one, then the doorman, and now Oliver. She didn't understand.

The kettle that Oliver had put on minutes ago started to whistle, so Oliver moved away into the kitchen to tend to it. Schuyler was about to follow when her attention snapped to movement out of the corner of her eye. At first, she thought she had interrupted Oliver while he was keeping somebody company. But an otherworldly chill set in when she realized the girl looking back at her was not a stranger at all.

Same Yosemite hoodie, same joggers, same wet hair.

The noise from the kettle seemed to shriek like an alarm. Schuyler blinked a few times, just to be sure, but the image never changed. She was looking into a mirror. But the face that stared back at her was not hers at all.

Different face, different hair, but same shocked expression.

As the kettle whistled, its shrill alarm fading, Schuyler fell down, down, down, and fainted to the floor.

THREE

SCHUYLER

Schuyler blinked awake once more. Disoriented, she tried to sit up, but Oliver was there and put a gentle hand on her shoulder.

"Hey, Sky," he said softly. "It's all right. Take it easy."

Schuyler realized he had carried her to a chaise lounge in the living room. A fireplace crackled nearby, and he had covered her in a faux-fur blanket. The sky outside continued to swirl with storm clouds, and rain pelted the glass walls. It had only gotten darker since she'd last seen the storm.

"You passed out," he said. "I hope it's not pneumonia."

Schuyler felt fine, especially now that she was curled up by the fire. But she remembered the stranger's face she had seen in the mirror and tried not to panic. "Ollie," she started, then stopped. This much she knew—she was in a different world. She, herself, was different. Looked different at least, but inside, she was still herself. How much did Oliver know about her? About her life? How much had things changed? How much of their shared history was still true?

"I'm not myself," she said finally.

"Did you hit your head?" he asked.

"No," she said. "I'm just . . ." How could she explain it? Her memories didn't line up. Why was Manhattan deserted? Why did she remember Oliver's last name as Hazard-Perry but the doorman said it was Golding-Chang? Why did she remember a home that wasn't hers? Her memories were like double exposures on a photograph. Which ones were real?

Oliver handed her a glass of water, and she sipped it gratefully. It helped her find the words. "Oliver, you have to listen to me. I'm not who I am."

Oliver smirked. "'Oliver'? You must be serious, then."

"I *am* serious! I'm Schuyler Van Alen . . . but I'm also not."

Oliver's eyebrows shot up in alarm. "What are you talking about? You're Schuyler Cervantes-Chase." He gave her an uneasy smile. "Is this some kind of game you're playing that you haven't told me about?"

Chase. As in Stephen Chase—her human father? Schuyler threw the blanket off her body and stood. Oliver didn't stop her as she went to the mirror hanging over the fireplace.

She saw the stranger's face looking back at her, just as before, but she realized it wasn't entirely different. The agency she modeled for, Stitched for Civilization, had compared her to a young Kate Moss—pale, thin, with bright blue eyes—but it wasn't what she saw anymore. While her new face still had her father's wide eyes and perfectly upturned nose, where her hair used to be blue-black and wavy, it was now dark brown and curly, and her pale complexion had become a warm, light tawny shade. And she looked fifteen years old again.

She met Oliver's gaze in the mirror, stunned. "Is my father alive?"

Oliver laughed. "You're joking, aren't you? Of course Stephen's alive. He was worried sick about you when you didn't come home for dinner. I called him a minute ago to tell him that you're safe here. You're in no state to be out in that storm any longer."

Schuyler could hardly believe it. As she knew it, her mortal father had died before she was born. He and her mother, Allegra Van Alen—also known as the angel Gabrielle—married and gave birth to her, the first-ever half-blood vampire, a *Dimidium Cognatus*. Allegra had broken an immortal bond with her soul mate, Michael, to be with him, and she had paid dearly for it.

"Does the name Allegra mean anything to you?" she asked.

Oliver jutted out his lower lip and shook his head. "Should it?"

Schuyler's suspicions were true. Allegra wasn't her mother, not anymore. Did she even exist? Schuyler's knees gave out, and she sat back down and stared at the fire.

"Are you going to faint again?" Oliver asked.

"No, it's just a lot to take in at the moment."

Oliver took a seat next to her and rested his elbows on his knees, looking into the fire too. She could feel how warm he was, he was so close to her. The simple act of being there with him was comforting.

"I'm glad you're all right," he said. "You're not hungry, are you?"

Did he mean *hungry* as in hungry-hungry or vampire-hungry? Human blood wouldn't be off the menu, even for a half vampire like her, but she wasn't craving any yet. She wasn't sure who or what she was anymore.

Feeding from a human wasn't so simple, and Vampire Code forbade humans from being abused or fully drained, but drinking their blood was an intimate affair called the *Caerimonia Osculor*—the Sacred Kiss. It bonded the human to the vampire forever, making the human their Familiar, giving not only their blood but years of their life.

The firelight softened Oliver's handsome profile. He looked just like the fifteen-year-old boy she had grown up with, except his features were part Asian, which made him even more handsome. Still, there was a sadness in his gaze. This was the same boy who at one time had given his own blood to her to make her well again when she was sick, and she knew instinctively that he would do it all over again if she asked.

This was one thing she needed to know. "Ollie," she said. "Am I a Blue Blood?"

He blinked, turned to her, then laughed. "*Duh!* Are you sure you're okay?"

A smile eased its way onto her lips. Oliver had the knack of making her laugh, especially when she needed it. At least some things hadn't changed.

FOUR

SCHUYLER

*S*chuyler decided she was hungry-hungry, more for the sake of returning to a kind of normalcy than because of any actual hunger, so Oliver led the way into the kitchen. It was modern, with ebony countertops and stainless-steel fixtures with a chic and sleek island table and stools in the middle. Schuyler had dual memories of sitting at this table with Oliver after school to do homework. The memories lined up like ghostly layers upon one another, similar but just different enough to stand out. Two worlds, Oliver from here, and Oliver from there, both looking at her the same way, with the same gentle smile, but it only lasted for a second before reality snapped into focus.

She took up her usual seat while Oliver finished making her a large mug of chai. The steam curled upward, and Schuyler inhaled the spicy cinnamon and cardamom aromas. He added a splash of milk, just as she liked it, and leaned on the counter, watching her.

He asked, "Schuyler, memory issues are no joke. Have you talked to a doctor? Like my aunt Pat? If anyone would know what to do, it'd be her."

Oliver's aunt Pat, known as Dr. Pat to the greater Blue Blood community, was a specialist in all things vampire related. But Schuyler shook her head. "I'm not sure this is within the realm of Dr. Pat." She forced her best smile. "But don't worry about me. It's probably temporary."

Oliver watched her carefully, like he was afraid she would topple over backward onto the floor, but he didn't press her about it. She knew she was acting strangely, and she didn't want to make him any more concerned, but she needed to find out what was real. Maybe when she did, it wouldn't feel like the world was a ship in the middle of a storm, rocking beneath her feet all the time.

"What happened to you?" Oliver asked. When his eyebrows cinched together like that, he looked like a puppy.

Schuyler couldn't lie to him, but she wasn't sure he could handle the concept that she was remembering another dimension. She wasn't convinced she could believe it herself.

"You have to trust me when I say I really don't know. The last thing I remember was leaving home for some reason . . . to do something. . . ." She realized with a start that this was true. She did remember leaving home but couldn't remember where home was. And she also remembered the battle with Lucifer as if it had happened just hours ago. How was that possible? "Then I woke up in front of the Empire State Building." She closed her eyes and tried to picture home. *Home.* But the rest of the memory failed her. Trying to recover it felt like she was trying to catch smoke.

Oliver worried his bottom lip with his teeth, looking pale. "Dr. Pat mentioned Regenerative Memory Syndrome all the time when dealing with new vampires, blackouts, and such."

"That must be it," Schuyler said, even though she didn't believe it and she was anything but a new vampire. "I'm sorry for scaring you. You're helping me, though, really. I know my questions sound so stupid."

"Not at all. Anything I can do to help. It's my job." It literally was the job of Conduits like Oliver.

"My parents," she said carefully. "Do they know about my true nature as a Blue Blood?"

"You said you were afraid they would get hurt if they knew about your abilities and what really went on in the world. You wanted to protect them. Have you told them now?"

"No," she said, and was surprised to realize she could answer truthfully. Everything Oliver was telling her was real. She remembered making the decision not to tell her parents about her abilities back when her fangs first appeared, the memory as solid as the mug of chai warming her fingers. Her life in this world was as real as the other one, the one in her memories.

But if both her parents were human after all, how was it possible that she was still a Blue Blood? Was she still Gabrielle's daughter? Why wasn't anything making sense? There were so many unanswered questions, and it made her head hurt trying to organize them all into a manageable order. Schuyler stared at her tea as if she would find the answers in the swirling milk.

"I think I know what else you need," Oliver said with a sparkle in his eyes. "You need a hearty helping of my family's special recipe—boxed mac and cheese."

Schuyler laughed with relief and agreed. He wasn't a chef by any measure, but at least he was capable of not setting the place on fire.

"So why is everyone wearing masks?" Schuyler asked as Oliver filled a pot and got the water boiling.

"You're joking."

"Humor me."

Oliver conceded. "We're in the middle of a global pandemic like the world hasn't seen in centuries."

Schuyler's eyes widened. "A pandemic?"

"A disease that leeches your blood. A year ago, when all this started, people were turning up dead on the street, drained of all their blood, and no one knew why."

"Silver Bloods?" Unlike Blue Bloods, Silver Bloods—dangerous Croatan—had no problem consuming their victims' blood entirely. The process was called Full Consumption, a total exsanguination and a treasonous violation of the Code of Vampires. Both Red and Blue Bloods alike were targets. The pure evil of the Silver Bloods' actions permanently transformed them into monsters. Schuyler had met one too many in her life and didn't want to meet any more.

Oliver shook his head. "It's not Croatan. It's a virus. Transmitted from person to person. It's not the Silver Bloods. Anyone can get it."

"What about the Coven? Are they doing anything to stop it?"

"It's new to everyone. Even to the most powerful Venators and the Regis." Veritas Venators were elite warriors who were tasked with protecting and keeping other Blue Bloods safe—the vampire secret police—and the Regis, the reincarnation of the archangel Michael, was the head of their Coven.

Though a Blue Blood's mortal body could die, their spirit and memory did not. For thousands of years, they were reborn into new bodies and carried on the legacy of immortality as the Coven led by the Regis. Their undying wisdom was a constant in the midst of the unexpected. Schuyler, though not immortal herself, used to find some comfort in the idea that very little could surprise an immortal mind. But the fact that the virus was something new unnerved her.

Schuyler tapped her nails thoughtfully on her mug. "What about your family? They're okay?"

"Thankfully. I've been home alone since the pandemic was declared, though. My parents were abroad—a ski trip in Switzerland—when countries started shutting their borders. Despite their best efforts, no one is going anywhere. I told my parents not to worry, to stay put. They're safer in the countryside than in the city anyway. Things started deteriorating quickly here not long after we learned what was happening. That was almost a year ago."

Schuyler knew that he meant the shuttered windows and locked-up doors. It must have been terrifying being all alone. "And the masks protect you?" she asked.

"For the most part. We're still not allowed to meet in large groups, though. Even going to Duchesne. We've been doing school online through Zoom."

"What's Zoom?"

"A video app. Blimey, you really did bonk your head."

"Yes, of course—how could I forget?" Schuyler said. Perhaps it was easier to play along with the craziness than try to question it.

"Anyway, classes are still going on. Nothing has really changed; we just get to learn calculus from the comfort of our own bedrooms. Or *not* learn calculus, as it's pretty hard to understand advanced math on a video screen."

By then the water was boiling, and Oliver added the noodles. Schuyler didn't ask any more questions after that. She let Oliver make her dinner while she churned over what he had said.

So she really *had* traveled forward in time to another world. But some things—a very few things, it seemed—were still the same. Take Duchesne—the elite private school that young Blue Bloods of Manhattan attended. Alongside Red Blood students, vampires like Schuyler were expected to learn how to be future leaders of the greater world. But it was still a high school like any other, complete with all the drama, aside from the added danger of Silver Blood attacks. If her current situation wasn't already a nightmare, reliving high school certainly would be.

The real question now was: Why? What made all of this happen? Could this be Lucifer's doing? Or had everything she'd thought she'd known before been a dream? The universe seemed like it was operating under a different set of rules. One thing was certain: She could talk to the current Regis, Charles Force, about her predicament. Surely he of all people would have some insight. But would he believe her?

Charles Force was Jack's father. With Michael's spirit, he was the guiding light for all the vampires in the city. But when the Silver Bloods had returned after years of hiding, he didn't want to believe it, and too many vampires died as a result.

Schuyler wondered if any of that was still true and if Charles would listen to her now. Would the reality of time travel be more or less convincing, especially coming from her? She was the half-blood daughter of his lost love in the old world. What would she be to him in this one?

Despite their tumultuous relationship, Schuyler had to trust that he would know what to do. She didn't want to think about what it meant if he didn't.

A pang of regret pinched her side. She would have been the one to tell him that his son was dead.

She blinked back tears and breathed. *One thing at a time*, she reminded herself.

A copy of the *Times* bearing the headline she'd been seeing all over town sat on Oliver's table, and Schuyler slid it over to get a better look. She wanted to think about something else for a moment, and finally she had the time and the energy to read the article.

DUNCAN DOMINATES DISSIDENTS

Mayor Aldrich B. Duncan signed an executive order Monday granting police full and complete power to detain any protestors found breaking the curfew on municipal property, claiming such acts of dissension to be a threat to the health, safety, and security of average citizens in the face of a global pandemic.

Candidate May Woldock, running in a tight race to replace Duncan this November, held a press conference admonishing the sitting mayor for his actions, saying the order is an example of "unchecked power and a step toward totalitarian rule." She further added, "The police should not be the mayor's personal hit squad to silence his critics." Opposing parties have repeatedly called for the mayor's removal from office since the pandemic first began ravaging the city. New York City alone has experienced a 200 percent increase in cases in the last month.

The Duncan administration is expected to open thirty clinics across the city.

Supporters for Duncan held a counterprotest at Woldock's private home, and a police report was filed for a broken window. Ms. Woldock was not available for comment at the time of publication.

A bowl of steaming macaroni and cheese slid into Schuyler's field of view. She tore her eyes away from the article and looked up to see Oliver smiling at her.

"You look so serious when you read," he said, and playfully pushed his index finger on the line formed between her eyebrows.

Schuyler shoved the paper away and sighed. "Either the world has gone crazy, or I have."

"The world doesn't seem so crazy to me, not when you're around."

Schuyler let out an airy laugh.

"Eat up. You'll feel better, I promise," he continued.

She did as he said, and he was right; she did feel better. The cheese powder from the mac-and-cheese box hadn't fully dissolved and the noodles were a little overcooked, but in Schuyler's unbiased opinion, it was one of the best meals she'd ever had. When she was finished, Oliver put the bowl in the dishwasher and poured her another mug of tea, but the ache and tiredness she had been carrying with her all day quickly took hold of Schuyler's body, and she yawned. She knew she needed to see Charles right away, but she could barely keep her eyes open. It was a miracle that she was still upright.

"You can sleep over if you want," Oliver said.

"That sounds wonderful, actually. Are you sure? I don't want to be a bother."

"Nonsense," he said. "You're pretty used to that guest room . . . or have you forgotten that as well?"

Schuyler managed a laugh, then bid him a good night and made her way alone. The guest room housed a king-sized four-poster bed with sheer georgette curtains flanking the canopy, and it had its own bathroom. She was too tired to wash up, so she removed the stack of pillows as tall as Mount Everest from the bed and kept only two for comfort—one for her head and the other to cuddle—and slipped between the satin sheets. Her hair fanned out around her as she looked through the windows from the bed.

The room had one of the best views of Midtown. Normally, the city lights illuminated the space with a steady pale blue hue, a surety of the world existing outside. But now the glass remained dark. The severity of the storm had passed, and only the gentle tap of rain on the glass made Schuyler feel cozy and safe. She didn't remember closing her eyes, but before she knew it, she was dreaming.

The dream began with a series of flashing images, like the shutter on a camera.

A woman's smile.

A paintbrush.

A windowsill garden.

An iron fire escape.

A key.

A vintage Mustang.

Sounds filtered in with the images.

Meat sizzling on the stove.

Jazz music drifting in from another room.

A man's laughter.

Pages of a book turning.

A ticking clock.

These things were not from her old life, the one she had known. They were from this new one, from this new world.

The images and sounds grew, increasing in speed and volume, until they reached a crescendo then went dark and silent. Schuyler found herself standing in a black void. Her heartbeat echoed in her ears. She sensed someone behind her and turned to see herself, her old self.

"We're both Schuyler," the old Schuyler told her. Her voice sounded far away and distorted, like she was speaking through a broken telephone. "There are many versions of us. Somehow, the timelines merged, and you're you, but you're not you. You're also me. In my world, my work is done. But yours is only beginning."

Schuyler blinked, and the old Schuyler vanished. More memories, new memories, flashed and merged with her old ones, fusing and separating and fusing again, like a spiderweb of paths through time and space.

Mother.

Father.

Schuyler turned around again, and Allegra now stood behind her. She glowed with heavenly light, but with a splintering sound, the light went out. "Wherever you are," she said, "you're still my daughter. You carry the light of Gabrielle. Perhaps the only thing that remains of my light in this world."

Schuyler wanted to ask, *What does that mean?* But her voice didn't work.

She tried to run toward Allegra, but her legs stayed glued to the darkness and started sinking. The darkness was going to swallow her whole. The black void crept up her legs, like veins, cold as death. It crawled up over her body, consuming her, but before it could cover her mouth, she screamed.

Schuyler startled awake and sat up in bed, panting.

Morning had come. The storm was gone, and in its place the sun shone brightly, promising a beautiful day.

Schuyler found Oliver was already in the kitchen, as if he'd never left.

"Morning!" he called cheerily when he noticed her walk in. He was in the midst of stirring a bowl of pancake batter, a smudge of flour on his chin.

The dream nagged at the forefront of Schuyler's thoughts as she took a seat at the island table. She still couldn't understand what it all meant. Was anything in her past life real? Any of her memories? Or was this a deconstruction of some cosmic game designed to toy with her emotions? Was that other Schuyler real? How many other Schuylers were in other universes? Was she trapped here forever? And what did the other Schuyler mean when she said, *You're not you. You're also me?*

Most of all, Allegra's cryptic message made her feel uneasy. How could the light of Gabrielle go out? Why couldn't dreams be literal and concrete and give helpful answers about anything?

"Feeling any better?" Oliver asked.

"Yes," she said, truthfully, but she neglected to mention her dream. She thought she had sounded crazy enough last night. She didn't see the point in worrying Oliver any more about it. "I think I should go home."

"But breakfast is almost done!"

"You're sweet, but my . . . my dad must be freaking out." It felt strange referring to her father in the present tense. She needed to see him for herself. "I don't want to make him wait any longer."

"You don't have to leave. You're safe here. I just sent out a grocery order for your favorite foods, and I've made arrangements for new clothes to be delivered, so you can stay as long as you'd like."

"No, thank you," she said firmly. "I really need to go home."

FIVE

SCHUYLER

*H*ome in this world was a loft in SoHo, on Wooster Street, near the intersection of Wooster and Grand. It was one of the remaining original artist lofts, which became more and more rare and expensive as the 1980s progressed and SOHO became gentrified. The place she called home, however, was in the designated SoHo–Cast Iron Historic District, and the white building in which she lived had been preserved.

The cast-iron architecture sat stubbornly on the block, sturdy and unmoving. Schuyler admired it from across the craggy cobblestone street, appreciating its tenacity. Very real memories of sitting on the stoop, eating ice cream with Oliver, and trying and failing to roller-skate on the sidewalk came rushing back. Graffiti colored the brick alley between buildings, a single-speed bicycle sat chained to a handrail, and a classic 1969 Mustang was parked in the street in front of the main entrance, exactly like the one she'd seen in her dream.

Earlier that morning, Oliver had given her back the spare key she had once given him, an official invitation to visit whenever he wanted, since she'd lost her own. It was brass, exactly like the one from her dream.

She let herself inside.

As was traditional in artists' lofts, the place was open and airy, with large windows capturing the sunlight. The walls were made of exposed brick, the high ceilings stretched with wooden beams, and vibrant deep-pile rugs adorned the pressed concrete floor, hiding dried paint drippings in dozens of colors. A large wagon wheel draped with Edison bulbs hung in the center of the combined living room and dining room space like a chandelier. Paintings and tapestries from all across the world covered every inch of available wall space, verdant houseplants grew unruly and free on any horizontal surface, and a delicately hand-painted stepladder coiled with fairy lights led to the mezzanine primary bedroom above. At the center of the room was a large blue sofa facing a television, perfect for family movie nights. Instead of plates, the dining table was littered with half-finished portraits and charcoal sketches. An electronic keyboard sat in the corner of the room, flanked by a Peruvian charango and a stack of sheet music. The entire apartment vibrated with color and life.

A large bookshelf sagging with hundreds of books divided the open floor plan of the loft, and from behind it came the sounds of someone moving through a kitchen: a clang of a pot on a stove and the usual *click-click-click* of a gas burner turning on.

She followed the noise and discovered a golden-haired man pouring ground coffee into a French press.

He glanced up when she came in and beamed. "Sassy Pants!" he said.

Schuyler stood glued to the floor, stunned. Her breath caught in her chest.

So it was real. Stephen Chase, her father, was alive.

In her old world, she'd seen him only in photos and heard stories about him. That Stephen Chase was dead, dead long before any events she could remember, a ghost in every way except for the imaginings that she had created while her mother was in a coma. On lonely nights, she'd talk to him, ask for advice, wish that he were there to tell her everything was going to be okay. In her fantasy, he was handsome, and strong, and warm, and now—standing before her in the flesh—he was all that and more.

He looked to be in his forties, with a stubbly beard and earnest blue eyes that gave the impression that he saw things about the world only an artist could see. He wore an old fisherman's sweater, plaid pajama bottoms, and slippers. And when he smiled at her, Schuyler could think of only one thing to do: She plowed straight into him, crashing into his body and wrapping him tightly in the biggest hug she could muster. It caught him so off guard, he almost toppled over. He smelled like paint thinner and soap.

"Whoa," he said with a laugh. "We just saw each other yesterday. You miss me that much, kiddo?"

"You have no idea," she said. "Where's Mom?"

As if summoned, a woman appeared, resplendent in a colorful kimono. She swept into the kitchen like a gorgeous tropical bird, graceful and otherworldly. She also looked to be in her forties, curvy, and tall, and effortlessly beautiful. Her dark hair was pulled into a high bun on the top of her head like a crown. Her skin was a beautiful mahogany that practically glowed in the morning sunlight. She smiled warmly at Schuyler, and Schuyler knew, deep in her bones, that this was her *mother.*

"There's my girl!" she said, and tenderly tucked a stray curl behind Schuyler's ear before moving to her husband's side and giving him a kiss on the cheek.

Schuyler's mother was Aurora Cervantes, a locally famous jazz singer. Later, Schuyler would remember her happy childhood as the only child of two loving parents, but for now, she marveled at how different this mother was compared to Allegra Van Alen. Most of Schuyler's memories surrounding Allegra were of the pale woman lying comatose in a hospital bed, cold as death. Schuyler had spent every Sunday, every holiday, every birthday, watching Allegra's face for any change, any sign of hope that she would return to her.

But Aurora Cervantes was vibrant, and warm, and humming with spirit. She was a mix of so many things, half-Spanish, part Chinese, with dashes of French and Jamaican. Schuyler remembered being very little and sitting on Aurora's lap, poking her little fingers on piano keys while her mother played around her, and laughing.

"Coffee, Ro?" Stephen asked.

"A dream come true!" Aurora said. She situated herself behind him, wrapped her arms around his waist, and rested her chin on his shoulder. "The most handsome painter in the world, making me the most exquisite cup of coffee? I must be the luckiest woman alive." Then she began to sing, and her husky voice filled the entire loft like the casting of a spell, electrifying the air in a way that sent goose bumps along Schuyler's arms.

Stephen hummed and swayed back and forth with her. Soon they were dancing and laughing, for no particular reason at all, and tears pricked at the backs of Schuyler's eyes. She had always wanted this life. She had always wanted parents who were happy together.

They were unburdened of the weight of heaven and earth on their shoulders, making life beautiful with art, free to live as people—regular, perfectly normal people.

She couldn't help but smile and laugh with them.

Her parents noticed this and paused, eyebrows raised.

"Something's wrong with our daughter," Stephen said with a grin. "You're not disgusted by our lovey-dovey antics? Not going to tell us to 'get a room'? Who are you and what have you done with our Schuyler?"

Schuyler knew it was a joke, but for a moment she thought of telling them the truth: that she wasn't entirely sure if she was the Schuyler they knew anymore. If she herself could barely believe it, they for sure wouldn't.

Unlike Stephen, though, Aurora sensed something else was going on. She went to Schuyler and wrapped her daughter in a hug. She smelled of Chanel perfume, and the silk kimono was soft under Schuyler's touch. After a moment, Aurora pulled away to get a better look at Schuyler's face. Her slender hand was warm as she gently tipped Schuyler's chin up.

Golden sunlight rippled around Aurora's head. "You look like you've seen a ghost, mi cielo," she said.

"I'm fine. I really needed to come home. That's all."

Aurora pursed her full lips but seemed satisfied with the answer as she grabbed a pair of matching mugs from the cabinet.

Meanwhile Stephen checked his frayed wristwatch then clapped his hands and rubbed them together. "All right, Sassy Pants, chop-chop. School's in five."

"I actually have to run out and talk to the Regis—" She stopped herself short, realizing she'd almost spilled the existence of her secret life.

Aurora looked puzzled. "On a school day? Absolutely not."

"Who's Regis?" Stephen asked. Luckily he assumed "Regis" was the name of a friend of hers.

"Someone we should know about?" Aurora asked, raising a shaped eyebrow.

"No. But—" Schuyler didn't know how to explain to a pair of humans that she needed to meet with the leader of a secret vampire league—or whether she should even try to explain this—so the words died somewhere on the way from her brain to her mouth.

"No buts, young lady," Stephen said. "Whatever is so important, I'm sure it can wait."

Schuyler wasn't so sure about that, but there was no room to argue. She hadn't considered that her parents still saw her as a teenager and not a half-vampire hero trying to save the world. Except she'd done that already. She'd saved the world. Her world, anyway. What was she supposed to do *here*?

Aurora tipped her head toward Schuyler's room. "Go on. I'll bring you some food. It's my turn to make breakfast today, so you'd better be hungry."

Where does one go looking for contact information about a vampire coven? Google, of course.

Perched on the edge of her bed, Schuyler scrolled through the list of results on her laptop when she searched for the name Charles Force, pressing her teeth into her lower lip as she went. After school, the first thing she would do would be to call him, or send him an email at least, asking to meet. She didn't want to think about the email she would send: *Hello, Charles. Do you believe in time travel?* She would have to work on it.

There were a few results on various job posting sites, but none of their profile pictures matched her memory of the silver-haired Regis. Although . . . was it possible his appearance had changed too? It wasn't out of the realm of possibility.

Someone as esteemed as Charles Force probably didn't need to post his profile on a job board site, so Schuyler tried another Google search, this time for Force Network, the multimedia corporation. Nothing. At least, nothing recent.

She was just about to click on a news article from seven years ago titled FORCE NETWORK PLANE CRASHES OVER ATLANTIC, NO SURVIVORS, but before she could, Aurora came into Schuyler's room with breakfast. Not only was her mother a talented singer, she was also an incredible cook. The smell alone was divine.

Schuyler closed the news article window quickly just before Aurora presented her with a steaming-hot plate of pan con chicharrón—a pork sandwich with red onions and sweet potato—with a side of yuca and a glass of juice. While Schuyler dug in, after realizing just how hungry she truly was, Aurora helped her get situated with Zoom, then kissed her squarely on the top of her head before leaving the room and closing the door behind her. It was a parent's instinct to make sure their child made it to school on time, virtual or not.

The subtle sound of jazz music drifted in from the living room, muffled behind Schuyler's closed door, just like her dream last night. The key. The Mustang. The music. It occurred to Schuyler all of a sudden that maybe it had been more than a dream.

While she ate, her thoughts drifted.

Schuyler's room (the only room besides the bathroom with its own door) was similar to the one she remembered having on the Upper West Side, with minor differences: dozens of Broadway *Playbill* covers taped to one wall, like *Hamilton*, *Les Misérables*, and *Wicked*, to name a few; Barbie dolls sitting posed next to graphic novels and manga on a bookcase; dirty clothes piled high in the hamper, waiting to be washed; a small closet consisting of mostly monochromatic black cardigans; blurry Polaroids, tacked to the corkboard, of her and Oliver making silly faces together and having too much fun to be able to keep the camera still long enough to get the shot.

The room was distinctly hers, but she felt older than the person to whom it belonged. She and Jack had been eighteen years old when they battled Lucifer. That was the last thing she remembered. Seeing her room now reminded her that in this world she was fifteen again. Three years' difference didn't seem like a lot of time, but to Schuyler it felt like an extra lifetime had been packed into her head. Déjà vu to the extreme.

It was also kind of funny. Would anyone suspect a musical theater fan of being a vampire?

Her first class of the day, English Literature, started on time, and dozens of little windows on the screen popped up as students entered the session, their cameras on and ready for attendance to be taken. Schuyler scanned for a familiar face in the crowd, human or otherwise, and spotted Oliver in a small window. She waved to him.

He privately messaged her: 😳

She replied with the same and smiled.

But she didn't recognize anyone else. No sign of Bliss Llewellyn or Mimi Force. As far as she could tell, her classmates were mostly strangers.

Everything was impossibly normal. No one pointed at her through their screen, shouting how she didn't belong there, or asked who she was. She was just another kid in school, exactly where she was supposed to be.

It was hard for her to pay attention as class went on. She'd already gone over all of Shakespeare's oeuvre the first time she'd been through high school. If her parents were expecting her to go to school, though, she would do it for them, but nothing was going to stop her from doing a little research of her own.

So Schuyler spent most of the class time searching for signs of another life. Someone out there must remember something, right? She couldn't be the only one. She didn't want to believe it.

There had to be some reason why she remembered another world.

She finally opened and read the article.

Force Network executive Maximilian Force Jr., 44, and his wife, Miranda Force née De Clare, 44, are presumed dead in a small plane crash that occurred while they were crossing the Atlantic Ocean, traveling from Heathrow Airport heading to JFK International, when tower control lost communication during the night as the plane disappeared from radar. Along with the Forces, a crew of three is also presumed to be deceased.

The couple was traveling in a private plane owned by the Force Network.

A source close to the couple mourns the loss: "They were a beacon of light for the community. Their grace and service to the greater good will be missed for a generation." News of their deaths has rocked the city.

Early investigations have not yet determined the cause of the crash.

The couple was scheduled to arrive at their home in Manhattan on Saturday morning but never made it. Searches are underway, but authorities with the Federal Aviation Administration say that severe weather will delay recovery of the bodies; however, some wreckage identifying the craft has been found.

The couple leaves behind two eight-year-old sons and a legacy of philanthropy.

So it wasn't Charles after all. Charles from her old world was married to Trinity Force, another Blue Blood. Whoever these people were, she didn't know them. Schuyler wondered if the name Force was common and if they were related in some way to the Force family that she knew. Regardless, this article wasn't what she was looking for.

For the rest of the school day, with Oliver's help reminding her what her class schedule was since they had almost the exact same courses, Schuyler spent most of her time searching for any leads, but she came up with nothing. No one.

The problem with secret vampire covens was that they were supernaturally good at staying secret. In fact, the Coven was so good at hiding, it was like they never existed—which, of course, was impossible. This was going to be more difficult than she thought.

After she signed off, defeated, her eyes aching with fatigue, she snapped the laptop shut.

She flopped back onto her bed and pressed her palms deeply into her eye sockets, massaging them so hard that pops of color burst behind her lids.

What she wouldn't give to cuddle with her bloodhound, Beauty, again, or go to a midnight horror showing with Oliver like they used to do, or—what was wrong with her?—even butt heads with Mimi Force one last time. She missed how things used to be.

She wanted to go home. To the *other* home. She still had people she cared about in that world, like her friend Bliss and her half sister, Finn. Did they even know what had happened to her?

How could she possibly have memories of two different worlds existing at the same time?

"Schuyler! Quesadilla time!" her father's voice called through the door. She could already smell the fresh aroma of smoked cayenne and peppers wafting in.

Schuyler joined her parents, her very real and alive parents, in the dining room, where they all ate together. They asked her about her school day and performed perfectly normal, loving parental duties. She should have been satisfied. She knew she should have appreciated that she had a good life now.

Yet she would never be able to rest until she got to the bottom of things. She needed answers, and she was going to get them. Tonight.

SIX

SCHUYLER

*I*t was late by the time Schuyler managed to sneak out of the apartment. She needed to be careful not to wake her parents, which was a feat all on its own, as the primary bedroom loft was open to the living room and had full view of the comings and goings out the front door. If she was caught sneaking out, she'd probably be grounded until she was fifty years old. So Schuyler opened the window in her bedroom, silent as a whisper, and climbed down the fire escape. She dropped to the alley ten feet below, adjusted the mask closer to her face, and pulled the hood of her coat up over her head, an anonymous shadow.

She needed to start from the beginning. Her best and only lead was the place where she had first woken up: in front of the Empire State Building. It was the one place she might find any clue as to what was going on or how she could get home.

Thankfully, the night was clear and cool. The full moon passed behind wispy clouds every now and again, casting a silver glow on the asphalt, but Schuyler's heightened senses made it easy for her to see in the dark. Mayor Duncan had instituted a citywide curfew that meant if anyone saw her out in the streets this late, she would be arrested, so she kept to the shadows. The last thing she needed was to make her one phone call to her parents. Only once did she have to hide behind a dumpster as a police cruiser rolled past, its blue lights flashing without the siren, but otherwise she made it to Thirty-Fourth Street without seeing another soul.

It was hard to believe that she had woken up in that very spot yesterday, knowing so little about what was happening. To be honest with herself, she wasn't sure she knew that much more now.

She stood on the same patch of sidewalk she'd stood on the day before and looked around. Fifth Avenue was devoid of any cars or tourists experiencing the city that never sleeps firsthand, and the streets remained quiet. She wasn't sure she'd ever get used to that part.

The Art Deco landmark loomed darkly overhead as Schuyler walked up and down the block. She wasn't sure what she was looking for, figuring maybe she would know it when she saw it, but so far nothing stood out from its surroundings. So much for that.

Schuyler sighed and looked skyward. With New York City having gone mostly dark, she could actually see the stars. In any other circumstance, seeing them for once might have been pretty. Now, though, they were just another harsh reminder that this world was wrong.

The wind kicked up, and the skin on the back of Schuyler's neck prickled. An ordinary person might have brushed it off as a chill, but she was a Blue Blood. She knew better.

Someone was watching her.

She played it cool, though. Showing her hand too early would be a mistake, so she walked. Footsteps followed her. Her heartbeat thrummed loudly in her ears, despite her best efforts to listen to whoever was behind her. They were a block away, maybe less, but they were definitely following her. Even when Schuyler used her incredible speed to cross the street, the footsteps sped up to match.

They were closer than ever. She could feel them, no matter how they tried to mask their presence.

Normal people didn't follow teenage girls down darkened streets for no reason.

But this was no ordinary person. No one should be able to keep up with a vampire. No one, except for . . .

Schuyler ducked into an alley and made a break for it. She jumped ten feet into the air, over a dumpster, and landed on a low dividing wall. The shadow followed. She jumped down to the other side and kept running, her sneakers pounding into the concrete. She was being hunted.

Thinking quickly without slowing down, Schuyler reached low and picked up a crumpled tin can from a garbage pile. She took off down the street once more. A looming shadow passed across a boarded-up storefront beside her. Schuyler turned sharply into another alley and jumped to a fire escape. As she did, she threw the tin can farther down the alley, and it clanged loudly, long after she had silently moved up the fire escape ladder and hidden within a pile of full garbage bags discarded on the landing.

She froze when the shadow rushed into the alley too, following the sound of the tin can. Her distraction had worked. Mostly.

Follow the sound . . . she prayed, hoping it would last long enough for her to escape.

Schuyler waited, her heartbeat thrumming furiously, and she

didn't dare to move. The figure was hooded and cloaked, impossible to recognize. They paused in the middle of the alley, directly beneath her hiding place. Their footsteps were soft and measured, and two silver blades gleamed, one in each hand. The daggers looked as long as Schuyler's forearms and sharp enough that anyone who was attacked with them would barely feel them slice. Whoever it was, they knew how to use them.

The worst part was their eyes. Even in the dark and from that distance, their eyes were unmistakable. They had a particularly silver glow, like an animal's caught in headlights. Schuyler's stomach heaved.

Croatan . . . Silver Blood . . .

The last time she had been chased down a dark alley by a Silver Blood, she had been a young vampire coming into her powers. She was not the same young vampire anymore.

The abomination that was the Silver Blood scanned the alley, their face still in shadow, but they never looked up. Schuyler held her breath, as if it would help. It might have.

For an agonizingly long moment, the Silver Blood waited, then eventually put away their daggers and took off in the opposite direction, dissolving into the night.

"You saw a Croatan? Here? Now?" Oliver asked, leaning over the table, his eyes wide.

Schuyler had run straight from the encounter with the Croatan to Oliver's apartment building. Luckily, the doorman, Freddie, didn't make a fuss like last time and just let her in. On top of that, Oliver had already been awake watching late-night television, so he was quick to make her feel at home with a steaming mug of herbal tea. The tea had cooled by the time she finished explaining everything that had happened.

"That's bizarre," Oliver said, shaking his head. "You're sure? I haven't heard of any Silver attacks in a while."

The easiest way for a Blue Blood to become Silver was to tap into their most basic instincts of greed and gluttony. Although they preferred to linger in the shadows, Silver Bloods weren't known to be subtle.

"I'm sure. It's hard to be wrong about this kind of thing."

"You're lucky you made it out alive."

Schuyler let out a breath of agreement, eyebrows raised.

"What sort of Silver Blood uses two daggers anyway?" he asked.

That was a good question, actually. Usually Silver Bloods were animalistic, relying on their teeth and raw strength to kill. She didn't know of any Silver Blood who used weapons.

An unsettling thought wedged its way into her mind, though: Maybe this world's Croatan were unlike anything she'd seen before. Maybe the creatures were . . . evolving.

"What were you doing out so late?" Oliver asked.

Schuyler chewed on the inside of her cheek. She still wasn't sure if Oliver could handle her explanation that she had memories from another world just yet. It was still too big, even for her to fully grasp. "Vampire stuff," she said.

Oliver furrowed his brow a little. "You're really worrying me lately. You were acting so strangely yesterday. Is something wrong?"

"You don't have to worry about me," Schuyler said. "Although . . . I could use your help."

"Anything."

"Do you still work at the Repository of History?"

"Yeah, but I haven't been there in a while. Since the pandemic, everything's closed, even that. It's like this all over the world, not just New York City."

A thrill rushed through Schuyler's body. The Repository of History was the headquarters for all Blue Blood record keeping. For hundreds of years, since the first vampires came to America, the Repository had contained the largest archive of their immortal history. Red Bloods who knew the vampire legacy, especially Conduits like Oliver's family, cared for the archives. It was a part of a Conduit's duty to help Blue Bloods. Maintaining the collection of vampire knowledge across the centuries was key to their continued survival. Oliver had been known to solve a mystery beneath the pages of a tome as thick as a brick.

"Do you think you could find some records for me?" she asked, barely able to contain her excitement.

"Being a junior bookkeeper doesn't exactly make me essential personnel, but . . . I could try! What are you looking for?"

"Anything by Lawrence Van Alen."

"I'm not sure who that is. Never heard of him before."

"You're sure? He used a bunch of aliases throughout history, through every reincarnation." Schuyler listed off all the names of his past lives. "Ludivivo Arosto, John Carver . . . you know, Metatron."

Oliver's face remained unchanged. "Sorry." He shrugged. "I stack the shelves, so I see the same names over and over, but I don't know who you're talking about."

Oh, right. She'd forgotten. Allegra didn't exist here, so it stood to reason that Cordelia and Lawrence wouldn't either. The Van Alen legacy was gone. As far as Schuyler could tell, Charles Force didn't exist here. What else was she going to get wrong?

As if on cue, Schuyler's stomach growled with hunger. Apparently the craving for human blood hadn't changed. She put her fist to her belly to quiet it, but nothing got past Oliver.

"When was the last time you fed?" he asked, concern etched all over his face.

Schuyler couldn't answer, her stomach was cramping so hard. The last time would have been before waking up in the street, but she'd been so caught up in everything since then that she'd forgotten to eat.

Oliver tipped his head boyishly, unconsciously exposing his neck to her. "I'm ready, if you need to."

"No," she said, wincing through the hunger pangs. They ebbed away, but the saliva still sat heavy on the back of her tongue. In this world, she hadn't performed the Sacred Kiss with Oliver yet. She wanted to keep it that way.

But she was so hungry.

Schuyler's eyes dropped to his throat, and her fangs started to emerge. Memories of the other world came to her: Oliver volunteering to become her Familiar so she wouldn't fall into a coma after refusing to drink from someone she didn't know, the taste of his skin and blood, the rush of being so close to him mentally, physically, spiritually.

But performing the *Caerimonia Osculor* with Oliver had been a mistake. The Sacred Kiss between a vampire and their Familiar was like walking a tightrope of risk. Becoming a Familiar created an unbreakable bond that was both a blessing and a curse: a blessing because Oliver had saved her life, and a curse because, as was the case with all Familiars, feeding from him drained years from his life. She couldn't do it to him again. He didn't deserve it. While the marks in his neck would close quickly, drinking his blood would leave a different, more permanent kind of scar behind.

Schuyler made her fangs retract and took a breath. "I can manage."

"Are you sure? I'm not scared."

"That's not it. I . . . I want to wait."

"I'll bring you some more blood pouches from the donation center. Guess I haven't been a very good Conduit if you've run out already."

"Oh, Ollie . . ." Schuyler said. "You're doing just fine, I promise. Things have been a little crazy lately, but it's not your fault."

"It'll take me some time to get you more, but if you ever change your mind about using me, you know where to find me."

Schuyler nodded, but the hunger had passed. For now, at least. Guilt wrapped a cold hand around her belly. She reached across the table and twined her fingers through Oliver's, and squeezed his hand. It was more than she could ever say at that moment.

Parts of her double memories overlapped in comforting ways. Her friendship with Oliver was a constant that she could clutch on to. The fact that he didn't know Lawrence, though, troubled her. Was Lawrence still alive in this world? She was eager to get some answers.

As if reading her mind, Oliver said brightly, "In the meantime, what say we go to the Repository and see if we can't track down this

Lawrence bloke together. You, me, a million or so books to comb through. How about tomorrow? We can meet after dark."

"I thought you said the Repository was closed."

"It is, but I bet no one would notice us. I admit, it'll be nice to be there again after so long. Who would have thought I would miss shelving books all day?"

Schuyler smiled. "That is an excellent idea. I can't wait."

Oliver's smile back made everything a little better.

SEVEN

SCHUYLER

*V*irtual school the next morning was almost unbearable. Schuyler needed to get some answers. Her meeting with Oliver that night at the Repository couldn't come soon enough. She kept checking the time, willing it to go faster. It was hard sitting still in her bedroom with only her stuffed animals for company.

When she went to Duchesne with other vampires, she had seen firsthand just how naturally school came to them.

Sitting in history class as an immortal soul reborn into a human body seemed really boring, even more so when it was online. For a reincarnated vampire with immortal memories, history was old news. Been there, seen that. And if a history book got it wrong, how infuriating would it be to convince people to correct it?

Schuyler didn't have that luxury. A half vampire like her wasn't reborn again and again over centuries. She had to learn history the old-fashioned way: all on her own. Granted, she'd gone through high school once, in another world, so the second time shouldn't be so bad.

She never used to mind. She actually liked history, even before she knew her true lineage. Humanity peeked its head out of the history books every once in a while, reminding Schuyler that people had been just that—people—forever. Thinking about it helped her feel like great figures in history had insecurities, hobbies, even a sense of humor. They seemed a little less intimidating after that.

History also, Schuyler believed, rarely changed.

That is, until European History, when their teacher, Dr. Perkins, began her lecture on Napoleon's rise to power. "And can anyone tell me what happened at the Battle of Eylau?"

The class fell silent.

"Yes, Schuyler?"

Schuyler leaned into her computer's microphone. Piece of cake—Napoleon was one of her favorite historical figures. He was a genuinely terrible person, but Schuyler had always found his story absolutely fascinating. "Napoleon overestimated his army's capabilities and underestimated his enemy's. For the first time in his career, Russian imperial forces successfully held him off for fourteen hours of continuous battle during a snowstorm, incurring massive losses on both sides, and it effectively broke Napoleon's winning streak. Napoleon didn't win, but he didn't lose either. Which in his book was a loss."

There was a pause and then her classmates erupted into laughter, all the tiny windows on her screen filled with mocking faces. Schuyler didn't know why. Voices cut in under the noise:

"Oh my God, is she drunk?"

"Girl, what are you talking about?"

"So cringe . . ."

Naturally, Schuyler's cheeks got hot. She didn't know what was going on.

"Everyone, please," Dr. Perkins said. "Quiet down. Enough of that. I'm sorry, Schuyler, but that's incorrect. Napoleon famously died at the Battle of Eylau. The Russian Imperial Army decimated his troops after Napoleon froze to death during the snowstorm. You must be confused. Napoleon's fall at Eylau marked the end of the French Imperial Age."

Schuyler's mouth opened and closed like a fish. She didn't know what to say. She knew she was right; she *had* to be right. The Battle of Eylau was one of Napoleon's most famous encounters with the Russians. Even people with only a passing knowledge of Napoleon knew about the famous snowstorm and how it nearly killed him. The Napoleonic Wars would continue for eight more years after it! She'd read about it so many times, she was sure of it!

But she blinked and she remembered that, yes, what Dr. Perkins had said was also true. Napoleon had died at Eylau; Napoleon had lived at Eylau.

Layers of reality lined up, and Schuyler knew that both events, Napoleon's defeat and death and his ability to keep on fighting, were somehow correct. The Schuyler from her previous life and the Schuyler she was here remembered both facts simultaneously. But she couldn't explain that anomaly, not in class.

Dr. Perkins continued with her lecture, but Schuyler felt like crawling into a hole. She was sure she would die of embarrassment. She'd never been laughed at in a class before. Her stomach churned like she was about to puke, and she wanted to cry, but she was too shocked to do anything else but slump low into bed, pretending she didn't exist.

She didn't speak another word in any other class for the rest of the day.

Schuyler usually didn't make a habit of sneaking out of the house, but extenuating circumstances called for some harmless teenage rebellion. Besides, if her parents found out that she was sneaking out to go to a *library* of all places, she doubted they would be too mad.

If everything went well, she'd find Lawrence's records, which hopefully could give her some insight into her memory issues. The man was meticulous in his record keeping, and the chances that the same thing, this living in two worlds, had happened to another vampire in history were slim but there. But now she had reason to believe that history was not the same in this world. First Napoleon and Eylau; what else was drastically different in this reality?

At least she still had Oliver. Seeing him was one of the things she looked forward to.

The Repository was a massive underground library hidden away beneath her favorite nightclub, the Bank, at the intersection of Essex and Houston, a block away from the famous Katz's Deli on the Lower East Side. The night was cold. Summer seemed to be having trouble deciding whether or not it wanted to leave just yet, so the waning hours of a September afternoon in New York City could either be unbearably hot and muggy or quite cool and dry, depending on the season's mood. Tonight it was firmly in the "quite cool" camp, almost as if fall had come early, so Schuyler had slipped on a black shawl, a large coat, and a chunky dark red knitted scarf. She'd almost left the apartment without grabbing her matching black face mask. Wearing one still wasn't a habit.

Oliver was already waiting for her outside Katz's Deli, bouncing on the balls of his feet and rubbing his hands together to stay warm. He was wearing a large olive-green parka over a mustard-yellow hoodie and jeans, complete with a black face mask like hers. When he saw her coming, he waved. Schuyler waved back but distractedly. She'd noticed that the famous Katz's Deli sat shuttered and closed.

"That's depressing," she said, gesturing to the boarded-up windows.

She had so many memories from another world, of hitting up Katz's after hours at the club with Oliver, loitering on the brick wall, sharing a couple of perfectly greasy latkes, laughing about nothing at all, not wanting to go home just yet because that would mean the night was over. Normally the place would be a hot spot for tourists standing in hour-long lines at all times of day. But just like her memories, Katz's had faded. This world was still so alien to Schuyler in so many ways. She wasn't sure she would ever totally get used to it.

As if reading her mind, Oliver said, "Pretty soon all this will be back the way it's supposed to be." He too looked at Katz's locked front door, the skin around his eyes tight.

"What makes you say that?"

Oliver turned to her. "You haven't heard? The treatments will start happening soon. Mayor Duncan approved the mandate today. They've opened special clinics all over the city for people to visit next week."

"That's great!" Schuyler said. She remembered reading about the clinics in the newspaper. The terrible pandemic had ruined so many lives. It was hard to believe such a thing could even be possible in the modern era.

"Yeah. It's huge," Oliver said, his gaze firmly on his shoes. "I can't wait." The way he said it, he sounded a little sad. A thickness had settled in his voice.

She looped her arm through his and stood with him for a moment. She knew he missed his parents terribly, and she understood how that felt, more than he would understand. Hopefully he would see his parents soon. She wanted to cheer him up somehow.

"Before you know it, we'll be able to do all the things we used to," Schuyler said.

Oliver smiled under his mask. "Remember all those summer days we used to spend at the Met? Running around the exhibits and trying to mimic the poses of the sculptures?"

Schuyler grinned too. "Ha! Yeah," she said. "Your Sphinx of Hatshepsut impression was uncanny. That *is* a thing, right? The Sphinx?"

Oliver glanced at her, amused. "Yeah, of course!"

Schuyler sighed, relieved. She couldn't be sure of anything anymore. "Come on," she said, tugging on his arm, tipping his head toward the club. "Let's get going."

They walked down the empty street together. As expected, the Bank too was dark and quiet, eerie for a nightclub. However, the nightclub next to it was thrumming with life.

Block 122 was one of the most exclusive nightclubs in the city. It boasted some of the most high-profile DJs performing every night.

If you had to ask how to get in, clearly you weren't going to get in.

Schuyler furrowed her brow. Apparently the rich and bored didn't care about social distancing or curfews. They didn't even try to hide the fact that the club was clearly packed. A couple of club goers wearing miniskirts despite the chill leaned on the wall by the entrance, smoking and glaring at Oliver and Schuyler as they headed for the door. Schuyler half expected to see Mimi Force among them. Mimi had been one of the club's most frequent patrons, some of her antics inside even making the papers.

Schuyler's heart felt as heavy as lead as she wondered if Mimi was okay in the other world. They used to hate each other, mostly because Mimi was jealous that her brother, Jack, had started dating Schuyler, but after Schuyler had saved her from a false arrest and blood trial, they came to a begrudging truce. Schuyler wondered how she would be dealing with Jack's death all alone in the other world. . . .

Just before she and Oliver passed Block 122's entrance, the door burst open, making them both stop in their tracks to keep from getting smacked right in the face.

A flash of golden-blond hair rushed in front of them, and time slowed.

Schuyler stood rooted to the ground.

Her heart leaped as she stared at the figure walking by.

It was Jack Force, back from the dead.

EIGHT

SCHUYLER

 ither Jack Force was alive or Schuyler was dreaming. And if
she was dreaming, she never wanted to wake up.

She couldn't believe it.

She had watched him die. But here he was, before her very eyes,
standing on the curbside and adjusting the cuffs on his jacket, his
back to Schuyler and Oliver. When he looked down the street, she
saw the familiar angle of his jaw, the sharp slope of his nose, the
perfect shape of his cheekbones.

Schuyler didn't realize she was squeezing Oliver's arm, even
after he made a noise of discomfort. She was pretty sure he was the
only thing keeping her upright.

Alive.

Jack was alive!

By some miracle, the universe had returned him to this world,
unharmed. The memory of his death was so fresh, so real, that
it could hardly be possible. She fought tears that burned her eyes
as her memory dragged her back to that moment: the gleam of a
sword, the distant sound of her scream as if it came from someone
else's throat, and Jack's eyes locked on hers when he faded.

She struggled to breathe, but only for a moment. He was there. *Her* Jack.

If he noticed her, he didn't show it. There were those bright, dazzling green eyes she knew so well, shining like a field in summer. His eyebrows were pinched with displeasure, though. Whatever he was thinking about seemed to be troubling him. He frowned and pulled out his phone from his coat pocket.

"What's going on?" Oliver asked, glancing back and forth between them.

"Jack," Schuyler whispered, unable to take her eyes from the boy she'd lost.

He looked as gorgeous as ever, in a blue Dior jacket, his blond hair brushed back from his forehead casually as if he had just come from the beach. He also looked sixteen years old again.

On autopilot, Schuyler rushed forward. A giddy feeling made her seem slightly crazed to herself, but she couldn't slow down. It was like she had just woken up from a nightmare, the adrenaline coursing as strong as a riptide.

"Jack!" she said, louder this time, coming around to face him.

At first he didn't react to hearing his name, but then he looked up from his phone.

She smiled through tears and said, "You should be dead." It was meant to be a joke. Those had been the first words she'd ever said to him all those years ago, in this exact spot, back when they were still strangers.

Before, he'd been the elusive golden boy at Duchesne, unattainable and aloof. It was right here, outside the club, that she had seen him get hit by a cab, but he had walked away unscathed. All of that felt like a lifetime ago now.

His green eyes looked her up and down, and then a small smirk spread on his face. "I think you've got the wrong twin, sweetheart."

It took a moment for Schuyler to process what he meant.

The entrance to Block 122 opened again, and her gaze drifted over his shoulder to another person coming out of the club.

Schuyler felt like she'd been seeing double for days, but now she really was. It should have been obvious. From the blond hair to the defined jaw to the gorgeous emerald eyes, everything was the same. Identical faces.

And then it clicked. She had been so focused on the impossible, she hadn't noticed the little details that didn't line up.

This wasn't Jack.

That was.

The real Jack Force.

Jack noticed what was going on and came over, curiosity twisting his eyebrows. Unlike his twin, who was dressed far more appropriately for a night at the club, he wore his usual Barbour tweed coat over a white oxford button-down and Ted Baker chinos. He looked just as he did when they first met at Duchesne: tall and athletic as always.

"Are you stalking my brother or something?" Not-Jack said, still smirking at Schuyler.

"Chill, Max, don't be rude," Jack said, coming to a stop next to him.

Max—that was his name—Jack's twin—ignored him and said

directly to Schuyler, "You know there's Strega fashion, and then there's just wearing rags, right?" His eyes drifted down to her outfit. Schuyler recognized the tone all too well, the snark unmistakably belonging to Jack's twin sister, Mimi, a blond hurricane made of pure spite. But, of course, he wasn't Mimi.

As they stood next to each other, the twins' similarities were uncanny. But the biggest, most apparent difference she could see was that Jack's eyes were softer, kinder. Max's had a sharpness, like a steel blade, ready to cut. The longer she looked, the more she noticed how wrong she had been all along. How could she have missed it before?

She took a faltering step backward, knees locked. "Who are you?" she asked. Her voice sounded so small. Everything was coming at her from all different sides, buffeting her like a whirlwind. Nothing made sense.

Jack was alive.

There were two of him.

And one of them wasn't nice.

There was no pity in Max's eyes. "Damn, what are you on?"

She ignored him. She turned to the other one. The one with the kind eyes. "Jack," Schuyler choked. "It's me."

Max rolled his eyes and looked at his phone again.

"Jack, it's me. It's Schuyler," she said. *It's me.* What else should she say? After everything they'd been through together. After everything they'd survived.

But saying her name didn't evoke any reaction. Jack's eyes searched hers. "Oh," he said. "Schuyler . . . from Duchesne, right?"

Max laughed coldly and shook his head dismissively. "You don't have to talk to her, Jack. Where's the stupid car?"

Schuyler couldn't take her eyes off Jack.

All she wanted to do was crash into him, hold him close, and tell him it was all going to be okay. But something held her back. Maybe it was the cautious smile on Jack's face, like he wasn't sure how to reply, or maybe it was the way he looked at her without really seeing her for who she was, for all they had been to each other.

This had to be the universe's idea of a cruel joke. Here was Jack, the love of a thousand lifetimes, back from the dead, and he'd forgotten her? Just like that?

"Take a hint and keep walking," Max said, waving his hand dismissively at her, like she was a fly.

A crowd had started to gather at the entrance to Block 122, watching the scene unfold. They had an audience.

"Don't you remember?" she asked Jack.

The way he looked at her then, the facts hit her straight in the heart. He didn't remember her, not like she remembered him.

She took another step back, slipping off the curb but not losing her balance. Jack's eyes widened. She didn't know why, not until headlights lit her up. Jack lashed out, grabbed her wrist, and yanked her back onto the sidewalk just as a red Range Rover screeched to a stop right in front of them. Max's car had arrived.

The crowd in front of Block 122 gasped and cried out, but she was safe.

If Jack hadn't acted when he did, the driver would have hit her straight on. She could have moved out of the way on her own as a vampire, but . . . did he know that?

He let go of her hand too soon as Max—hardly reacting to the near accident—opened the rear door to the SUV and climbed in.

"Come on, Jack."

Jack gave Schuyler a lingering look and a slight nod before he followed his twin into the car. He shut the door, and Schuyler watched, shocked, as the love of her life drove away.

"Jack!" she yelled, way too late. It was no use. He was gone.

Oliver appeared at her side, breathless. "Are you okay?" he asked.

No, Schuyler was not okay. Not in a million years. She turned and marched down the sidewalk.

Oliver called after her, "What about the you-know-what?"

With an apologetic wave, Schuyler didn't stop walking. "I can't do this right now. I'll talk to you tomorrow."

She didn't have to turn around to know the look of disappointment on Oliver's face.

As she walked, she shivered, but not only from the cold, and she hugged herself. Why didn't Jack recognize her? Why didn't he know who she was?

And what if he would never love her the way he had?

What if they would never get that back?

What then?

Schuyler didn't walk home. In fact, she wasn't paying attention to where her feet were taking her at all until she looked up and realized that she was near the Brooklyn Bridge. The bridge, unlike the rest of the city, was illuminated against the dark night sky, making the suspension towers stand out like beacons in the night.

She was no longer worried about the curfew. She wasn't worried about anyone bothering her out here. Perks of being a vampire.

More than anything, she just wanted to be left alone. She walked along the bridge and stopped to lean on the railing, taking in the view of Lower Manhattan. The wind sliced all around her, but she didn't care. Her gaze drifted to the dark water below as she began to feel sorry for herself.

Living with double memories was about as fun as taking a pickax to your frontal lobe.

Ever since that day she'd woken up in the street, Schuyler wasn't sure about what was real and what was not. Her memories kept vacillating, sometimes changing so quickly, she felt like she was arguing with herself.

Did I ever live on the Upper West Side? Yes, with Cordelia. No, I've always lived in SoHo. With Mom and Dad. Right, with Mom named Allegra! Aurora, a jazz singer. I need to take Beauty for a walk! I've always wanted a dog, but my cat, Belle, died last year. But I've never had a cat. Why can't I find my Chucks? I don't wear Chucks. Where's the seashell bracelet Jack gave me in Egypt? I've never been to Egypt. . . . Am I kidding?

It made Schuyler want to tear her hair out.

She'd had a lifetime of memories in this world too. She'd found dozens of shoe boxes full of photographs that proved she had lived a life here with her mother and father. There were family vacations, such as last year's summer-long road trip across the country along Route 66, and smaller moments: her waving to them in the audience at a school play when Schuyler had the role of Tree #2 in *Little Red Riding Hood,* learning to ride her bike down the street with her dad assuring her that he was still holding on to the seat even though he had already let her go, curling up on the couch with her mom Aurora brushing her fingers through Schuyler's hair as they watched trashy reality TV.

But she also remembered her life with Allegra: falling asleep in a stiff chair next to her hospital bed and staring at an old photograph of Stephen near a vase full of dying roses.

Two versions of her memories bundled into one brain made it feel too full, like her head needed to be wrung out and hung out to dry.

Jack existed in both of these realities too, shimmering versions of himself overlapping in her mind's eye. Golden hair, emerald eyes, killer smile. All the same, except in the ways that mattered.

Seeing Jack in the flesh had been like jump-starting a car engine—memories had unlocked, like somewhere deep down she had been protecting herself from the inevitable shock of it all. Now she had memories of Jack in this world, knew that he was the captain of the lacrosse team, that he spent his lunch periods in the library, and that he always got the lead in the school plays.

And then she'd blink and remember that in this world they hadn't even known each other. They'd never even spoken. Here he was the most popular boy in school, and she was the weirdo with only one friend at Duchesne. Just like in her old world, before she and Jack had met.

She wished she could talk to him.

That was what she missed the most, simply talking with him, lying in bed late into the early morning, when all she could see of him was the curve of his cheekbones in the darkness, his voice growing soft and airy as sleep took hold of him. To know if he was still awake, she'd whisper "I love you" and smile when his response was a deep sigh, one reserved only for dreamers.

To have him back in her arms would be everything.

What else was she supposed to do? Give up? She had to know if he remembered dying, if he remembered fighting Lucifer, if he remembered *anything*. If he didn't, it'd be back to the way things were before.

He'd still have everything, and she would be . . . Schuyler.

In another world, they had been together for years, going up against every power that tried to break them apart. They'd been happy.

Schuyler had imagined their whole lives stretched out before them, spanning decades of a future together, traveling the world before settling down and making a home someplace safe and secure, a paradise of their own creation on earth. Except she'd killed Lucifer and let Jack die.

If she had been given the chance to return to her old life, she wasn't sure she would take it. In her old world, Jack was dead. When she closed her eyes, she saw it happen all over again, reliving the same brutal shock of dread she'd felt when the demon cut him down.

It had happened then. It couldn't be undone.

But in this world, Jack wasn't dead—*Jack wasn't dead!* And that alone had to be enough. He had a second chance. *They* had a second chance. There could still be a happily-ever-after. Hope was enough. Wasn't it?

So, was this paradise?

Was this the heaven she had won them?

Was it some kind of afterlife?

She wished there were a half-vampire self-help book that could give her some guidance:

What to Expect When You're Expecting to Suck Blood
The Seven Habits of Highly Effective Vampires
How to Win Back Your Not-Dead True Love and Influence People

She slumped over her arms on the railing and sighed.

Her phone buzzed with a new text in her pocket. She couldn't imagine who might text her other than Oliver. She expected to see a message from him asking if she was okay, but instead she saw a message from a blocked number.

Meet me @ ROH

- VV

Schuyler stared at the phone for so long, the screen went dark.

ROH. The Repository of History, obviously.

But VV—what did that mean? She twisted her lips as she racked her brain, but she didn't know anyone whose name started with the letter *V*. Then she realized: It wasn't a name.

Veritas Venator. An immortal truth seeker. One of the elite secret vampire force.

Someone from her old world had come knocking.

NINE

SCHUYLER

ithout delay, she went straight back to the Bank. Just as before, the nightclub that hid the Repository was dark and locked up, and Schuyler wondered if she had been wise in coming here. It was so late that even Block 122 was closed for the night. No sign of any drunk wanderers looking for the next party, no sign of Oliver or anyone at all.

For all she knew, the Repository could have easily been moved. It had happened before in times of crisis. But when she tried to message the mysterious sender for more information, no response came. The text was the only thing she had to start out with.

The heavy steel front door to the Bank was locked, so Schuyler jumped, higher than was humanly possible, to the second-floor balcony. There she managed to ram open the flimsy glass door and duck inside.

She blinked a couple of times and her eyes adjusted to the low light. Dust permeated the air in the club, which always had a thickness that reminded her of leather booths, sticky floors, and stale beer. The building was eerily quiet as she made her way downstairs, past the empty stage, the bathrooms, and toward the basement, where the owners kept kegs of local brews and bottles of liquor, all while she listened for any sound of movement besides the soft tread of her sneakers. But nothing seemed amiss. She walked through the secret door hiding in the wall and took the narrow stone spiral staircase that wound down, several floors deep into the underbelly of Manhattan.

As she went, she mentally kicked herself. This was a bad idea. What was she thinking, coming here alone? She had gotten so caught up in the moment, still stinging from the encounter with Jack and that impostor Max, foolishly, and didn't stop to consider that maybe the person who had sent the message could be a Silver Blood luring its prey. Her desperation for answers had blinded her.

But it was too late to go back now. By the time she had concluded that she was an absolute moron, she had already reached the bottom of the stairs and stood before the door to the Repository.

Schuyler reached into her pocket, withdrew her phone, and turned on the flashlight.

The door was made of gold, ebony, and platinum. It stood ten feet tall and was wide enough for an SUV to drive through with room to spare. She traced her hand over the fretwork and read the Sacred Language inscribed above: INGREDIOR PERCIPIO ANIMUS. *Enter to gain knowledge.*

Schuyler let out a breathy laugh. The Latin word *animus* was often translated as "mind" but could also mean "memory." *Enter to gain memory.*

Though the light of her phone was too weak to reach the very edges of the atrium, Schuyler was able to see what she was looking for. Clearly, in the dusty floor leading to and from the Repository, there were footprints. Someone had been here, and recently.

The air shifted around her, the atmosphere changing ever so slightly, feeling full.

Schuyler spun around. A cloaked figure stood behind her. Another appeared on her left, and then another on her right, melting out of the dark. They had been hiding, waiting. She should have listened to her instincts. It was a trap.

A flash of something—a blade—and Schuyler's phone fell out of her hand as she ducked and dodged, the *shhhhrink!* of steel slicing through the air, just barely missing the fabric of her coat. Schuyler wheeled and danced away from blades as they came out from the darkness, stabbing and slicing with laserlike speed, but she moved quickly, and each attack missed. To the human eye, she would have been nothing more than a blur. But these attackers weren't human.

The stairs were open. She ran for them. But a fourth figure leaped down from above and landed in front of her, blocking her exit.

Before they could raise their weapon, though, Schuyler lashed out, grabbed her attacker by the wrist, and twisted. Their blade fell from their fingers and Schuyler caught it in midair. She spun it around and aimed the blade at their chest, but she stopped when she felt another blade press into her side. They had produced a second weapon from their cloak.

Double blades . . .

The two of them stood, frozen for a moment, at a standoff.

She panted, heart racing, ready to kill, and stared into the hooded figure's shadowy face. This was the one who had followed her the other night.

Slowly, the knife at her side pulled away and the shadow figure raised their hands to surrender. "I yield to the blood of Gabrielle. I'm sorry. I had to make sure you were who you were. I'd know those moves anywhere, any world." The hood dropped and Schuyler finally saw her attacker.

"Kingsley!"

Kingsley Martin—darkly handsome, chiseled, and dangerous—was a trusted Venator and Silver Blood turned good. In a way, a Silver Blood really had been waiting in the shadows.

Was he still the same Kingsley she remembered, though?

Kingsley cleared his throat expectantly and glanced down at the blade she still held to his chest. She was so relieved to see a familiar face that she almost forgot that she had been going to kill him. She gave his dagger back to him apologetically, and he waved to his three compatriots. They returned to their posts, melting back into the shadows.

"Good to see you too, Schuyler," he said with his usual smirk. "I see you got my message."

TEN

SCHUYLER

When Kingsley led Schuyler through the door and into the Repository, she was immediately struck by the familiar scent of chalk and aged parchment. The library air hummed with history. Despite being underground, the Repository was well lit and cozy. Aubusson rugs warmed the stone floor, and banker's lamps emitted a comforting glow, revealing thousands of shelves of books from all across the world, some as old as time itself, shelves that stretched high up into the rafters seventy-five feet tall.

"She's here!" Kingsley called to another hooded figure standing in a nearby alcove. "Tell the others to redraw the sigils. Protect the Repository. We can't let them know where we are."

The figure dashed away, and Kingsley addressed Schuyler briefly over his shoulder as he walked. "Welcome to our humble abode. We've managed to keep a low profile by ramping up security. On your account, we had to make a few changes. All that's missing is a red carpet."

"Who's 'we'?" she asked.

"Let's play one hundred questions over drinks, shall we?"

She had to jog to keep up with his pace. "You owe me a new

phone, the least you could do is answer my questions," she said, brandishing the shattered screen. It had broken during the scuffle.

"Sorry about that," he said. "Just be thankful it wasn't your skull."

"Good luck explaining that to my parents. Why did you chase me the other night?"

"I thought you were one of *them*."

"I thought *you* were one of them!" Though she wasn't quite sure who "them" was. "Why did you stop anyway?"

"You could have been leading me into a trap!" he retorted.

"Well, I thought you were going to eat me," she huffed.

"I think we're even, then. Come, I'll explain."

They weaved through the aisles, taking a right, right, left, right, left so many times that Schuyler lost track and got disoriented. It was said that the library housed ten million books. Schuyler wouldn't have been surprised if there were even more. A person could get lost in the maze looking for a title if they didn't know where to go. Thankfully, Kingsley knew exactly where he was going.

The reverential silence of the Repository, as quiet as a cathedral, always made Schuyler think of wizened old monks hunched over their illuminated manuscripts.

However, now in this world, the Repository was mostly abandoned. The books remained, but Red Blood Conduit staff were unusually absent. Even at this hour, humans should be walking the aisles, always on duty, like guards at Buckingham Palace. In their place were half a dozen or so vampires. Schuyler spotted the telltale *illuminata* that made their skin glow in low light, akin to the moon shining on a recent snowfall. A handful of them watched her warily from desks scattered about the library or from lookouts on the bridges that stretched between catwalks high above. They kept a curious eye on her as she followed Kingsley deeper into the great hall. She didn't recognize anyone.

"I heard the Repository was closed," Schuyler said. "Because of the pandemic."

"As far as anyone else is concerned, it's still closed. It's for the best, believe me."

Before she could ask any more questions, Kingsley brought her to a break in the maze. It opened up into a makeshift classroom with rows of desks facing a chalkboard on wheels. The chalkboard was dirty, having been erased and reused so many times that it had a pale smear of spent chalk under hastily written text, timelines, maps, and strange symbols that Schuyler didn't recognize.

"Welcome to Parallel Universes 101," Kingsley said, gesturing.

He unclipped his cloak and tossed it onto a front-row desk to reveal he was wearing a black oxford shirt, the sleeves rolled halfway up his forearms, ripped jeans, and Doc Marten boots. For a vampire cop, he certainly never dressed like one, even in her old memories. He always looked seventeen. Because Kingsley was a Silver Blood, he was enmortal, unable to go through the regular cycle of Blue Blood reincarnation, and never grew old. He was the closest thing to a Hollywood vampire that you could find.

They had first met when he posed as a high school student at Duchesne in order to investigate a series of Blue Blood murders. Funnily enough, at the time Schuyler had been one of his prime suspects. Thankfully the real culprit had been caught, and Kingsley remained an ally ever since.

He looked much the same as he did in Schuyler's other world—long, dark hair, intense black eyes when not in vampire mode, punctuated with a roguish grin. *Handsome* was too clean a word. He was one of the most skillful Venators the Coven had ever known. Cocky yet charming, he proved that Silver Bloods could be reformed, even though they were still cursed. Like all Croatan, he could change his silver eyes at will, which was what made vampires like him so dangerous. By the time a person saw those eyes up close, it would already be too late.

Kingsley had fought alongside Schuyler and Jack against Lucifer in the final battle; he had even killed Lucifer's brother Leviathan himself, and she considered him a dear friend.

Kingsley pulled at a drawer beneath one of the desks and produced some amber liquid in a crystal decanter and two whiskey glasses. He poured the whiskey into one glass, then glanced at Schuyler by way of offering her some, but she shook her head. He shrugged and set the decanter down.

"How is any of this possible?" she asked.

Kingsley pressed his lips together and gave her a withering look. "Schuyler, we're vampires. Do you really think this is so out of the realm of possibility?"

"Okay, but parallel universes are like something out of science fiction."

"Believe me, if I didn't know what I do, I'd be inclined to agree with you." Kingsley raised his glass to her and said "Cheers" before tipping his head back and downing the drink in one gulp. He cringed and hissed. "The whiskey in this world is terrible. I'll never get used to it."

"Wait." Schuyler held out her hand, as if pressing pause on the conversation. "You know about the other world? You . . . remember?"

"Bingo. I woke up here, same as you, but a year ago in this timeline."

"How did you know I'm remembering another world too?"

"Being a Venator has its perks," he said. "Always got an ear to the ground; it's instinct at this point. Good job disarming me back there, by the way. You should really consider becoming a Venator someday. Oh, wait, you *were* in our old world. Sorry, memories are faulty."

"Answer the question."

Kingsley conceded. "I saw the signs, the storm, felt it." Schuyler remembered distinctly. Those purple clouds. She'd thought it was lightning. Kingsley went on. "I sensed the energy rift and rushed to the Empire State Building, but I was already too late. You'd left by then. I waited around to see if anyone else would follow after you, mostly keeping watch for any shady folks looking for trouble. Of course, I didn't know it was you who had come back, not until I was outside Block 122."

Heat rushed to her cheeks. "You were there? You saw Jack?"

"I did." Kingsley looked grim. "That's how I knew to contact you."

"Tell me what you remember," she said. "I need to know everything. What's the last thing you remember from the other world?"

"Well, to sum it up: Lucifer was defeated, Jack died, the Blue Bloods' exile on earth was over. Blah blah blah, you know the story. And then *bam*, next thing I know, I'm lying facedown in an alley with the worst hangover in the world. At least, seeing as we vampires can't get hangovers, I can only guess that's what it felt like. I was seeing double for weeks."

"Double memories?"

Kingsley nodded. She wasn't going crazy after all! Someone else knew about the other world! She had to tamp down her excitement, but her heart was galloping like a horse at the Kentucky Derby. She meant to take it slow, ask one thing at a time, but the details spilled out of her like a waterfall.

"Why'd you call me here? Where is everyone? Where are the Conduits who take care of the Repository? What's going on?"

"Lucifer is back."

Three words. That was all it took for Schuyler to feel like the world had dropped out from underneath her. Her veins ran cold at the thought of it. "How?" she asked. "We killed Lucifer. I struck him down with Michael's sword."

Kingsley pointed a finger. "Ah, but *Schuyler Van Alen* killed Lucifer. *You* are Schuyler Cervantes-Chase."

Kingsley went to the chalkboard and flipped it around to the other side. He erased a corner and drew a circle.

"Imagine, if you will, this is one universe. Everything you've ever known, everyone you've ever loved, existed in this circle." He drew another circle, like a tight Venn diagram, but just barely out of alignment. "This is the universe you're in right now." He pointed to the space where the new circle didn't overlap with the first one. "Some things in this universe are the same because they share the same part of the circle, but this right here is a fissure in space-time—"

"You really need to get out more. . . ."

"I live in a library. What else am I supposed to do but read? Don't interrupt. Where was I? Right—anything that didn't happen in one universe happened in another, and vice versa. Like, a person flips a coin in one universe and get heads, another gets tails. You choose to eat cereal for breakfast in one, and scrambled eggs in another." He made a little X-mark in the spot that didn't overlap and wrote YOU ARE HERE like a map at the mall. "Lucifer is dead in one, and alive in another."

"All right, then why am I remembering things differently? How can I remember something that happened in another universe?"

"I haven't settled on a name for it yet, but for now I'm going to call it a Superimposition. Universes in layers."

"I've never taken you for a scientist."

"I'm full of surprises." Kingsley saluted with his empty glass.

"So I've somehow tapped into the memories of a Schuyler that existed in another reality. An alternate dimension. I'm not really Schuyler but just another version of her?"

"Exactly. A shared consciousness. Something must have happened and the universes collided. Just like you, I remember being Kingsley Martin *there*, but I also remember being Kingsley Martin *here*." He jabbed his chalk into the board for emphasis.

The pieces were starting to come together. "My dreams and memories! Two worlds overlapping!"

"Now you get it. *Superimposition*. You were always smarter than you looked."

"I'm still having a hard time distinguishing the two worlds."

"Give it some time. It's not every day a person's consciousness passes through dimensions. It'll get better, I promise."

"Could there be other universes? More of us?"

Kingsley shrugged. "For every single choice, every roll of the dice, every outcome, there could be a million alternatives. All possibilities exist. A multiverse."

"Like Max Force being born instead of Mimi."

"Ah yes, Max. He's a real peach, isn't he?" Kingsley said, laughing despite himself.

"You and Mimi used to date. . . . Do you and Max have the same bond?"

With a tip of his head, Kingsley said, "Let's save that conversation for another time."

Schuyler reeled for a moment. To think, in other universes another Schuyler could be an evil Silver Blood, or a boy, or dead, all because of a choice made in one universe branching out into more. It brought to mind a single snowflake setting off an avalanche.

"What happened to Schuyler from this world?"

"You *are* Schuyler from this world. You just happen to have a few extra memories stacked on top, like a layer cake. It's how you know me, even though in this world we've never actually met."

"How did this happen, then?"

"I've asked myself that question so many times, but I don't know. I'm a Venator, not a theoretical physicist. This is my best and only guess. I doubt we'll ever really know for sure. It would take a huge amount of energy to cause anything like this, nothing we've ever seen before. Maybe your anguish about Jack opened a rip in space-time. Or maybe it was you killing Lucifer to begin with. Who knows? Let's just call it magic." He poured a third drink and cringed as it went down.

"Then how am I a vampire in this universe? Both my parents here are human and alive."

Kingsley hummed. "Now, *that* is interesting. Are you one hundred percent sure there isn't something your parents aren't telling you?"

"They're human. They're . . . normal." Even as she said it, she wasn't convinced either.

How else could she be a vampire? Vampires were always born, never made. At least, that's how she thought it worked. Now she wasn't so sure. Could a half vampire come from nowhere?

She chewed on those thoughts for a moment, but something else bugged her. "So everything I had with Jack isn't real anymore. He doesn't know me at all."

Kingsley nodded solemnly. "It sucks, doesn't it? As far as I can tell, only you and I passed through the Superimposition. I'm not sure why. I remember dating Mimi in one world, and I was happy and she was safe, but here I . . ." He trailed off as his gaze went somewhere far away, then cleared his throat and focused on Schuyler. "It doesn't matter. She's gone. As far as I can tell, I can trace this universe's singularity back to one event. As we used to know it, Michael and Gabrielle defeated Lucifer and banished him from heaven. In this universe, Lucifer killed the archangels in the Battle of Heaven before man walked the earth."

Schuyler could hardly believe what she was hearing. "God's strongest soldiers against evil, defeated? The *archangels* are dead? And Lucifer won?"

"Ready for that drink now?"

Schuyler put her hand to her forehead, shocked. It explained so much. Bliss never had to be born, because Lucifer didn't have to hide from the archangels. And if Gabrielle was dead, Allegra wasn't Schuyler's mother. "Wait, the archangel Michael—Charles Force . . ."

"Finito," Kingsley finished for her. "The Uncorrupted are gone."

"Then who's leading the Coven? I haven't been able to find anyone."

Kingsley smirked, as if it amused him. "Lucifer is Regis."

Schuyler felt very small all of a sudden. Her plan to convince Charles about her predicament had been torn to shreds. "Why couldn't I have merged with the universe where the only thing different was what I had for breakfast?"

"Welcome to the club."

"So then who is he? Who is Lucifer?"

Kingsley hugged himself tightly. "He goes by the name Aldrich Belphegor Duncan."

ELEVEN

SCHUYLER

"Wait, Duncan is Lucifer? As in the *mayor of New York City*?" Schuyler felt like she'd been hit over the head. Her ears rang loudly.

"Evil and politics really go hand in hand, don't they?" Kingsley mused. "As if he wasn't evil enough, Duncan is also a descendant of the richest slave owners of the Confederacy. As far as I can tell, Lucifer is the key to all of this. At first, Lucifer was weak. He was badly wounded after the fight against Michael and Gabrielle. So his rise to power was slow, but precise, as he reincarnated his soul into new bodies. As he grew stronger, he divided us, divided our loyalties, and split the Coven into two factions. Either you were with Lucifer or you weren't. We weren't. And Duncan wiped us out." Kingsley began to pour another glass of whiskey. "He came after the Red Blood Conduits first. And then the Blue Blood dissenters. And then everyone else."

Schuyler stood up so quickly, the chair scraped loudly on the stone floor, and she paced back and forth.

She asked, "Does he know about me? Has he ever sent anyone after me?"

"You wouldn't be standing here right now if Lucifer knew you existed."

That statement wasn't as comforting as Kingsley probably intended. Her thoughts went to her family. The very real possibility that Stephen or Aurora could be captured by vampires and killed at any moment tied her stomach into knots. And Oliver! He could be in danger, even right this second. He knew so much about the Blue Bloods, but he was still human, and being a Conduit was like walking around with a target on his neck. There was so much at stake. Pun definitely intended.

A realization hit her like a truck, stopping her in her tracks. "The pandemic. It's not a disease. It's other vampires, isn't it?"

Kingsley nodded and drank. "The Blue Bloods who sided with Lucifer feed mercilessly, draining anyone they like. Blue Bloods have always had a deep-seated hunger, and Lucifer opened the buffet." Kingsley's eyes turned glassy, and it wasn't because of the booze.

"What's this treatment, then?"

"That's the bit that worries me the most. Something big is coming down the pipeline. Whatever it is, the treatment isn't what it seems."

"You don't know what yet?"

"I'm working on it."

"Why hasn't anyone been able to stop him? Where's the rest of the Coven?"

"You're looking at it." He spread his arms wide. A pair of vampires sitting in a set of high-backed armchairs glanced over.

Schuyler stared at him incredulously. "There's like . . . ten of you!"

"We're all that's left."

Schuyler's jaw dropped.

"We know things can be different. We know we can defeat him since we did it once before, and we're not giving up until the last of us is dead." He let out a halfhearted chuckle. "It's ironic, isn't it? That I, a cursed vampire, have become a vampire hunter. We do what we can to save humans, but . . . until Lucifer is defeated, it won't stop. Ever."

The reason he had called her here became clear. "You need me," she said.

"Frankly, we need all the help we can get. So having you, the blood of Gabrielle—the person who already triumphed over Lucifer—on our team isn't half bad."

Schuyler started pacing again while Kingsley watched her soberly. The fact that he kept saying she was the blood of Gabrielle felt like a fool's hope. If Gabrielle was dead, who was Aurora?

The thought of her parents getting hurt was too hard to handle. The people she loved most didn't deserve this. And innocent humans would get hurt if she did nothing. As Schuyler paced, she chewed on her thumbnail. One thing still ate away at her. "Just because I killed Lucifer once . . . what makes you so certain I could do it again? If he was strong enough to kill the archangels, how could I possibly stand a chance?" Her voice cracked, and she swallowed thickly.

Kingsley nodded. "I know it's a lot to ask of you, but what other choice do we have?"

That wasn't good enough. The odds were stacked against them. She felt like she was standing at the base of a mountain, and she needed to push a boulder up a sheer cliff face. Nothing made her feel smaller than that.

How much more would she have to sacrifice, only for it to mean nothing all over again?

Schuyler stopped pacing and held herself tightly. "Hypothetically, if I fail, what would happen?"

"It's the end of the world. The end of time. If Lucifer wins in one universe, he wins in them all," Kingsley said. "His victory negates everything we did before."

All of it. For nothing. Jack would have died for absolutely nothing. Rage flared hot inside her belly. No matter how many times she thought she won, evil would always find a way to return. She wanted to scream, to punch something, to throw her hands in the air and give up. But deep down she knew she couldn't, and that was the worst part.

"I can't . . ." she said weakly.

"You're the blood of Gabrielle," he said. "You're the last—"

She rounded on him, her anger boiling over. "Stop! If what you're saying is true, I'm not Gabrielle's daughter! I'm not special, there's no prophecy. I can't defeat Lucifer, I'm . . ." But then she stopped, midsentence, rendered immobile as her dream came back to her. She repeated Allegra's words softly. *"Wherever you are, you're still my daughter. You carry the light of Gabrielle. Perhaps the only thing that remains of my light in this world."*

Kingsley went to her side. "Gabrielle spoke to you?" he asked. A crease between his eyebrows deepened with concern.

Schuyler blinked away hot tears. Her voice barely rose above a whisper when she said, "I thought it was just a dream. I didn't know what she meant at the time."

Kingsley rested his hands on her shoulders and squeezed. His hands were rough, dry, and callused, but warm. Schuyler looked up to see him smiling, and his dark eyes danced in the light of the Repository.

"Schuyler," he said softly. "It's okay. Just breathe."

She did, and it came out like a shuddering gasp. She inhaled again, and it was easier this time. Kingsley squeezed her shoulders again, reassuringly.

"Gabrielle merged your consciousness for a reason," he said. "It's clear now. Somehow Gabrielle knew she would die in this world. She knew how to stop Lucifer and waited for the right moment to act. We of all people should know heaven works in mysterious ways."

Words were too complicated for Schuyler for a moment, but eventually she said, "I hope so. And I'm sorry, Kingsley. I shouldn't have snapped at you. I just feel so alone."

"I know how it is," he said. "But you're Gabrielle's daughter in every universe. You beat Lucifer once before. You're not going to fail. She believes in you. I believe in you. And you're not without backup. You've got me. We can do this."

"How many times am I going to have to kill him?" It was starting to feel futile.

The corner of Kingsley's mouth lifted. "I like to think of it as fighting for the light rather than fighting against the dark. It's easier to fight for something, rather than against it. You light a candle when you want to see; you don't try to put out the night."

A smile made its way onto Schuyler's lips. He was like an older brother, someone who saw her for who she was and who she could be, even though he could be so arrogant. "You're really cheesy sometimes, you know that?"

"You could say it's my only redeeming quality."

Schuyler smiled wider and shook her head. If what he was saying was true, she couldn't do nothing. "I guess, seeing as I'm the only remaining spirit of Gabrielle, it's up to me to put things right."

"Hell yeah, you are, and hell yeah, you will, rookie," Kingsley said with a wry grin.

Schuyler took a deep breath and pushed back her shoulders. *Be strong and brave.* "What do you know so far?"

Kingsley called for a Blue Blood nearby to bring out the map and files while Schuyler helped him put a couple of the desks together. Shortly after, the Blue Blood returned with a giant map of Manhattan. Red markings were already drawn all over it, with notes and dozens of giant Xs in almost every neighborhood on the island.

Kingsley put his finger on an X. "These here are all the locations of the blood clinics funded by Duncan's administration. The rebels and I have scouted out every building, watching carefully for who comes in or out. There's absurd amounts of Blue Blood activity at each one of these sites, swarming with Duncan's cronies. I think if we find out what they're doing in these clinics, we can put a stop to Lucifer's grand plan. They build them fast, though; construction is almost overnight, so it's like playing Whac-A-Mole trying to keep up."

The image of Kingsley—the fallen Angel of Vengeance and a super soldier—playing Whac-A-Mole on Jenkinson's Boardwalk in

New Jersey jammed into her head, and she would have laughed if the reality of Croatan activity didn't scare her so much.

"All you do is watch?" she asked.

A devious little smile played on Kingsley's lips. "Well, *mostly*. Occasionally, we do what we can to slow things down and add a little . . . *chaos* to the mix."

"Like what?"

"It makes sense you haven't heard. Duncan's got a pretty tight grip on the media these days. I think it's more fun if I show you in action anyway."

Schuyler wasn't sure what he meant, but she couldn't stop the little thrill of excitement that jumped through her body. "You sound like a vigilante."

"You can be one too. Meet me in south Harlem tomorrow."

Even though she felt vastly unqualified to sneak around like a spy in the movies, one thing was clear: Schuyler couldn't sit back and do nothing.

With a firm nod, she set her jaw. "Let's stop Lucifer."

TWELVE

SCHUYLER

aiting for Schuyler on the fire escape when she returned home was a small teal cooler. A note had been tucked into the handle. The first thing she noticed was a cartoon drawing of Oliver's face winking at her. His note read:

Special delivery for my BB
Love,
   Ollie

"*My BB,*" *huh* . . . Schuyler thought with a small, amused smile. Inside the cooler were twenty packages of red blood sealed in plastic, stacked in neat rows, each of them labeled with stickers of either A, B, AB, or O. It reminded Schuyler of the juice packs that teachers handed out at soccer practice when she was a child. Oliver had come through! She hadn't realized how hungry she was until now. Her appetite had evaporated when Kingsley told her that Lucifer was back. But when she saw the fresh red blood now, her stomach clenched in anticipation.

She slinked inside her room and silently slid her window

shut before she twisted the cap off one of the packets and drank. Although feeding from packets didn't have the same effect as drinking from a human's veins directly, it still satisfied her needs without taking on a Familiar or accidentally hurting someone. She sighed with relief when the blood flowed down her throat, better than a cool glass of lemonade on a hot summer day. She saved half the packet for later and slid the cooler under her bed to keep anyone from stumbling upon it.

She heard her parents moving quietly around in the living room, no doubt thinking that Schuyler might still be asleep. So she got dressed in her pajamas—simple plaid pants and one of Oliver's oversized hoodies that she'd "stolen" from his closet—and went to greet them.

Stephen was in the kitchen at the stove, cooking up a couple of eggs and toast, while Aurora stood in front of the television, watching the news with a furrowed brow and the remote pressed thoughtfully against her chin. She looked at Schuyler when she heard her come in.

"Good morning, mi cielo," she said, smiling softly. Then she frowned and pushed Schuyler's hair back from her forehead. "You look exhausted. Did you get any sleep?"

Schuyler wrapped her arms around her mother, taking in that familiar smell of Chanel, and lied. "I'm okay, Mom. Only nightmares." *Nightmares come to life, more like* . . . Now that she was going to help Kingsley, she wasn't sure when she would get a full night's sleep next.

Aurora kissed the top of her head and rested her cheek there while they stood together, watching the television.

The news anchor was in the middle of a telecom interview with mayoral candidate May Woldock. She was a thin white woman in her late sixties, with straight gray hair to her chin and a navy blazer, smiling politely at the camera.

"Now is the time for action," May Woldock said. "I fully support Mayor Duncan's plan to treat all citizens by the end of the month."

The news anchor went on. "I'm surprised, Ms. Woldock. You've been a staunch critic of Aldrich Duncan's policies for some time—"

"What policies we disagree on is not the issue here. We—all of us, as red-blooded Americans—need to consider the livelihood and safety of our family, friends, and neighbors during one of the most dangerous public health crises of our lifetime. That's why I fully support the view that everyone should visit the nearest clinic when it opens. We need unity, especially in these interesting times—"

Aurora turned off the television. She'd apparently heard enough. "Interesting times we live in, indeed." She sighed.

Schuyler's insides felt like sludge. If Duncan's schemes with the clinics went through as planned, though, no one would be safe. Whatever they were doing in them, it couldn't be good. Lucifer having total, unchecked control as leader of the Coven was a worst-case scenario, and it was already happening. People were going to go to these clinics and they were going to get hurt.

Schuyler worried her bottom lip with her teeth and asked her mom, "You and Dad are being careful, right?"

Aurora tipped her head lower to see Schuyler's face and rubbed her back affectionately. "Of course, sweetie. What's wrong?"

"The clinics. I want you to stay away from them, okay?"

Aurora scrunched her eyebrows together. "What makes you say that?"

"I've got a bad feeling about them, so please just stay home."

Aurora looked at Schuyler for a long moment. "What are you worried about?" she asked.

"I don't want you going out alone too, especially at night, okay? It's not safe. Double-check the locks at night and don't answer the door if you hear a knock but you're not expecting someone and—"

Schuyler stopped herself short. How was she supposed to explain that vampires like her didn't have to follow arbitrary rules that had been spread by Hollywood? Garlic had no effect, the sign of the cross was nothing more than a hand wave, and running water wasn't a protective barrier. If a Blue Blood, especially one under Lucifer's influence, wanted to get you, they would. The Vampire Code used to establish a balance between people and vampires existing together, but Lucifer didn't care about the Code. To him, humans weren't worth preserving.

The mere idea that Aurora, or Stephen, or Oliver could be the next victim sent a chill down Schuyler's spine. She couldn't bear to think about it. Worry ate away at her insides like acid.

Aurora's brown eyes swept back and forth, gazing into Schuyler's deeply, as if trying to read her. Schuyler searched for any sign of otherworldly origins, but all she saw was the warm, loving gaze of a concerned mother worried about her daughter. After a breath, Aurora tucked Schuyler's curls behind her ears and said, "If there's something you want to tell me, you know you can talk to me about anything."

Schuyler highly doubted that. She needed to keep her true

nature a secret. It was better for her parents to think she was just a normal girl, even if she truly wasn't. It would keep them safe, and that was what mattered. Schuyler finally had a family, and she couldn't lose them again.

"Breakfast time, my beautiful ladies!" Stephen called as he brought a steaming plate of scrambled eggs to the table. Stacks of toast and fresh fruit slices were already waiting for them. It was the perfect distraction. Schuyler pulled away from Aurora and took a seat at the table.

She ate in silence while her parents chatted, and when she was done, she excused herself. School was starting soon.

"Schuyler," her mother said gently before Schuyler could go. Her eyes lingered for a breath, as if she was working out what to say before she settled on "Have a good day."

Schuyler nodded and gave her best smile.

Schuyler poured the rest of the blood pouch into an opaque water bottle so it would be easier to hide the true contents and logged in to school for the day. As expected, she saw Oliver in his window. He mimed drinking, and she nodded appreciatively. He smiled and gave her a big thumbs-up, beaming wide. Seeing him again made her feel better, honestly. What would she do without him?

She had considered telling him about Kingsley and his hideout at the Repository, but that would bring up so many questions about her double memories and the other world, she wasn't sure how to say it just yet. She promised herself that she would tell him later.

For now, she would have to be satisfied pretending to be a normal girl having a normal day at school, and act as if what she was drinking out of a water bottle wasn't human blood. Normal things.

Class started as Dr. Perkins began her lecture with a chipper "Good morning, students!" and Schuyler settled into her bed, her laptop tucked onto her lap. As she took another swig of blood, another student window popped up on the screen.

"Nice of you to decide to join us today, Mr. Force," said Dr. Perkins. "Now, where was I—"

Schuyler choked on the blood in her mouth, sputtering and coughing. She gagged with watery eyes, but she couldn't look away. It really was Jack. There was no mistaking him for his twin this time. Of course he was a classmate!

Stephen's voice called through Schuyler's closed bedroom door. "Are you all right in there, Sassy Pants?"

Schuyler was thankful that she already had a habit of keeping herself muted on Zoom. She was coughing so badly, no wonder her father thought she was dying. "I'm fine!" she managed to say, her heart still racing. Her eyes landed back on the screen.

Jack was in his bedroom, a bed neatly made behind him. Books lined a bookshelf next to a few of his lacrosse trophies, which he used as bookends, and what looked like ancient Roman centurion shields hung on display above his bed. A nightstand near his bed also had a stack of books on it, ones whose spines had cracked from use. Early morning sunshine streamed in from a window near his desk, and his head was turned, his chin resting on his hand as he looked outside.

Immediately Schuyler opened a private message to Jack, but her fingers hovered over the keys. She wasn't sure what to write. How could she even begin?

She had so many questions for Jack. She didn't want to flat-out ask him if he was still a Blue Blood, just in case he wasn't, and he'd think she was even more crazy than she was acting.

But the ache to talk to him was almost unbearable. She debated about whether or not she should reach out. They were strangers again, but she couldn't stop herself.

She typed several versions of *hey*, with some followed by an excessive amount of exclamation points to emphasize friendliness and some with an absolute absence of exclamation marks to convey casualness. What if he thought she was a stalker? She typed and erased her message so many times that she realized she was acting like a lunatic. She held down the delete key one final time and twisted her lips, trying to decide what to do next. Maybe she was overthinking everything.

She settled on a casual *hi, Jack* and hit enter.

Jack noticed her message, peeling his eyes away from the window. He looked at her face on his screen, and then he started typing. It felt like her heart was about to burst out of her chest. She stared at him. His cheeks were full of color, his eyes full of life. She wanted to reach through the screen and touch his face.

Her hands shook as she watched the little dots bounce as he typed a response. It took only a few seconds, but it felt like ages, and then the words appeared.

I remember you. Schuyler could have jumped for joy. But then he added: *You almost got hit by my car. Are you okay?*

Schuyler's stomach dropped as she tried to mask her disappointment. *Do you remember anything else?* She hit the enter key a little harder than she meant to.

No. Did I do something?

There was no sign of his remembering her in the way she cared about. His face was neutral. The way he looked at her through her screen said everything she needed to know.

Schuyler slumped low into her bed. She wasn't sure what to say. She wanted to remind him about the life they had had together, about their battle against Lucifer and the Silver Bloods, about the Venators, and the wolves, but she remembered what Kingsley said. That Jack wasn't like them. He didn't know.

So she typed: *No, nothing.*

A cold, hard reality crushed her heart. They were strangers again.

She would have cried if she wasn't so furious. Why was this happening to her? Was this some kind of joke? After everything she had done, this was what she got for it? To be forgotten by everyone she loved? Was some higher power getting a real kick out of her suffering?

What if the universe had a giant bright-red reset button, and it had been pushed, and Schuyler was one of the few in this world who remembered the truth?

Just when she thought she had caught a break, fate pushed her back down again, reminded her of her place. Who was she to think she could have ever had a chance with the incredible Jack Force? The universe was making her pay for her hubris.

He didn't reply again for a long minute, but eventually he sent:

I'm sorry that I left in a hurry last night. I haven't been feeling like myself lately.

What's wrong?

Have you ever woken up from a nap and felt like you're still in a dream? Nothing seems wrong, but nothing seems right either.

Yeah, actually. I know exactly what you're talking about. It just about summed up her current experience.

It's been like that, just all the time. Nothing makes sense anymore.

Schuyler paused for a moment. What if Jack was experiencing the same thing she was, seeing and feeling two conflicting lifetimes and not being able to understand? It would explain a lot. Dying in one world might have scrambled his memories in another. It wasn't the first time his memories had been tampered with.

Maybe Jack needed help remembering. If he had a push in the right direction, he might be able to remember *her*.

She typed and sent, *If you ever want to talk about it, I'm here.*

Thanks, Schuyler. That means a lot. Maybe later.

They didn't talk for the rest of the day.

In this world, Schuyler had Ollie, she had living parents, she had a loving home, but the one thing she wanted, the one thing she needed most in the world, she didn't have.

She didn't have Jack.

She was going to have to change that.

THIRTEEN

SCHUYLER

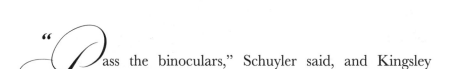

"Pass the binoculars," Schuyler said, and Kingsley handed them over.

After sundown that day, she and Kingsley had met in south Harlem near one of the mayor's special clinics on 116th Street, the construction of which had just been completed earlier that week. They had chosen a hiding spot on the roof of one of the high-rises near the clinic, a perfect vantage point from which to see all the comings and goings out of the unassuming and frankly boring-looking building. Pigeons cooed in their nest nearby, snoozing comfortably, and the street below was empty, as expected. They'd been scouting out the place for hours, and Schuyler's fingers had gone cold.

Schuyler used the binoculars to focus on a couple walking down the street toward the building, but they passed it and turned the corner.

Schuyler sighed and handed the binoculars back to Kingsley. "You never told me that this was going to be so boring."

Kingsley's smile was bright in the dim light. "Thought the life of a Venator was going to be thrilling all the time? Why so eager to jump into the fray?"

Schuyler shrugged. "I need to stop Lucifer already. I feel like we're so behind. People are dying. The longer we wait, the worse it'll get."

"I like your spunk, but charging in without any information is the absolute best way to get yourself killed, rookie." Kingsley put the binoculars up to his face as a car came down the street, its head-lights illuminating the pieces of garbage picked up in a gust of wind. But it went on down the road, leaving the street vacant once more.

Kingsley blew out a raspberry with pursed lips. "I thought we had something there."

Schuyler grinned. "You used to be so formal in our other world. You've changed."

"For the better, I hope."

"Your sarcasm and charm are growing on me. Makes it easier to trust you, for one."

"Trusting people makes you do stupid things."

"I trust you, don't I?" She knocked him gently with her elbow.

"Big mistake. Big. Huge."

Schuyler squinted at him. "Was that a *Pretty Woman* reference?"

"Look, you can only read so many historical vampire texts in a row before you go crazy. The Repository has a surprisingly large collection of romantic comedies from the nineties."

Schuyler giggled and Kingsley smiled. He handed her the bin-oculars again so he could be free to take out a bag of peanut M&M's from his leather jacket pocket. Schuyler held out her hand and he poured a couple into her palm. She appreciated the forethought. She'd never been on a stakeout before.

"So when we first met at the Repository and you said you wanted to add a little chaos to the mix . . . what exactly did you mean?"

Kingsley put up a finger. "I'm so glad you asked. How about a little demonstration, seeing as we've got some time?"

Schuyler continued eating her M&M's and watched as Kingsley fished around in his leather jacket for a moment before revealing a piece of paper—an old receipt, Schuyler noticed—and a pencil. He started drawing a series of symbols on the back of the receipt. "Everything in the universe is made of energy. The ancients had a word for it: chaos—the primordial state of matter. Harnessing that energy is what transforms it from potential to kinetic energy."

"What are you drawing?" she asked.

"These are called sigils. For thousands of years, pagans used to draw these symbols as a method for focusing the chaos energy in a way that could be useful. Drawings could be as simple as a protective circle traced in the dirt around a campfire or as complex and wide scale as city streets. People used to draw sigils on their homes to protect against lesser demons, harness spirits, even attract luck. By using the right sigils in the right order, I can focus intense amounts of energy into one place and . . ." The lines Kingsley had made on the paper began to glow. He held up the paper just in time for Schuyler to see it burst into flames, crumbling into ash, as if he'd taken a match to it. In seconds, it was gone. Kingsley coughed, swatted at the air, and brushed the ash onto his leather jacket. "Voilà. Magic. It's literally chaos. Chaos magic, to be precise."

Schuyler raised her eyebrows, impressed. "So you're a wizard now?"

"Of course not. Anyone can do it. You just have to know the right patterns."

"I seem to recall you had a certain penchant for black magic in the other world. *Materia acerbus*, right?"

Kingsley smirked. "*Materia acerbus* is kind of old-school, don't you think? Besides, chaos is more my style."

Schuyler chuckled and popped another M&M into her mouth. "This new world surprises me more and more each day. . . ."

"How are you adjusting here so far? Are the memories starting to even out?" Kingsley asked around a mouthful of chocolate.

"It's getting a little better, but . . ." She trailed off, distantly thinking about Jack. "I just want things to go back to the way they were."

"I know."

Schuyler buried the lower half of her face deeper into her scarf. "Do you ever think about the people we left behind?"

Kingsley went quiet for a moment and then said, "All the time."

"Have you tried getting back?" she asked.

"The Repository has a lot of arcane knowledge, but our particular situation hasn't been recorded before. I'm not sure there is a way back. Besides, you forget, this *is* our world. We've just got a sneak preview into the multiverse."

"Don't you miss it, though?"

Kingsley was still for a second, then said softly, "You learn not to get too attached to anything when you're immortal. Things come into your life, then go. People too. The best way to break your own heart is to forget that. What's gone is gone. Getting hung up on it is a mistake."

No one had ever thought a half vampire was possible until she had been born. When she inevitably died, hopefully a long time from now, there was no knowing what would happen to her soul, not like a Blue Blood, who knew that rebirth was just around the bend. But even if she was immortal, she wasn't sure she could ever harden her heart enough to let the people she loved go. It made for a lonely existence.

She couldn't help but imagine that while she faded from time after her death, Jack would go on without her, maybe one day forgetting her forever.

"I miss him too, you know," Kingsley said, as if reading her mind.

Schuyler tried to play it cool. "Who?"

"Jack. I wish I could have helped. You shouldn't have had to go through it alone."

Schuyler nodded solemnly. "Thanks."

"But stay away from *this* Jack, and that brother of his while you're at it."

"What, why?" Schuyler spat out.

Kingsley put the binoculars up to his face again and said, "I don't trust them. Call it an instinct."

Schuyler scoffed. "You're paranoid."

"It's kept me alive this long, hasn't it?"

It was a rhetorical question, one Schuyler wasn't going to even try to answer. "How do you know, though? You've talked to them?"

"To Max. I wanted to know if he remembered me. If my bond with Mimi was the same here as it used to be." Kingsley cleared his throat. "I was wrong. I'd forgotten he's not Mimi. Mimi is gone. So is your Jack. I just don't want you to get your hopes up. Things aren't the same in this world."

"I can't give up."

"I've been exactly where you are now, a whole year's worth of lying awake from not knowing. If you trust your heart too much, thinking you know somebody . . . I just don't want you to get hurt."

Before she could respond, Kingsley leaned forward, peering through the binoculars.

"We've got activity," he said in a hushed whisper.

A large semi truck pulled up to the clinic and two hulking figures emerged from the cab, both wearing workmen's jumpsuits and caps. Even from where she was, Schuyler saw the glint of silver in their eyes as they moved around to the back of the trailer and opened the doors.

She didn't take her gaze off the two Silvers as they unloaded hospital beds, wheeling them into the clinic one by one down the ramp and through the front doors.

"Well, well, well," Kingsley said with a sneer. "Two familiar faces. Definitely some of Duncan's henchmen. I've seen them at other sites before. I call that one Eenie and the other one Meanie."

"You really need to get out more," Schuyler said. She took the binoculars from Kingsley and focused in on the new arrivals. No doubt they were Silver Bloods. Both Eenie and Meanie had a similar scowl that would be scary enough even without their eyes shining like coins.

"How many beds does a clinic need?" Schuyler asked.

"We've already recorded about a hundred beds getting dropped off in there during the week. See? This is why recon is important. Note-taking is next to godliness."

She knew he was trying to make a joke, but she wasn't in a laughing mood anymore. "What is all that? It looks like medical equipment."

They carried in boxes that were labeled with the names of the different kinds of supplies one might find in a hospital, like IV drips, and oxygen masks, and syringes. Everything looked so ordinary . . . but the fact that there were Silver Bloods carrying them into the clinic was what made Schuyler's skin crawl.

"We've been seeing this a lot," Kingsley said. "They're stocking up; it's almost like they expect half the city to be living in these clinics long term. They've got enough IV drips, for example, to last a decade, by our calculations."

"That's insane."

Kingsley shifted beside her, rummaging in his leather jacket once more. "They look to be following a tight schedule. How about we interrupt their route?" He held up a piece of plain white chalk, his eyes alight with mischief. "Stay here," he said, and before she could stop him, he dropped off the roof and into the alley. She stopped herself from calling out to him and revealing their location. Instead, she put the binoculars to her eyes again and watched as his shadow moved down and across the street. He paused, his back pressed up against the broad side of the truck, and peered around as the two Silver Bloods walked into the clinic, oblivious to Kingsley's presence. Kingsley looked up at Schuyler's spot on the roof, gave her a thumbs-up, and then disappeared around the front of the truck.

Schuyler watched, waiting with bated breath, searching for any sign of Kingsley, but he wasn't in sight. She kept scanning back and forth between the spot where he vanished and the clinic, praying that the two Silvers wouldn't come back out soon, but with each passing second, she grew more anxious. What was taking Kingsley so long?

Schuyler couldn't take it anymore. She had to go down there. What if he was in trouble? With a groan, she pushed away from the edge of the roof and rushed downstairs. She tried to keep as quiet as possible, crouching low when she emerged from the building. Eenie and Meanie had both come back to the trailer and were unloading more supplies. She hoped they were too busy to hear her heart beating.

Just before she was about to cross the street, Kingsley reemerged from the front of the cab, running straight for her. He didn't look surprised to see that she had been about to follow him, but he didn't slow down, even when he got closer.

"Time to go," Kingsley whispered, and kept running. Schuyler followed and looked behind her just in time to see the truck begin to glow, the telltale markings of Kingsley's drawing burning hot on the cab's hood. The sigil pattern grew brighter and brighter until Schuyler couldn't bear to look at it anymore, and then with a great *KA-BOOM!* the semi truck exploded, sending a shock wave that pounded her eardrums. The trailer launched into the air, smoking like a fireball, and crashed back down to the street with a thunderous noise. She was too amazed to care. She had stopped in her tracks, staring at the smoldering semi truck, her mouth hanging wide open.

"You *have* to teach me how to do that," she said.

Eenie and Meanie emerged from the clinic, yelling and moving through the smoke. Before the two henchmen could see them, both Schuyler and Kingsley were long gone.

FOURTEEN

SCHUYLER

*S*chuyler couldn't wait any longer for Jack to reach out to her. She needed to see him now.

Kingsley had to be wrong. Completely giving up on Jack would be a mistake. He had to remember something. She wouldn't rest until she knew for sure. Besides, this was Jack and she could never turn her back on him, no matter if he remembered her or not. There had to be a trigger to unlock his memories. Of course, she didn't know what that trigger would be yet, but she would try everything and anything she could think of. The first step would be to simply talk to him again.

During class, Schuyler had done some internet sleuthing and found that the entire school's schedule was posted online for students to use. Even though students and staff were restricted from meeting in large groups indoors, outdoor sports practices were still going on as long as proper safety measures were taken, and the lacrosse team was to have its practice from three until six in Central Park at the Great Lawn near the baseball fields.

Jack was the boys' varsity-team captain, and rain or shine,

plague or not, he would be there. Fortunately for her, Kingsley had given her the night off to get some sleep.

After school, Schuyler texted Oliver. *Up for an adventure?*

His response came back almost instantaneously. *Where to, Mr. Frodo?*

She grinned at her screen, texted him the time and place, and slipped on a change of clothes for the trip. Summer weather fought with its last remaining strength to give what was possibly the last warm day of the rest of the year. The sky was bright; the clouds, fluffy and inviting. If the weather was to be taken as a good sign, she was optimistic and hopeful.

"Heading out?" Stephen asked as he spotted her from behind an easel near the window. She paused at the door.

"Only for an hour or two. I'm meeting up with Oliver in the park," she said. "I promise I'll be home for dinner."

"Okay. Do you have your phone? Your keys? Your mask?"

Schuyler nodded yes to all of those things and opened the door.

"Good girl," he said. "Love you!"

"I love you too, Dad," she said, her heart doubling in size, and then she left. She was sure that hearing those words from her father and saying them back would never get old.

Her hands shook with anticipation as she walked from SoHo to the Upper East Side and found Oliver waiting for her like he promised.

He leaned casually on the low stone wall near the Metropolitan Museum of Art, his head tipped back to catch the rays of sunlight peeking through the still-green American elm tree branches. When he heard her coming, he stood up straight, and she could tell he was smiling behind his mask.

"So, you want to tell me what shenanigans we're getting up to, or are you going to keep it a mystery?" he asked.

"I need to talk to Jack Force."

Oliver rolled his eyes. "Really? That guy? Why?"

In the other world, Jack and Oliver had hardly gotten along, even before Schuyler got trapped between them. They were like an unstoppable force versus an immovable object: Jack was the golden child; Oliver, the soft-spoken geek with a penchant for reading books. It appeared that in this new world, they were also at odds with each other.

Oliver kept talking. "Is this about the other night at the club? He's never once talked to you before. Why do you want to talk to him now? Think of him like an alien, living on a completely different planet. He barely even knows we exist." He didn't mask his contempt well.

"It's just talking, Ollie," Schuyler said. "If he ignores me, then I guess I have my answer." She didn't want to even think about what she would do if that happened. She started walking into Central Park, not waiting for his response.

"Okay, but what's the question?" Oliver asked.

"It's . . . a long story."

Oliver jogged to catch up to her. "Two kinds of people exist in this world," he said, holding his hands out, palms up, like he was measuring weights. "There's Jack Force. And then everyone else. If you haven't noticed, we are everyone else."

Schuyler sighed, but she wasn't slowing down. "It's . . . complicated."

"Come on, Schuyler. Let's do something, literally anything, else. Why are we wasting our time on this?"

Schuyler stopped in her tracks and spun to face him. "Please, Ollie. I don't need another person in my life telling me not to talk to Jack."

"Isn't that a sign? What do you see in that guy, honestly?"

Schuyler shook her head and kept on walking. Oliver wouldn't understand. "I told you, it's just talking. Nothing more."

"Right, sure."

Oliver didn't complain the rest of the way, though she was pretty sure he had plenty more grumblings he was keeping to himself, which was fine by Schuyler. She needed a friend right now, not another obstacle in her life. With Kingsley's help, maybe she'd be able to properly explain it all to Oliver soon—once she was better able to understand it herself.

While they walked, she had time to get her heartbeat under control. But the closer they got to the field, the more she felt sick. Excitement-plus-nervousness was an awful combination. She tried not to imagine the multitude of ways this conversation could go and focused on getting to the field.

Soon the pair arrived at the Great Lawn, and, just as expected, Schuyler spotted a cluster of lacrosse players wearing blue and red practice pinnies, doing a sprinting drill and tossing a ball between them in a complicated pattern while managing to stay six feet away from one another. To Schuyler's untrained eye, it was like a magic show, trying to keep track of the ball, but the team moved so quickly, it was hard to keep up. The players wore masks under their caged helmets, so at first it was almost impossible to tell who was who, but Schuyler carefully scanned the group until she found Jack. His stride gave him away.

He juked and weaved through the course, leaping expertly over sticks and volleying passes like a professional. His uniform—loose white shorts, blue pinny, and long-sleeve T-shirt—showed off his sculpted calves and thighs, putting the marble Greek statues in the Met to shame.

Coach blew the whistle, and practice was over. Jack air-fived his closest teammates and headed with the rest of his team to pack up their belongings and go home. Schuyler knew this was her chance and walked over, clenching her fists to make her hands stop shaking.

When Jack took off his helmet, his blond hair was wet with sweat, but he shone like sunlight. He did a double take when he saw her coming. She could drown in those soft green eyes.

"Oh, hey," he said. Behind his mask, he looked uncomfortable, like he didn't know what to say. His gaze darted around nervously.

Schuyler kept her distance, Oliver hovering behind her protectively, and she tried to ignore the feeling that maybe Jack hated her in this world. A person didn't look at someone like that unless there was reason to. She brushed the thought aside. She had come too far to give up now.

"Hey, Jack," she said, a little breathlessly, like she was the one who had just finished lacrosse practice. "Do you have a minute? I wanted to talk. Face-to-face."

"About what?" he asked.

"That thing you mentioned the other day, about feeling like you're stuck in a dream."

Jack's eyes flicked to his teammates, as if he was worried they would overhear; then he tipped his head, indicating that he and Schuyler should move away. She signaled to Oliver to wait for her and followed Jack to a nearby oak tree, still keeping a safe distance. To Schuyler, that distance spanned miles.

Schuyler wrung her hands together. Her palms had gotten sweaty. "Are you having dreams? Visions? Seeing things that make you feel like they should be different but they're not? Like another reality."

"Y-yeah," he said, amazed. "How did you . . ."

The skin prickled on Schuyler's arms, and quick as a blur, she caught a lacrosse ball aimed right at the side of her head. It had shot at her like a bullet, the breeze ruffling her curls. The hard rubber stung her palm, but otherwise she was fine. Her vampire reflexes had saved her from getting a black eye. Or worse. Jack looked, shocked, at the person who had launched the ball.

"Max!"

Sure enough, Jack's twin, Max, took off his lacrosse helmet, looking smug as he whirled his stick in his hand, making wide arcs as if it were a sword. He was wearing a red pinny, putting him on the opposite practice squad from Jack. He tipped his head at Schuyler, his eyes flashing, and said, "Impressive."

"What did you do that for?" Jack barked.

"What? My hand slipped."

Schuyler was thankful that the mask hid most of the blush

growing hot on her face. "I didn't know Jack had a jerk for a brother," she said.

"I didn't know Jack was friends with Spirit Halloween witches." If Max had long hair, he would have flipped it over his shoulder. Just like Mimi. No matter which world she was in, Mimi would always be Mimi.

Schuyler bit back her frustration. This was not how this conversation was supposed to go. But just like in the world before, Jack's sibling always felt the need to run interference. She squeezed the rubber ball so tightly, it creaked in her grip.

By then, Oliver sensed trouble brewing and stepped in. He protectively grabbed Schuyler by her upper arms. "Come on," he said, guiding her away. "You don't want to get on Max's bad side. And you already are. He's a *beeyotch*."

Blood roared in her ears like a raging river, but she didn't fight Oliver. With each step, the roar in her ears was replaced by a simmering boil.

As they walked, she overheard Max scoff and say, "Who was that? Does she even go to our school? She looks like she doesn't belong here."

"That's Schuyler," Jack said. He sounded forlorn.

Without stopping, Schuyler turned around and threw the lacrosse ball at Jack, who caught it easily but watched her go, saying nothing else.

"Another one of your many groupies," Max sneered, and narrowed his cold eyes at her. "Let's go, bro."

Schuyler turned forward once more and kept walking with Oliver, her teeth clenched hard to stop herself from screaming.

FIFTEEN

SCHUYLER

That night, Schuyler had another dream.

She stood on a beach at nighttime, her bare feet sinking into soft, dry sand. An ocean stretched out in front of her, the water wide and calm, black as obsidian. The stars were so bright in the sky, they glittered like diamonds. The world was still and quiet; not even the waves on the sand were audible. A shooting star streaked overhead. Then another—then a million more. All the stars fell, winking out of existence, cascading down like a waterfall, until there were none. There was only darkness and fire.

The sky folded in on itself, empty into empty, nothing into nothing, forever falling into itself in perpetual black. The only light came from a new dawn.

Schuyler blinked and Lucifer appeared, standing on the water, his white suit glowing against the darkness. Aldrich Duncan. The sun rose behind him. He walked toward her, his feet barely making a ripple as he did. She tried to run, but she couldn't move.

He held his hand out to her, fingers gently curled, and he smiled at her.

"Child of Blood and Blessed," he said, his voice resonating

all around her, rattling her bones. "Rejoice with me. It is done."

He snapped his fingers and she spun against her will, her back now to Lucifer. A blast of heat crashed into her face, nearly knocking her over.

Schuyler choked on smoke and fear.

Before her, New York City burned. The roar of carnage. Buildings like skeletal remains crumbled to dust. Within the smoke, a dark giant moved through the carnage. Curled obsidian horns, great leathery wings, a flaming sword clutched in enormous claws. She had seen this being before, in her old world, and it was now more terrible than ever.

The destroyer.

Abbadon.

The demon turned its flaming red eyes upon her and raised its sword.

Schuyler jolted awake, a scream stuck in her throat.

It was still dark outside. The only noise came from her ragged breathing. Her T-shirt clung to her back with sweat as she sat up, grounding herself in reality. She was in her room, in her bed, safe. But the dream had felt so real. She held her head in her hands.

Even though she wanted to believe it was just a dream, she couldn't help but fear that it was so much more.

SIXTEEN

SCHUYLER

Schuyler went to the Repository later that evening after school and found Kingsley hunched over a large tome, reading by soft lamplight. A few other Blue Bloods lingered in the shadows, resting between their duties as patrols guarding the Repository from Duncan's henchmen. But Schuyler didn't really know any of them even though she'd been visiting the Repository almost every single day. Of course she'd tried to introduce herself, but the other Blue Bloods found any excuse to walk in the other direction or pretend like their blade sharpening was much more important than getting to know her. They didn't trust her yet. Kingsley told her as much.

She didn't blame them. In the other world, if a strange Blue Blood whom she didn't know suddenly showed up, saying that she'd killed Lucifer in another timeline, would she have trusted them? The best way to earn that trust, Schuyler figured, was through defeating Lucifer again—easier said than done with the odds stacking ever higher against them.

When she found Kingsley at his desk in his classroom, another Blue Blood was standing beside him in mid-conversation, but he looked over when she approached. She knew his name was Bowman, and that was the extent of it. A stern crease appeared on his brow, and he put his hand on the short sword at his side as if in warning. Schuyler gave him a smile, but it didn't seem to ease the tension.

"I'll keep you posted, sir," Bowman said, and stepped away.

"Yes, thank you." Kingsley didn't look up from his book, but he heard her coming. "Speak of the devil. If it isn't Schuyler Cervantes-Chase!"

"Talking about me?"

"Only good things. Where have you been?"

"I have school. And parents now, which is nice, don't get me wrong. But I can't stay here long. I need to get back soon." *To protect them*, Schuyler finished in her head.

"Fair point," Kingsley said. He marked the page with a ribbon and closed the book with a loud thud. When he looked at her, he frowned. "Are you all right?"

She knew she looked tired.

The nightmare she'd had last night had rattled her so deeply, she hadn't been able to get back to sleep. She had to nurse copious amounts of coffee all throughout the day in order to stay awake in school, which had surprised her father. She wasn't usually a coffee drinker, but he'd made sure to keep her mug topped off. His little vampire vigilante was growing up. He didn't even know the half of it.

The day might have been more bearable if she had seen Jack. But his face had been missing in all three of the classes they had together: English, European History, and calculus. The only sign that he was even present was a little black box on the screen with his name on it, his camera and microphone disabled. She hadn't been able to speak with him again since their meeting at the park.

With a heavy sigh, Schuyler fell into an empty chair and told Kingsley about her nightmare. He rubbed his chin thoughtfully as she spoke. When she was done, she took a breath, feeling a little better knowing that she had told someone who would believe her.

"Did you have these kinds of dreams when you first experienced Superimposition?" she asked.

"Occasionally, but nothing like what you're seeing. Mostly dreams about Mimi." Pain darted across his face. Schuyler chose not to pry.

"You don't think what I'm seeing is . . . something more than a dream, do you?"

Kingsley's expression turned grim, but he tried to hide it. He looked at her and smiled, though it didn't reach all the way up to his dark eyes. "I'm sure it's nothing to worry about."

Schuyler wanted to believe him, but she knew he had said that for her sake.

"What were you two talking about just now?" Schuyler asked, tipping her head in the direction Bowman had disappeared.

"Some activity at a clinic that's worth paying attention to," Kingsley said. "All across the island, there's movement. Bowman was just giving me his report."

"Anything I can do?"

"Sit tight, keep your head down, and pay attention. I can't have you running off into trouble."

Schuyler sighed. "Okay. But only because you asked nicely."

Kingsley winked at her.

Just then, Bowman came back, looking frazzled. "Sir, it's confirmed," he said to Kingsley. "Operation Argenti is underway. Duncan's lieutenants are on-site."

Kingsley had already risen to his feet, bracing himself on the desk. "Where?"

"The Seaport."

Schuyler had no idea what they were talking about. "Operation Argenti? What's confirmed? Lieutenants?" she asked, but Kingsley didn't answer. He gathered his cloak and his weapons from under his chair, the color already draining from his face.

"Kingsley," she said, her voice tense. "What's going on?"

He looked at her for a beat, his lips pressed into a thin line, and said, "I think perhaps this is something you should see for yourself."

SEVENTEEN

SCHUYLER

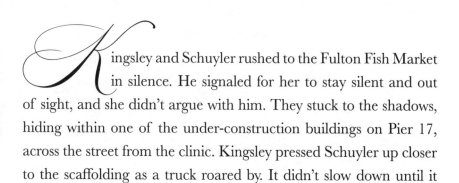

ingsley and Schuyler rushed to the Fulton Fish Market in silence. He signaled for her to stay silent and out of sight, and she didn't argue with him. They stuck to the shadows, hiding within one of the under-construction buildings on Pier 17, across the street from the clinic. Kingsley pressed Schuyler up closer to the scaffolding as a truck roared by. It didn't slow down until it came to a stop right in front of the squat white building, where a dozen or so of Duncan's men were coming in and out of the doors.

"Is this the Operation Whatever?" Schuyler whispered.

"Argenti," Kingsley corrected, not taking his eyes off the building. With his hood up, he looked about as stealthy as one could get. "And yes. My team intercepted some documents that were passing between clinics, all written in code, but the one thing we could decipher was the name Operation Argenti. If Duncan's lieutenants are here, this is exactly what we're looking for."

"His lieutenants?" Schuyler asked. She'd only ever known Lucifer to work with other demons, like Leviathan. She didn't know anyone or anything else he might have on his side, let alone a being powerful enough to be considered his second in command. She got her answer soon enough.

When the truck pulled up to the clinic, half a dozen of Duncan's men attended to hauling the boxes from the back. A voice carried across the street.

"See to it that these are stacked and labeled correctly this time."

Schuyler's heart nearly stopped. She'd recognize that voice anywhere. The tone was all she needed in order to identify it, especially since its owner had nearly taken her head off with a lacrosse ball.

Max Force stood watch with his arms folded over his chest, supervising the entire unloading process. There was no mistaking it; he was in charge. Kingsley tensed beside her. She couldn't move either.

Max continued. "When we open, I'd better not see anything out of order, or we'll tear your throats out ourselves. Isn't that right, Abbadon?"

From the shadows stepped the familiar form and face of Jack Force. "Whatever you say, Azrael." He looked grim, but there was only one reason he'd be here.

Duncan's lieutenants.

The Twin Angels of Death and Destruction.

Jack was working for Lucifer.

Kingsley wrapped his hand over Schuyler's mouth and whisked her away before she could scream.

Schuyler shrugged Kingsley off once they ducked into a burned-out movie rental store on Water Street. They were far enough away from the clinic, a couple blocks west, and far out of earshot, so Kingsley didn't stop her when she screamed with rage.

She couldn't believe it. This had to be a trick. That couldn't be Jack. It wasn't possible. Not Jack. Not her Jack. He would never. He *was* Abbadon of the Dark in her world, but he had fought for the Light. Alongside Michael and Gabrielle's kin.

But Michael and Gabrielle did not exist in this world.

In this world, there was only the Light of Lucifer the Morningstar.

She whipped around and stared at Kingsley, searching for answers on his face.

He stood in the dim light, shoulders slumped, but he looked more defeated and sad than she did. There was only one reason why.

"You knew," she gasped. "You knew Max and Jack were working for Duncan."

He nodded once.

"How long?" Her voice shook with raw emotion.

"Not long. I had my suspicions, but . . . now we know for sure."

"You're wrong!" Tears welled up in the corners of her eyes.

"I specialize in information and intel. I had reports, but no concrete proof until now. I thought they were just part of the Coven, lower-level members. Now you've seen it for yourself. These are facts, Schuyler. The Force twins are Lucifer's chief lieutenants."

"Maybe it was someone using *mutatio*! It could have been someone disguised to look like Jack."

"You know that's not what this is."

Kingsley was right. She was desperately grasping for answers when the truth was staring her right in the face.

"Max I could believe, but Jack?"

"Hey now, Mimi was on our side in our world," he said curtly.

"But . . . but—Jack isn't a traitor. He would never—"

"Your old Jack, maybe. But this world's Jack? He's got a different agenda."

Schuyler put her cold hand to her forehead. She felt like puking. "When were you planning on telling me?"

"Only when I had the facts. I promise, I wasn't trying to keep you in the dark on this. I thought it was best if you saw it for yourself. Then you'd know the truth."

Schuyler's fists shook as she paced back and forth on the scorched carpet. The whole world had gone to hell, and she was helpless to do anything but watch as the love of her life joined Lucifer's cause.

Taking her anger out on Kingsley would be a mistake; Schuyler knew that. It wasn't his fault.

An idea struck her. "Maybe this isn't real! Do you remember in the other world when Jack and Mimi tricked Lucifer into thinking they were working for him?"

Kingsley shook his head. "This is different. Max and Jack . . . they're in it for real."

Kingsley looked spooked, and if he looked spooked, Schuyler knew it was for a reason.

"So then this treatment that Duncan is approving . . . they're giving it out?" Schuyler asked.

"It's a trap. Don't you see? The treatment isn't real. Mortals were so scared of the so-called virus, they tried to shut down the world to save themselves. But Duncan used their fear against them and told them a treatment was available, but only at his clinics. People will go in, but they won't come out. In this universe, vampires really live up to the stereotype: They're bloodsuckers. All of them."

"Why, though? Why are they working for him? Why is Jack working for him?"

"The Force twins are powerful."

"How powerful?"

"*Scary* powerful. In our old world, there was some level of restraint, an unwillingness to unleash their true potential for fear of what they could do. Here, the rules have changed. Lucifer has tapped into their instincts. They're still Twin Angels of the Apocalypse. We've heard whispers of some kind of scheme, and if I'm right, which I usually am, it's going to be big. Under Lucifer, they're just waiting for the word; then it's showtime."

Schuyler clenched her jaw. It was hard to believe that the boy she had watched practicing lacrosse with his teammates in Central Park the other day was a harbinger of the end of the world. But she had seen what he could do, seen him in her vision as Abbadon. Black wings, horns, eyes red as blood, New York City in flames. Whatever this Operation Argenti was, it had everything to do with the clinics and hurting people. But to believe that Jack would willingly join Lucifer . . . It was a lot to take in.

"Waiting for what? Why not have them end the world now?" Schuyler asked.

Kingsley worked his jaw. "I don't know."

She had already lost Jack once when he died; now she was losing him again to Lucifer in a way that was somehow worse than before. Schuyler used to think Jack's dying was the worst thing that could happen, and yet the universe was giddy to prove her wrong yet again.

Schuyler shook her head. "I can't give up on Jack. I just can't. There has to be a way that I can make him remember. He *will* change."

Kingsley scoffed dismissively. "He's not the same Jack that you knew, so good luck with that. And if he's anything like Max, you're better off without him," he muttered.

"No, I don't believe that! He's different. He's *good*; I know he is."

"Jack Force isn't the Angel of Destruction because he makes it rain kittens and hail snow cones."

She rounded on Kingsley, the words coming out hot. "You're one to talk! You don't become a Silver Blood because you're a saint, and yet you got a second chance."

Kingsley's dark eyes flashed with anger. "Because I *wanted* to change. I asked for forgiveness. I repented for my sins, and I am still paying for them."

"But you won't give anyone else the same opportunity."

Kingsley looked at her from under his brows, simmering. "You tried talking to Jack, didn't you?"

Schuyler looked away, ashamed, but Kingsley saw right through her.

He took a step forward. "You talked to him when I specifically told you not to! What did I say? I said stay away from him."

"How was I supposed to know that he was Lucifer's lieutenant? But even then, it's Jack!"

"He's not your Jack anymore! When will you understand that?"

Schuyler's face burned. "Would you really feel the same way right now if it were Mimi?"

"But she's not here. He is."

Mimi Force was Jack's twin and Kingsley's lover in the other universe. Mimi didn't exist in this one. But Mimi and Max were the same person. Same soul, different wrapping. Couldn't Kingsley see that?

"Mimi, Max, it doesn't matter. If you can't allow people to change, then you damn them for eternity!"

Pain darted across Kingsley's face. He had been alone in this world for too long, had lived centuries witnessing too much death and suffering repeating themselves throughout history. Schuyler knew he had been hurt in ways she couldn't understand. He huffed noisily through his nostrils. "I'm trying to protect you."

"Well, ask me next time if I want or need protecting."

Neither of them moved for a long moment, staring at each other across the ruins of the store. Kingsley was the first to move. He dragged his fingers through his long hair and sighed.

"So this is the remaining light of Gabrielle, huh? It takes a lot more than I thought to put out her fire."

He said it like a compliment, and Schuyler took it that way. The dense air between them had dissipated.

"Have you even tried talking to Max?" Schuyler asked.

Kingsley tipped his head to the side. "I tried. Several times, in fact. But he's lost. I've followed him all over town, seen his true nature, his ruthlessness in action. He's committed to the cause. Lucifer has a grasp on his spirit somehow. I'm not sure what else I can do."

"We can't give up. If there's a way to get to them, we have to find it. Did you ever stop to think that maybe the two of us were sent here to help them? To turn them toward the Light?"

A pinprick of light caught in Kingsley's eyes. Even in the dark, she could tell he was smiling. "Maybe you're right." He sighed loudly.

Schuyler allowed herself to smile too. "Is Max as much of a pain as Mimi was?" she asked.

"More," said Kingsley.

"Which means you still love him, don't you?"

"Even more than I ever did."

"My condolences."

Kingsley laughed heartily and Schuyler smiled wider.

"All right. If we're going to save them, we'd better start planning soon," Kingsley said. "There's not much time left. Lucifer's plans are almost complete."

"Teach me some more chaos," Schuyler said.

PART TWO

A FEW MONTHS EARLIER . . .

MR. FORCE, IF YOU'RE NASTY

YOU POOR, SIMPLE FOOLS. THINKING YOU COULD
DEFEAT ME. ME, THE MISTRESS OF ALL EVIL!
—MALEFICENT, *SLEEPING BEAUTY* (1959)

EIGHTEEN

MAX

The nightclub music thrummed with a deep, industrial bass. The underground hot spot Terminal was Manhattan's latest exclusive watering hole, open despite the Red Bloods' fear of the plague.

Situated in an abandoned subway station in the Meatpacking District, the club could only be found by those who knew about it. It wasn't advertised; there was no sign on the street, no paparazzi. If you knew about it, you were *supposed* to know about it. A-list actors, runway models, foreign royals—wannabes all the same—were always clawing at the gate to get inside. They wanted what they couldn't have. The music was earsplitting, and inside, blood flowed as freely as liquor. Hundreds of bodies writhed and crushed into each other, captured for a moment of frozen time by strobe lights, hypnotically dancing to the beat, drenched with sweat, and lust, and hunger. Auto-tuned lyrics commanded them to *dance, dance, dance,* and they listened, even if they didn't know why. Red Bloods were so easy to compel, it almost wasn't fun anymore. *Almost.*

Maximilian Reginald Force III watched them all from his VIP table situated high on a metal scaffold, lounging above the masses like a king at court. He sat sprawled on the red leather couch with one male and one female human on each side. They couldn't keep their hands off him, grabbing the straps of his sparkling Louis Vuitton harness and pulling them in every which way. He had had to remove his Dior blazer; otherwise they would have torn it with their grubby little fingers. He liked both men and women, really anything on the spectrum, so long as they were pretty. He liked pretty things. He smiled, satisfied, as he reaped the rewards of his hard work. Being a Blue Blood vampire was terribly exhausting.

His fangs out, he drank from his handsome male plaything, an up-and-coming actor who had just landed a role in a popular super-hero franchise. He could taste the supplements the actor was taking to bulk up for the spandex costume, and his blood tasted like plastic, but it was still good. When he'd had his fill, Max wiped the spot of red that had pooled at the corner of his mouth. The man slumped into him, barely conscious, but still gripped on to his chest as if asking for more. Max turned and kissed the woman—a skinny model—hungrily, and sighed with want. She smelled like mango lotion. She stretched her neck for him, and he sank his fangs deeply into her throat. She let out a small gasp, and her eyes rolled up to the back of her head before she went limp. Max's mouth dripped with her blood, hot and sweet, and he smirked. He cleaned his lips with the back of his wrist as she fell into his lap like a rag doll.

Max's memories of heaven had faded with every new mortal body his angelic soul possessed, but he guessed that this was the closest he'd been in a long time. He felt so alive.

"Skinny humans always pass out too quickly." He sighed. "I

should go for more professional athletes—like a running back, or a swimmer, maybe. More blood in them. And tastier too."

His attention landed on his brother, Jack, who was sitting on the far side of the couch with his arms folded over his chest, looking somber and troubled. He stared at the glass table full of empty cocktail glasses in front of them without really seeing anything. He didn't have a human to drink from.

"Thirsty?" Max asked.

Jack looked like he'd eaten a lemon and didn't seem to notice Max was talking to him.

"Earth to Jack Force!" Max had to shout over the music and kicked his twin with a polished oxford shoe right in the ankle.

Jack jerked with a start and glared at him. "Are you done yet?" he asked.

"Done? I'm just getting started. The night is young!"

Jack huffed and went back to studying the invisible spot on the table, his brows knitted together in thought.

"Oh, come on," Max chided while pushing the Red Blood man's face away. He had stuck his tongue into Max's ear and was getting annoying. "Quit bumming me out. Have some fun, why don't you? You're like a teetotaler in a speakeasy."

"I told you, I didn't want to come tonight."

"As if going out is *ever* your idea."

Jack was usually the more introverted of the twins, hardly the life of the party, but tonight he was especially withdrawn. Max admitted now, though, that his dear twin brother was totally killing the mood.

Max absolutely lived for parties. These days, while waiting for Lucifer's orders, he was desperate for any kind of action. He missed going to school, purely for the sociability of it. He loved to see and he loved to be seen. At sixteen years old, he commanded any room he walked into. A boy as beautiful as Max parted crowds, drew stares, and attracted Familiars eager to spill their blood at his feet, all of it as easy as snapping his fingers. Pale, blond, and handsome, he expected the world to bow to his every whim.

If it didn't, he would *make* it bow.

Max often noted that if Jack wanted to, he could have all of Max's success, but Jack was stubbornly set on being a bore.

As twins, they were inseparable. They had been twinned souls in heaven, reincarnated together on earth as a pair when they fell—two halves of the same soul. They shared the same face, but they were opposite sides of the same coin.

"What's wrong with you?" Max asked, narrowing his gorgeous eyes.

Jack shrugged. Max could see the muscle working in his jaw just like their father's used to do, when their father was alive, of course.

"I'll share," Max offered. He gestured to the model, who stirred slowly awake in his lap. She could have passed for any drunk girl at a party, the way her hair hung loosely in front of her face and she stared vacantly. "You can take this one. She's definitely your type."

"She's almost drained," Jack said.

"So then we'll get another. There're plenty to be had."

Jack's focus drifted across the throng of humans pulsating to the beat of the music. Max knew that his brother wanted to take them; he felt it. He and Jack were connected so deeply to each other on a spiritual level. The craving poured out of Jack like lava: scorching hot, unstoppable, and entirely natural.

"This isn't normal," Jack said, still looking at the humans.

"Of course it is," Max reminded him. "Humans want to be controlled. They are terrified of existence and want to be told what to do. God put them on this wretched planet to figure out life without any guidance. And maybe He put us here to give them that guidance, show them their purpose." He stroked the young model's cheek and flashed his teeth, smiling sharply as his emerald gaze landed on her neck.

Jack stood up so suddenly that the empty cocktail glasses in front of them rattled and one fell and shattered on the floor. "I'm leaving. I'll see you at home," he said, and then disappeared without another word into the crowd.

"Fine! More for me, then!" Max called out, but Jack was already long gone.

Why Jack refused to drink completely baffled Max. They were *vampires*. Everyone wanted to be them, whether they admitted it or not. Blue Bloods had everything that mattered in the world: money, beauty, power. They wanted for nothing, and yet Jack wasn't happy.

His attitude had totally zapped all the fun. It was such a buzzkill.

What was his brother's problem?

Max was the older twin, but Jack always acted more mature. He hardly ever liked having fun in the same ways Max did.

Max scowled. His mood had soured, even though the young actor had started raking his fingers through Max's golden pompadour and kissing his neck with renewed energy. Max closed his eyes and breathed deeply, and the male Familiar's Comme des Garçons cologne washed over him. The actor smelled of smoky liquor and sweat, with a hint of fear—*delicious*. Compulsion couldn't erase the human's natural instinct. Max kissed him again, tasting the human's fear, bitter like dark chocolate.

He kissed the model next. Her fear was already waning, flickering like a candle about to go out. She was too weak. They both were. *Humans are always so weak . . . so boring.*

Max took what he needed from them, then joined the mass of humans on the dance floor. The wet heat of the crowd surrounded him like an embrace. He didn't need Jack to have fun. This was everything he ever wanted, ever needed, he told himself. So he danced, one with the music, taking it all in. *More. More. I want more.*

Max moved to the rhythm of the beat, basking in the thrum of sound and energy.

A body pressed up against his.

In the strobe lights, Max caught only glimpses of dark eyes, broad shoulders, and shiny black hair. He was strikingly handsome for a human and taller than Max, but only by a fraction. Max's heart raced with desire.

The man wound his strong hands around Max's waist, and they moved together, pressed into each other. Energy radiated off them as they danced. Max twined his fingers through the stranger's hair. Though the music made it hard to hear, the man leaned in, and his words, hot in Max's ear, cut through the noise of the club.

"Thought I'd never find you . . ." the stranger said.

He smelled of leather, and whiskey, and burned sugar, and something else—like a place on a map Max couldn't quite put his finger on.

Max didn't know what the stranger was talking about, and frankly, he didn't care. He liked being wanted and sought after. There was no time to ask for the stranger's name because the crowd swelled and consumed them both, pulling them away from each other. In the next second, the stranger was gone, having disappeared into the crowd. The smell of him still lingered, though only in Max's thoughts.

Even though Max searched, he couldn't find any sign of him. The stranger had vanished.

Nineteen

MAX

Max's back slammed into the floor mat with a heavy *WHUMP.*

Jack stood over him, looking down at his handiwork. He wasn't even out of breath.

Max groaned in frustration and rolled onto his knees. Jack had always been better at judo; in fact, he had been better than Max at most things ever since they were little. It didn't matter how many times they'd been reborn; Jack—the Angel of Destruction—was always the best. What made it worse was that Jack never rubbed Max's face in it. If he did, maybe it wouldn't have been so annoying.

Jack turned and walked to the edge of the mat and said, "Again."

Max rose to his feet. Every morning, before dawn, the twins sparred in their home gym. Training, even for vampires, was necessary; being an out-of-shape bloodsucker would really put a damper on the whole affair. Besides, Lucifer would never allow his right-hand soldiers to be slouches. It had become a little ritual for the twins to test each other's strength and abilities, each one's skills comparable only to the other's. Max always felt like he was a half step behind his brother, though today Jack was acting particularly ruthless.

Max bounced on the soles of his bare feet and shook out his shoulders. He was tired of hitting the floor.

Jack wiped his nose with the back of his wrist.

Max took that as an opportunity to attack, grabbing for Jack's wrist and swiping in for a kick. Jack countered with a simple reversal, and Max found himself flat on his back again, staring up at the ceiling.

"Again," Jack barked.

Was this payback for making Jack come out to the club last night?

He should have known Jack wasn't in the mood to party. Jack had arrived home just as Max was coming down the grand staircase, and when asked where he'd been all day, Jack, being Jack, didn't want to talk about it. He shut himself in his room and would have stayed there if not for Max's taunts, promising that he himself would get into trouble (or rather cause trouble) if he went to Terminal alone. Only then had Jack finally relented and come to the club, not because he wanted to, but because Max did. After their fight at the club, Max didn't get a chance to talk to Jack. It had been the biggest one they'd had in a long time, if one could even call it a fight. When Max had arrived home in the early morning hours, full and drowsy, all the animosity he had originally felt toward Jack had evaporated. Jack seemed to feel otherwise.

"You're slow," Jack said.

Max kept his reasons to himself. He wasn't ready to talk about the fact that the man from last night still lingered on the outskirts of his thoughts. How could a mortal even do that to someone like Max? In fact, when Max had fallen asleep that night, the last thing he thought about was how the man's hands were on his waist while they danced. They were so strong and sure of themselves. He knew he shouldn't have filled up on that actor and model earlier in the night; otherwise he could have tasted the stranger, and maybe then his mind could rest. He always wanted what he couldn't have. He hadn't slept well because of it, tossing and turning, awake at every hour.

Jack raised his fists, staring down Max with a cool look.

Max got to his feet once again.

"One more round," Max said, "then we should go, or we'll be late for our meeting with Duncan."

With incredible speed, Jack put him down on the mat once more, as if having the final word.

The Force mansion on Fifth Avenue on the Upper East Side was enormous, especially given the fact that only two people lived in it. The scale and grandeur of their neoclassical home, smack in the middle of one of the most expensive real estate zones in Manhattan, was a testament to their family's wealth, money as old as money could be.

Most people who were lucky enough to walk into their sweeping entrance hall—fashioned like the palace at Versailles, with gilded cornices, vibrant red carpet, a vaulted ceiling, and high-warp tapestries—wore the same expression: pure awe. But since the accident that had killed the twins' parents, not many visitors had come through the mansion's front doors. Memories still lingered in their home like a scar, half-lived-in, half-empty. It served as a vicious reminder of tragedy.

Maximilian and Miranda Force had been esteemed Blue Bloods of their time, and when they died in a plane crash somewhere over the Atlantic, thousands of well-wishers and mourners filtered in and out of the mansion, bestowing gifts and words of kindness to the little orphan boys they had left behind who had not yet come into their powers as Blue Bloods in their own right. But with each passing day, fewer and fewer visitors came through the front doors. The boys grew into the house, filling up the empty corners by living their lives.

Along with the home gym, the mansion had a small theater, bowling alley, and swimming pool, everything to keep two teen-age boys entertained and happy. Jack's and Max's rooms were on the third floor of the east wing. Their parents' old primary bedroom was on the opposite side in the west wing, but it hadn't been touched in years. Max didn't like to spend too much time on the landing leading there; it still felt off-limits.

The one place of his parents' that didn't feel off-limits as much as it used to was his father's study.

Max, already dressed and waiting for Jack, sat in his father's burgundy leather chair with his feet kicked up on the grand oak desk. He read over some of the documents he would be presenting to Duncan at their meeting today.

As the firstborn, Max had inherited his father's name, so he felt it was his responsibility to maintain the Force legacy.

Spacious, opulent, and imposing, the office was reminiscent of an old hunting lodge, with deep maroon wallpaper, brass lighting fixtures, and a high, coffered ceiling made of reclaimed wood from an old Scottish castle. Bespoke cherrywood bookcases packed with leather-bound history books stood opposite a stone fireplace, where—on chilly nights—a crackling fire within would cast an orange glow over plush antique leather chairs, arranged perfectly for occupants to warm their feet. Opposite Max's desk were glass-paneled French doors that opened out to a balcony high above Fifth Avenue, giving him a full view of the Metropolitan Museum of Art. The morning light cast a pleasant streak across the large antique Persian rug in front of the window.

The wall behind the desk was dedicated entirely to hunting trophies—mostly deer plaques—that, when Max was a child, inspired the absurd image of a stampede of deer having tried to ram through the plaster only to get stuck. Max had left his father's office mostly unchanged, choosing not to redecorate to his own taste, as if to keep it preserved for his father when he returned. He never would return, of course. Not in this lifetime.

Max always associated the smell of smoke and firewood with his father. He spent so much time in the study, it felt like his father had never really left.

Max didn't feel like it was properly his space yet even though he used it for most of his duties as Lucifer's venerated soldier. It was as if he was wearing his father's old suit and hadn't grown into it. He was playing dress-up with destiny.

Max supposed that Jack would be much more suited for the study. He had been their father's favorite then, and he was Lucifer's now. Jack was the Angel of Destruction, and destruction always came before death—the sword piercing the skin, the disease destroying the cells, a plane crashing to the sea. Death was secondary.

But Max had worked too hard to give it all up.

Max was ranked higher than Jack in Lucifer's army after years of grinding to prove that he was worthy of Lucifer's attention, and it made Max feel proud. He had always cared about his status more than Jack did. His position as Venator, chief enforcer of the Coven, was a job he had desperately wanted and took very seriously. He had worked for the title. He wanted to be strong. Lucifer knew that.

Duncan had chosen Max for a reason. His plan had been put in motion, all thanks to Max's ambition.

Max sorted through another one of the papers and did a double take when he saw the date. His stomach sank and went cold, like he'd been shoved into the ocean carrying a cannonball.

Oh.

Right then, Jack appeared in the doorway, dressed exactly like Max in all black, in accordance with the customs of Lucifer. He was freshly showered, his hair still not totally dry, but he was ready to go.

Max looked up from his documents.

"I forgot," he said, aghast.

Jack's gaze was narrow, heavy with accusation. "You forgot." With that, he clenched his jaw and left.

TWENTY

MAX

*M*ax and Jack stood at attention, facing Mayor Aldrich Duncan's empty desk, waiting.

Mayor Duncan's office was situated in City Hall in the heart of the Financial District, with a spectacular view of City Hall Park. On the inside, the building was swarming with vampires.

Currently, Duncan's office was empty. His Majesty, the Prince of Heaven, Lucifer Morningstar, was late. Duncan had a penchant for pure white decor, everything from the steamed high-pile carpet to the large alabaster desk to the single lamp shooting a bright white light down upon the white stationery on the desk neatly arranged in perfect symmetry.

The brothers had a standing appointment to meet with Duncan bright and early each week to give reports and updates on the Coven's activity. As Venator, it was Max's responsibility to see Duncan's plans executed without failure.

They'd been standing for a long time, not willing to break the silence in case Duncan arrived. The clock on the wall ticked loudly. Max fought the urge to unbutton the top button of his shirt to loosen the cut of his collar.

How could he have forgotten the date? One of the most traumatic events of his life, and it had simply slipped his mind. How was that even possible?

Max glanced at Jack out of the corner of his eye, trying to get a read on him, but Jack remained as aloof as ever.

Ever since Max was appointed Venator, Jack's temper had come out more often. But this time it was entirely Max's fault.

He had completely forgotten that yesterday was the anniversary of their parents' deaths. He'd left Jack to visit their graves alone. He should never have urged him to come out to the club last night.

Of course, Jack had let him figure out his mistake on his own. It might have been better if Jack had just punched him in the face and been done with it. But Jack was far more patient than Max could ever hope to be, and making him suffer like this was a special brand of torture.

Jack must have sensed Max's stare—he pulled his shoulders back and stood up straighter.

The fastest way to tell the Force twins apart was to look at the way they styled their hair. Max favored the wavy pompadour, but Jack hardly ever bothered to brush his hair, and it always looked good. Max took great care in making his hairstyle seem effortless, sculpting the stray hairs meticulously to give the impression of ease. If he didn't, it would be a mess. He was secretly envious that Jack could get his hair to look that good without even trying.

In contrast to the office's pure white decor, the boys were expected to dress all in black. Lucifer expected his chief lieutenants to look their best at all times, and the fact that Jack could do it without even trying was a bitter pill for Max to swallow.

Max was about to say something to Jack, anything, when all of a sudden the door behind them slammed open and in strode Aldrich Duncan, Regis of the Blue Blood Coven—Lucifer the Morningstar, Prince of Heaven, Archangel of the Dawn. And he was covered in bright red blood.

He was tall and broad chested, with the chiseled face of a golden-era movie star. He wore a perfectly tailored white suit from Harrods, now ruined like a Jackson Pollock painting. Even without the blood dripping from his chin, his black hair and pale blue eyes made Duncan hard to miss. Charm and charisma radiated off his body, and one got the sense that he was in charge before he even opened his mouth to speak.

Jack and Max watched him, following him only with their eyes, as Lucifer circled around to his desk. He opened a drawer, took out a white handkerchief, and cleaned off his fingers one by one, inspecting the nails. Blood had settled into his cuticles.

"Apologies for the delay, boys," he said, his voice deep and resonant. "I had a late breakfast." He grinned, the gore on his face making a macabre mask.

"Very good, sir," Max said automatically.

Jack didn't say anything, his face flat as stone.

Duncan continued cleaning his fingers, scrubbing away at his fingernails, and said, "You both look well. Healthy. You've been feeding?"

"Yes, sir, we have. Thank you, sir," Max said.

Jack, again, didn't say anything. Max looked at him warily, but Jack remained silent.

"And your summer tutoring sessions—you're keeping up your studies?" Duncan asked. He either didn't notice or didn't care about Jack's silence.

"Nothing but straight A's, my lord," Max said.

Duncan's straight white teeth stood out starkly against all that red when he smiled. "Excellent. You know, your father always said that it was so important to him that you two get your education. It was one of the last things he ever said to me, as a matter of fact. It has been my duty to see his last wish through, to the fullest extent possible. I expect nothing but the best from you two. Your grades are to remain exceptional; I won't tolerate any less. There will be no uneducated vampires on my watch. Even if that education does have to come from dirty Red Bloods." He chuckled as he wiped his face with the handkerchief, but the blood was thick and it only smeared. "But we work with what we have, don't we, boys."

Max nodded. "Yes, of course, my lord."

When their parents died, it was revealed that Duncan had been named their legal guardian. He'd taken both of them under his wing when they had desperately needed it. He let them stay in their family home, living independently and as comfortably as they wished, but managed their finances, seeing that the house staff was paid well and their food taken care of. He ensured that the Force boys were never in want of anything.

Lucifer was as good as their father now. Which was part of the reason Jack's disrespectful behavior was so rankling at the moment.

"A vampire's greatest ability is not his speed or his strength, but his mind," Duncan went on. "The mind is superior to everything;

lesser beings don't know this. It is the key to order above chaos. It is why we are meant to rule the world."

Max glanced at Jack, but Jack's expression remained blank. Whatever he was thinking, he was keeping it to himself. But Duncan had moved on.

"Back to business. What news of the clinics? Are we expecting any more delays?"

"The clinic openings are on schedule," Max said. He stepped forward and handed over his file.

Duncan's smile was luminous as he flipped through the papers, scanning them quickly. His fingers left rusty-red streaks of dried blood behind. "Perfect. I cannot be any more impressed."

Pride swelled in Max's chest.

Aldrich Duncan dropped the file on his desk and said, "You know, my angelic brother Leviathan initially had concerns about my choice, designating you two as my as chief lieutenants. He said anyone was better than two sixteen-year-old Blue Bloods, two newly cycled no less, who haven't even reached their full power yet. And what am I thinking by risking putting a junior at Duchesne as the chief enforcer of the Coven, as the linchpin to our victory?" His pale eyes landed squarely on Max. His voice had been calm and cool, like ice on a frozen lake. But there was a hidden depth that chilled Max to the bone. "What do you think of that?" Duncan asked.

"I think Leviathan underestimates the almighty power of the Twin Angels Abbadon and Azrael," said Jack.

Both Duncan and Max looked at him.

The room was quiet for a moment, but then Duncan's warm

smile broke the tension. "I am inclined to agree, Abbadon," he said to Jack.

Lucifer never smiled at Max like that.

After Lucifer had offered him the job of Venator, Max often had a thought that he dared not entertain, but in that moment, it came back to him like a punch in the gut: Did he get the job as Venator because Jack had declined the offer first? He raised his chin defiantly.

"Good work. You are dismissed," Duncan said.

They took the drive home in their chauffeured Range Rover in silence. Max's hands always shook after meetings with Duncan. Lucifer still frightened him. He had that effect on people, especially Max. He sat with his hands pinned under his armpits to hide them from Jack. He was a coward in so many areas of his life.

He couldn't wait to stop being one, couldn't wait to be strong again, like the angel he once was. There was just one final step that he needed to take. *Soon.*

The next stage of Duncan's plan was almost ready.

Max hadn't told Jack about it yet, but he expected that he would get the offer within the next few days. As Venator, he was the obvious pick. He wasn't sure what Jack would say anyway. Would he try to stop Max? Would Jack join him if he asked? Max imagined Jack would find out eventually. Duncan's plan was already in motion, and Max intended to see it through.

Jack was staring out the window at the passing city, his eyes scanning the empty streets. The silent treatment was getting boring.

"Where did you disappear to this morning?" Max asked.

"I told you, I went home."

"You didn't tell me that at the club. I heard your bedroom door open at four a.m."

"I went for a run," Jack said with a shrug. "Couldn't sleep."

It made sense. Jack had always been that way. If something was troubling him, he'd run somewhere and blow off some steam. He said that running was like meditation, and he could go for miles not thinking about anything. Max couldn't blame him for wanting to get out of the house last night. How could anyone sleep when it was the anniversary of their parents' deaths?

Swallowing his pride, Max said, "I'm sorry you went alone . . . to the cemetery." He made a point not to look at Jack, turning his head to stare out the window. He wasn't sure he was strong enough to see Jack's expression.

"You should have been there," Jack said. Something that sounded an awful lot like contempt lined his voice.

Max glared at him. "I just said I was sorry! What else do you want from me? Do you want me to get on my knees and beg your forgiveness?"

Jack sighed and faced the window again, a muscle in his jaw throbbing. "You're such an asshole."

Max snapped. "I've clearly got a lot going on practically running the whole Coven, if you haven't noticed. I have almost ten million hospital beds that need to be set up, millions of dollars' worth of equipment that needs management, and a bunch of Silver Blood morons who don't know how to do anything themselves! I miss one death anniversary, and suddenly I'm the asshole. There aren't even any bodies there, Jack! They buried empty caskets, and you want me to cry over an empty grave."

Jack's eyelids fluttered closed, and he put his fist to his mouth. Whatever he wanted to say, he was holding himself back.

Max caught himself too, knowing he'd gone too far, and clamped his mouth shut. He slumped back into the seat and frowned. His jealousy had gotten the better of him. The notion that Lucifer still preferred Jack after all this time ate away at his insides like acid, and he didn't know how else to purge himself of it.

They didn't speak for a long while until Max said, softer, "I'm sorry. I should have been there for you."

"He's never going to replace him, you know," Jack said. "Aldrich. No matter how hard you want to believe it . . . he's not Dad."

"I know."

"Do you?" Jack scrutinized him for a moment, and Max shook his head, tired of the conversation. They didn't say anything again until the driver pulled up to their building. Max was the first out the door, followed by Jack. They entered their large, empty house and went straight to their rooms. Max was excited to get out of this dull monochromatic outfit.

When he got to his bedroom door and Jack got to his, Jack spoke up, which made Max pause.

"Have you been having . . ." he began, but he trailed off, as if unsure how to finish.

Max fussed with his silver cuff links, eyebrows cinched with curiosity as he let Jack find the words. Jack licked his lips and shifted his weight on his feet.

"Have you been having any weird dreams lately?"

"No. I don't dream at all."

It was true. Max never dreamed. When he did sleep, he embraced the dark void and then woke up, simple and clean. His answer seemed to trouble Jack, though, and he sighed, making his blond bangs flutter off his forehead.

"I guess we can't all be that lucky," Jack said, and turned to go, but stopped short and added, "What were you doing awake at four anyway? When you heard me leaving?" A teasing glimmer danced in his eyes.

Max rolled his own and managed a smile. "How am I supposed to get any beauty sleep if you're making so much noise sneaking out of the house?"

"You really need all the beauty sleep you can get. In fact, you should be asleep twenty-four/seven, you need it so badly."

"A comedian! Don't quit your day job."

Jack's smile split wider, warming his eyes even more. Max felt a little better, watching his brother disappear into his room. He knew he had to make it up to him somehow, but at least they were on a better footing than they'd been on earlier.

They could never hate each other, not really.

Although Max liked to try.

Twenty-One

MAX

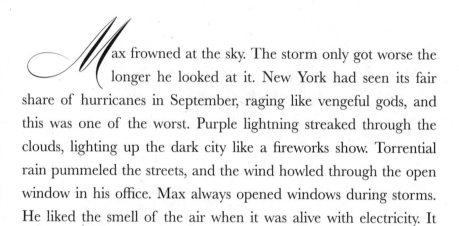

*M*ax frowned at the sky. The storm only got worse the longer he looked at it. New York had seen its fair share of hurricanes in September, raging like vengeful gods, and this was one of the worst. Purple lightning streaked through the clouds, lighting up the dark city like a fireworks show. Torrential rain pummeled the streets, and the wind howled through the open window in his office. Max always opened windows during storms. He liked the smell of the air when it was alive with electricity. It made him feel alive too.

But in all his years of watching, he'd hardly ever seen a storm like this. The climate had gotten worse over the centuries. Max had seen it change through hundreds of eyes, but this was different. This storm was . . . unusual.

The storm was causing delays at one of the clinics.

For days, they had been dealing with a series of setbacks all over the island, with clinics either being vandalized or broken into. At first there were only minor crimes, like broken locks on doors and such, but with more and more clinics being built, there were more and more instances of vandalism and theft. If Max didn't know any better, he would have thought it was sabotage.

One of his Blue Blood wardens, a man named Thomas, had arrived to report the bad news while Max stood at the window, watching the clouds swirl.

"The building in the Seaport is damaged," Thomas said. "The electrical wiring seems to have caught fire and—"

Max's thoughts churned like the storm. He spun around. "How long a delay does this cost us?"

Thomas's eyes darted around the room as if he were looking for an answer Max would want to hear. "A week? Perhaps more."

"We don't have a week. You have five days."

"Yes, sir, it's just . . . the lightning. Rather, we think it was lightning. . . ."

"You think?"

"The building was fine, and then there was this bright light—"

Max's patience was running out. He pinched the bridge of his nose with his fingers, trying to quash the pain blooming behind his eyes. If he had known being a Venator was just a glorified managerial position, overseeing a horde of brain-dead vampires who didn't know the difference between right and left, he never would have applied for the job. "I don't care what you think, Warden Thomas. Just get it done."

"Yes, sir," Thomas said, bowing slightly at the waist. His raincoat glistened with water in the light from the fireplace.

"Hesitation from anyone will not be tolerated. Lucifer orders, we obey. Understood? Operation Argenti will only be the beginning of a brighter future. Everything will change, but first I need you to do your goddamn job. Get the clinics operational, and we won't have any more problems."

"Yes, sir. The humans don't stand a chance, sir."

"As it was meant to be. Dismissed."

Warden Thomas left in a hurry, as if he couldn't get out of Max's office fast enough.

Max too wanted to be done for the day. Since the storm started, he'd had a splitting headache that he was sure would cleave his skull in two. Now it was only getting worse. The stress of being Lucifer's right hand was starting to fray the edges of his sanity. Managing Blue Bloods was a lot more work than he'd thought.

On his way out of the office, Max passed Jack in the entrance hall. Jack had been reading and walking at the same time and looked up when Max went by.

"Trouble with another clinic?" he asked, tipping his head to Thomas's retreating back as the man disappeared out the front door.

Max didn't slow down as he climbed the stairs. "A Venator's job is never-ending."

Once in his room, Max felt like he could finally breathe.

Max kept his room dark at all times. It helped ease the head-aches. He took off his shirt and tossed it into a corner of the room, then kicked off his shoes. The rain was louder here, clattering against the glass. It was the perfect sound to fall asleep to.

Just as he was about to throw himself onto the mattress, Max noticed that the window was cracked open and the curtains bil-lowed in the wind. He hadn't left it open. Puddles of rain trailed back and forth across the floor. Someone had been here, and who-ever it was had left the way they came.

Max's heart raced. He flicked on the light. An envelope had been left on his bed. It was addressed to Azrael. To him.

His fingers tingled as he opened the letter. Inside was a small piece of parchment, no larger than an index card. On it, written in neat script, were the words:

MF,
You're better than this.
XO
KM

TWENTY-TWO

MAX

You're better than this.

The note stared up at Max from its place on his desk.

He had taken his morning coffee in his office, but he sat looking at the note for so long that it had gone cold. He had his chin rested on his folded arms as he leaned upon his desk, willing the note to make sense.

Those words had stuck with him all night. Just who could KM be? He didn't know anyone with those initials. Katherine? Karolina? Kyle? Kevin? Angelic or mortal, no one that he knew fit.

Who did this person think they were? Who were they to say they had any idea who *he* was? Who could pretend to know anything about him, let alone think that he could be better than he already was? And how could they sneak into his room several stories off the ground and leave a note in his bedroom with his name on it?

The morning after the storm had become bright and sunny, almost taunting Max with how beautiful the day promised to be.

"You look rough."

Max looked up to see that Jack had let himself into his office. He was dressed in a tank and loose sweats for their usual sparring match, but his eyes were heavy and dark. He stood half in the door-way, half in the hall, like a specter coming to haunt his twin. His hair didn't have the usual lift, and bags shadowed his eyes.

"Speak for yourself," Max said. "You look like you've been hit by a bus."

"Don't you know that's the latest fashion?" Jack said with a sardonic grin. "Are you ready to spar?"

"In a minute. What are you doing here anyway?"

"I can't find my cigarettes. Have you seen them anywhere?"

"Your . . . cigarettes?" Max said slowly. He wasn't sure he'd heard Jack correctly.

"Yeah, I . . ." He mimed slapping a pack on his palm, like it would somehow manifest in his hands. Jack furrowed his brow as he did so. "I thought I had some. Didn't I?"

"You've never smoked a day in your life."

"Really?"

Max scrunched up his nose like he could already smell the putrid, sticky tobacco trapped in the fabric of his clothes. "Ew, Jack, no! It's gross, and I'm glad you don't. Are you sure you didn't dream it?"

Jack pressed his lips together and sighed. "Right. Just a dream." He didn't seem convinced. His attention landed on Max's desk and the letter. "What's that?"

It was Max's turn to sigh. "I'm inclined to think it's some kind of practical joke."

Jack picked up the letter. His eyes flicked over the words several times before he flipped it over in case there was anything on the back. There wasn't, but it made Max smile because he had done the exact same thing. They truly were brothers.

"KM?" Jack said. "Kingsley Martin, of course."

Max sat up ramrod straight. "Who?"

"Oh, come on. Kingsley Martin. Don't you remember?"

Max gestured impatiently because obviously he didn't.

Jack dropped the letter back onto the desk. It slipped on a pocket of air and came to rest right near Max's hand, light as a feather. He leaned forward, bracing himself on the desk, his eyes blazing. "He betrayed Aldrich centuries ago. He's dangerous. He was also your best friend."

"What in heaven and hell are you talking about?" Max had risen to his feet, every muscle in his body charged.

Jack blinked, as if snapping out of a daze, and reeled. His eyes went round and wide. "That's . . . Why did I say that? I don't know what I'm talking about."

"Yes you do. How do you know this person?"

Jack shook his head and ran his fingers through his hair. "I don't know!"

Max slammed his hands on the desk. "Goddammit, Jack! Focus. Why do you think he's my best friend? I have never heard of him."

"Yes, you have, he's . . . he's a Venator. He's—"

"No, he's not. I know every single one of our Blue Bloods." Max narrowed his eyes. "What is going on with you?"

Jack turned and walked away a few steps, pressing his hands into his face. Max stared at him, his brow furrowed. Jack hadn't been acting like himself for the past few days. At first, Max had noticed the smaller details, like Jack looking at their house as if he were seeing it for the first time or Jack not knowing where they kept the spoons in the kitchen. Their whole lives, Jack had been the sensible, level-headed one, never the one to make a scene or cause a commotion. People always used to tell their parents that they wished they had a child who was as soft-spoken and well-behaved as Jack, always Jack. Never Max.

Seeing his brother start to unravel unnerved Max. He hoped it wouldn't get worse.

Jack's attention fell away to the window. His stare could have spanned thousands of miles. But then he took a breath and dragged his hands down his face. Whatever had just happened, it passed. The panic in Jack's eyes ebbed away, and he glanced back at Max.

"I must have dreamed it."

"You've been doing that a lot lately," Max said pointedly. Jack's relationship with reality was shaky at best.

"You think I'm crazy."

"I admit the thought has crossed my mind."

"I'm *not* crazy!" Jack pointed his finger as he said each word. "I am just . . . I don't sleep well anymore; I don't feed. I sense Lucifer's power growing, and it . . . must be affecting me." He looked out the window again.

"Why didn't you say anything?" Max asked.

"You have enough to worry about. I'm fine."

Max let out a long, low breath. The uptick in the break-ins and the vandalism was weighing on him. Jack's mental health was one more thing on his plate. "When was the last time you fed on a human?"

Jack gave a noncommittal shrug.

"Then it's time. Maybe then you'll have a chance to relax and enjoy the fruits of our labor for once."

The muscle in Jack's jaw pulsed, but he nodded.

Max folded his arms across his chest and looked his brother over. "Maybe it's for the best that you didn't become Venator. With everything you're going through . . . I'm not sure you would have been able to handle it."

Jack's lip curled in disgust. "You don't even know how much—" He clamped his lips tight and didn't finish his sentence.

"What, Jack? Say what you want to say."

"Nothing." Jack turned and headed for the door. "I'm going back to bed."

"No school, then?" Max coolly called after him, but if Jack heard him, he didn't answer.

Max sat back down at his desk and traced the card with his finger. One thing was certain, he wasn't going to tell Duncan about this note until he knew for certain what to do about it. If Jack was right and this Kingsley person really had written it, Max needed to be smart and strategic.

He brought the note to his nose. It smelled like burned sugar.

TWENTY-THREE

MAX

"I need a drink," Max said, flying into their home library, finding Jack exactly where he expected him to be, sitting in his usual window seat, reading. The setting sun cast him in shadow.

As usual, the school day at Duchesne had been uneventful. Teachers had assigned homework, but Max would rather read even the dullest of vampire intel than study the likes of chemical structures and equations. He was itching to get out and do something that made him feel alive.

Even though school had started again and he was back at lacrosse practice with his team, he missed being able to surround himself with people. No matter what, Max always felt like he was standing in an empty room, shouting, and no one could hear.

One headache that had been invading his every waking moment was particularly worrying.

There was a group of rebels trying to undermine Duncan's plan, and they were getting better at their job.

This underground resistance was growing more confident,

choosing larger targets and making grander moves, but their demands were still unknown. The clinic at the Seaport was only the beginning. A clinic on the Upper West Side had been leveled almost entirely; all that remained was a pile of bricks and dust. It was as if the building itself had disintegrated. When Max had arrived on the scene, he found that all the buildings nearby were unscathed, even their windows still intact. If he didn't know any better, he might have thought it was magic.

However, there had been a break in the case. A clue had been left behind.

Max had shifted piles of broken cement idly with his foot while the cleanup crews began to rebuild, and he'd found a piece of brick with a strange chalk mark on it, barely legible in the dust. Three curved lines and half a circle, the rest too damaged to decipher . . . Perhaps writing of some kind?

No way had it been a part of the clinic before this; Max had been to the site and had never seen any kind of markings like it. It was too peculiar to ignore. He kept the shard in his pocket, a reminder that his work was never finished, and as long as these acts of sabotage kept happening, he would never sleep.

Still, he kept his efforts to find KM and these saboteurs to himself. As Venator, it was his job to investigate and suss out any opposition to the cause. Aldrich Duncan would not be burdened with his subordinates' failures.

The clinics were almost complete, almost ready to open; they were so close to completion, and Max had been working almost night and day to see that there would be no more interruptions, not from anyone, especially from these phantoms bent on trying their hardest to stop him. It was even more important that he get a drink, now more than ever.

"If you want something, there're some bottles of frizzante in the fridge. The import just came in," Jack said. He flipped the page of his book, not looking up. Whereas Max was the extroverted type, and always yearned to be the center of attention, Jack would often choose to sit in a corner by himself and read at parties. Max always thought that was terribly dull and never understood the appeal. How could anyone sit still for that long?

Max came over and yanked the book out of Jack's hand. It was some story about Russian brothers—already Max didn't care. It was so typical for his brother to choose something extra boring to read. Jack sighed loudly as Max snapped the cover shut. "I'm not talking about sparkling water."

"Then go out." Jack snatched at the book, but Max held it out of reach.

"Not without you."

"Why?"

"Because I'm trying to be nice. You need a break as much as I do, so I'm politely inviting you to come to Block 122 with me."

Jack sighed loudly. "I told you not to worry about me."

"I can't help it. I'm the older brother, so I'm supposed to worry about you."

"Are you always going to hang those two minutes over my head?" Jack smirked. There was the brother he knew and loved.

"Get dressed. You'll thank me later."

~ ~ ~

Max threw back his shot and leaned on the bar. He liked the taste of tequila and how it burned on the way down his throat. While he couldn't get drunk, he could at least enjoy the simple pleasures of tasting liquor.

The music wasn't so much music anymore, but a constant, hypnotic drone. Blinking lights and deep bass permeated the entire club. The DJ bobbed his head to the mix, sequined dresses sparkled in the lights, and dozens of bodies danced on the dance floor.

Max tipped his head back, soaking up the energy of the room, and smiled. This was his temple, a refuge from the world.

He had lost track of Jack in the crowd, but that was the point. Max and Jack had different approaches to the game. Jack was off doing his own thing, probably with a girl in a hallway somewhere, finally letting loose and taking his fill in privacy. Max took a lime wedge from the bar and sucked on the sour juices as he caught the gaze of a girl standing on the other side of the bar. He grinned when she looked at him under her long lashes, the red of her lipstick standing out against the paleness of her skin. Max's eyes drifted to her throat, and his mouth watered. He needed a chaser after taking such a strong shot, something sweet and satisfying. These humans should have known to stay home, should have known what waited for them in the dark.

A warm, strong hand rested upon his, and before Max could realize what was happening, he had been whipped onto the dance floor. Leather. Whiskey. And the smell of something else too, all too familiar, even in the dark of the club. The stranger had found him again.

The song changed and picked up tempo, matching the beat of

Max's heart. All thoughts of the girl at the bar melted away. Whoever this stranger was, he knew how to move, drawing Max in as if he were the only person that mattered in the universe. Max grinned as he danced, draping his arms over the stranger's shoulders and losing himself in a moment of pure, basic hedonism. Max couldn't keep his hands off him, and the stranger held on like he was afraid to let go, afraid that the clock might strike midnight and their night would end. They pressed up against each other, cheeks almost touching, and Max's hands wanted to be everywhere at once. The stranger was broad shouldered and lithe, his biceps firm beneath the soft texture of his shirt. He was sturdy, like a pillar, and grounded. Max's head swam with yearning.

Their lips hovered inches from each other's face. The stranger took up the entirety of Max's field of vision: the curve of his cheek, the straight slope of his nose, the glint of his teeth. If it were possible, Max could have drowned in all of it.

The stranger spun Max around and pressed Max's back up against his front. The whole club seemed to fade away, like they were the only two people left on earth, surrounded by faceless ghosts.

"We know each other . . ." the stranger said in his ear, still swaying to the music that had become a muted afterthought.

Max could barely speak. "From where?"

He answered with a touch to Max's chest, his fingers pressing firmly on his breastbone. Max's heart hammered, and he was positive the stranger could feel it.

"Remember." His breath tickled Max's neck, sending a shiver down his spine.

An invisible hole punched through Max's chest and made his

fingers go numb, and it only got wider, as if desperate hands were tearing it open. He clutched the front of his shirt with his fist and notched his fingers into the stranger's hand. All the air had left his lungs like he'd sprung a leak, and sweat trickled down his back. The club ahead of him seemed to narrow with pinpoint focus, tunneling with no way out except forward. His heart felt like it was imploding like a black hole.

He closed his eyes and forced himself to breathe. Just breathe.

What was happening? What was wrong with him?

No one had ever made him feel this way.

Lucifer's voice echoed in the back of his mind. *You don't need anyone,* he'd said to Max. *You don't need anyone but me.*

Max's lungs started to work properly again, and he inhaled deeply. He willed himself to get back in control, even if every atom in his body tried to resist.

This stranger had touched a part of his soul and rattled the lock on it.

Something in his belly twisted, and the invisible hole in Max's chest sealed up. He felt sick all of a sudden and pushed away, breaking free of the stranger's embrace.

He needed to get out of there as fast as he could.

That stranger was no mortal Red Blood.

Max would never admit it, but he was shaken. He put his walls back up, steeled his heart, and did what he was best at: pretending.

Jack saw him heading for the door and shot him a confused look. The second their eyes met, though, Jack knew that there was no room for questions—it was time to go.

Max burst out of the club, not caring that he'd nearly knocked over a couple on his way. And when the girl named Schuyler mistook him for his brother, it wasn't even on his radar. His mind buzzed like a swarm of bees as he masked his confusion with snark, but all the while willing his heart to return to a normal rhythm. He barely even noticed when the girl stepped out in front of his car and Jack saved her. He just wanted to go home and go to sleep and forget.

And that night, for the first time in what felt like forever, he dreamed.

In the early hours of the morning, Max sat in the dark, hunched over his computer, typing different spelling variations of the name Kingsley Martin in Google. Nothing. No one.

Your search did not match any results. Try different key words.

Max dug his fists into his eyes, scrubbing furiously. He shouldn't have been surprised—no matter how many times he searched, the engine yielded the same tauntingly blank page.

If Kingsley Martin did exist, and he really was KM like Jack said, why would he risk coming to Max's house and leaving a note for him? Was he cocky and confident in his own skills to keep one step ahead of Max's reach? Could he be behind the attacks on the clinics? Or was KM, perhaps, a moniker for a group? Maybe Jack really was going crazy. Or was, at least, wrong.

One thing was for certain: Kingsley Martin did not want to be found.

"Or he really doesn't exist," Max muttered to the infuriatingly unhelpful search screen.

No, he had to exist. Jack wouldn't make up a name to mess with him. Kingsley Martin had to be out there somewhere.

He'd dreamed about it.

This was the third night in a row that Max had woken up from a dream of chasing a figure down a long tunnel. His heart pounded so fast, it was almost like he'd actually been running, and it got him too wired to go back to sleep. It showed in the circles under his eyes.

Over the past few days, Max had sent a team of Blue Blood agents to gather intel from various factions across the island, interviewing any potential witnesses who might know the name, binding them to utmost secrecy. Modern methods were getting him nowhere. Max needed to do this the old-fashioned way: get people talking.

So far, no one had found anything. And as the sun rose that morning, he expected that today would be the same, but along with his breakfast delivered to his office came an envelope from one of his agents. Max tore it open and scanned the document, finding the name Kingsley Martin and tamping down his beating heart.

According to the intel, Kingsley Martin was definitely real and definitely a threat.

But Max's vindication was short-lived when the brief went on to say that there wasn't much information beyond that. Nobody knew who he was or where he lived. People called him a ghost, a rumor, a myth, while others claimed to have met him—to have seen him in the shadows. How could Kingsley know as much about the clinics as he did? Was he the mastermind? Was he the leader of the rebellion and the letter he sent a calling card? How dangerous was Kingsley Martin?

Max couldn't give this information to Aldrich. There wasn't enough to move on. He would only be presenting Aldrich with a problem, not a solution, which would look like Max was asking for help. He couldn't afford to seem like he wasn't in control, even though it was true. Desperation wasn't a good look.

For once, Max would take a page out of Jack's book and be patient.

Kingsley Martin would be found soon enough.

TWENTY-FOUR

MAX

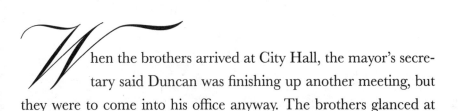

hen the brothers arrived at City Hall, the mayor's secretary said Duncan was finishing up another meeting, but they were to come into his office anyway. The brothers glanced at each other before being let inside.

Already standing in Duncan's office was Warden Thomas. The warden glanced at Max with a sour expression, lifted his chin, and continued his conversation with Aldrich, who remained seated behind his desk, his fingers steepled. He wore a dark pin-striped suit, the one he often wore for television appearances. Duncan's eyes landed on Max for a brief moment before returning to the warden. Max's stomach dropped. This couldn't be good.

"As I was saying, my lord," Thomas went on, "I thought you should know that the clinics are under attack."

Max felt like throwing up.

Thomas, in his warden uniform, with his shoulders thrown back and his head held high, looked like a general standing at attention. He was a dark-haired, middle-aged Blue Blood, graying at the temples, and hailed from one of the lower families, one of the lesser angels when they fell.

Duncan rose from his desk slowly, came around the front, and perched on the edge. He looked at Max. "Is this true, Venator? Is what Warden Thomas here says about Operation Argenti accurate?"

Jack stiffened at Max's side, but Max couldn't move.

Duncan continued. "He's provided enough evidence to show that these are no accidents, that these are targeted attacks, in particular the fire at the Seaport. The warden says that you dismissed him and that he doesn't have . . . *faith* in your judgment."

Thomas lifted his nose haughtily at Max. Max's heart had lodged in his throat. He didn't know what to say. Fortunately, Duncan didn't ask him to speak.

"Thank you, Warden," Duncan said. "You came to me feeling that I deserved to know about the lack of leadership displayed by your superiors. I understand your discontent, I truly do. . . . You saw mismanagement and you decided to act. It was a very brave thing to speak up." Duncan tapped his fingertips together thoughtfully and stared at the white carpet. He was barefoot.

"My greatest wish is to see your vision come to fruition, my liege," Thomas said, looking smug.

Duncan sighed, tipped his head toward Max and Jack, and said, "Blue would be awfully hard to wash out, wouldn't it?"

Thomas looked at Max and Jack too, his eyebrows cinched curiously. But he didn't have time to react.

Duncan lashed out, grabbed Thomas around the throat, and lifted him off the floor. His fingers pressed deeply into Thomas's neck, so hard that his knuckles turned white. There came the distinct sound of bones cracking as Thomas's eyes bulged and he thrashed, grabbing uselessly at Duncan's hand. He made a terrible gurgling sound as he gasped for air.

Duncan's face transformed into a mask of pure rage. When he squeezed, Thomas squeaked like a mouse. "You distrust your superiors, yet it is on my authority that those superiors are chosen. Therefore you distrust me."

Thomas tried to shake his head, to say anything, but he was turning a deep shade of navy. Drool slid out from the corners of his mouth.

Duncan sneered. "You think you are above Azrael, the Angel of Death, and you forget your place. Your insolence will not be tolerated in my kingdom."

With that, he snapped Thomas's neck and let go. Thomas dropped hard to the white carpet, dead.

No one spoke or moved. A lock of Duncan's hair had fallen onto his forehead, and he pushed it back into place as he moved to stand in front of the window. Overlooking the city, his hands clasped behind his back, he said nothing for a long while. His toes clenched over and over in the deep-pile carpet, as if he were soothing himself.

"I'm sorry you had to witness that, boys," Duncan finally said. "Hopefully a few years of rebirth will make Thomas see his error."

With a deep breath he turned to face them, and Duncan's handsome visage returned with the politician's smile.

Try as he might, Max was unable to speak. His mouth had gone as dry as the Sahara, but his tongue couldn't form words anyway. It was tying itself into knots as if it were afraid that it would be ripped from his mouth for saying the wrong thing.

Max couldn't stop staring at the body on the floor. Duncan had killed the man like it was as easy as breathing. He knew the stories, same as everyone, but seeing the reality of them rocked Max to the core. He clenched his fists tightly behind his back, desperately hiding his trembling hands.

"Well?" Duncan finally said. His voice was level, measured. It chilled Max down to the bone.

Max tore his gaze away from the murder scene and cleared his throat.

"I didn't . . ." Max started, stopped, and then started again. Heat rushed to the back of his neck, like he'd been slapped. "I didn't want to trouble you, sir. Most of the clinics are almost up and running. I considered it a nonissue. I had it under control." He needed to show Lucifer that he was not weak and that he was worthy of the power he had been given. He couldn't be like that body on the floor, worthless, less than worthless—nothing.

"'Most' clinics . . ." Duncan repeated. He let Max's own words linger in the air heavily for a moment. Max didn't dare move a muscle. "Do you know who is behind this?"

"I . . . need to investigate further." That was a lie. Kingsley Martin—if he really had betrayed Lucifer all those years ago, what would stop him from doing it again now? But Max needed to wait. He promised himself he wouldn't bring it up to Lucifer until he had proof that what Jack had said was real. He couldn't be made to look like a fool chasing a ghost, especially not now.

As if sensing the lie, Duncan looked Max over, scanning him up and down. Max stood a little straighter, hoping he could mask any hesitancy Duncan was looking for. His pale blue eyes stared as if they could peer right through Max's skin, and Max's skin crawled like it was covered with a million ants.

"Is there something else that you're not telling me?" Duncan asked.

Words failed Max again. He should tell him about the letter from KM. Aldrich Duncan would know how to deal with traitors. Max's eyes landed on the body on the floor once more. *Clearly.* Telling Duncan might be the answer to all his problems. But something held him back.

You're better than this.

Max was taking too long to respond, and Duncan glared at him down the length of his sharp nose. His eyes, cold as frostbite, glued Max's shoes to the floor.

Just as Max opened his mouth to say something, Jack stepped forward.

"No," Jack said. "There's nothing else." It was the equivalent of diving into the path of an oncoming bullet aimed straight for Max's head. "My brother is the best Venator we have. He's working tirelessly to complete your mission. I have no doubt that he will see it through to the end."

Max couldn't afford a sigh of relief.

Duncan regarded Jack warmly, softening at Jack's assurance. "So it would seem. I don't want any more delays. I'm granting you full control over my hellhounds; use them, if you have to, as backup. My hounds will be able to track anything that stands in our way, including these rebels who don't know when the battle is already won." Duncan moved around to his desk once more. "We are doing God's will. Make sure the plans for the Silver Legacy are intact."

Jack flinched at the words *Silver Legacy* and looked at Max, eyes wide. Fortunately for him, Duncan hadn't noticed.

Max bowed his head and said, "Yes, Master."

Duncan smiled at Max then, but any warmth there might have been in his eyes for Jack disappeared. "Do not disappoint me."

"I won't. You have my word."

"Good. When the Red Bloods flood into our clinics in their desperation for a cure to this plague, we will be waiting for them. One by one, we will trap and harvest the humans like cattle. We can keep them alive for years with enough of these modern medical devices. They will return to their original purpose on this earth: serving as fuel for our crusade. And after they die and we deliver their souls back to God, we will reclaim the world for ourselves. As it was meant to be."

The true vision of Lucifer's work, on full display. First New York City, then the rest of the United States, and then the world. Why kill the humans when you could keep them in a vegetative state for years, constantly feeding upon them forever? One day the world would know, and by then it would be too late. Lucifer was going to rule. And Max was going to do everything in his power to make sure it happened. It was what he was designed to do in heaven, and he wasn't going to fail on earth.

"As it will be done," Max and Jack recited back, bowing together.

"Dismissed." Jack and Max turned to go as Duncan called out, "Someone come in here and clean up this mess." He waved vaguely at the corpse on his office floor. "And, Jack . . . ?"

The brothers paused. Duncan casually flipped through a few papers on his desk.

"If you would stay behind a moment?"

Jack glanced at Max briefly—no doubt seeing a mixture of fear and curiosity on Max's face, he wondered what Aldrich could possibly want to talk about alone—before Max saw himself out of the office. There was no use in defying Lucifer's will.

After a few minutes, Jack emerged from Duncan's office, looking sallow, and the brothers left the suite, silently waiting for the elevator to take them down to the lobby. Max's hands shook even though he clenched them into fists so tightly his nails cut into his palms, bringing the blue blood up in little crescents. Jack pushed the button to call the elevator while Max loosened the tie around his neck. It felt like it was choking the life out of him.

"What was that about?" Max hissed, keeping his voice low. "What'd Aldrich want?"

"Doesn't matter." Jack stared at the illuminated numbers above the door.

"It looks like it matters. You're pale as hell. What was it? What did you talk about?"

Jack didn't answer.

"Did he say anything about me?"

Jack managed a weak smile. "Believe it or not, Max, not everything is about you."

Max's cheeks flushed. Jealousy was a vicious beast in his gut. "Why do you always have to do that, anyway?"

"Do what?"

"Talk over me in front of Aldrich! I'm a Venator. I'm capable of handling the heat. I don't need to be saved all the time."

"Right, I'll keep that in mind."

The elevator doors opened. The twins entered, and Jack hit the button for the lobby. Max leaned on the handrail as the doors closed and the elevator descended. He wasn't sure he could keep his balance. It always took him a moment to get his bearings after dealing with Duncan.

"You lied to him back there," Max said. "Why?"

Jack shrugged. "I didn't lie. I just didn't tell him everything."

"That's not lying to you?"

"No."

Max huffed. "I should have told him about Kingsley. Maybe then he would have turned his attention to the real enemy."

"That wouldn't have worked, and you know it. Besides, Kingsley is only one person. There's no way he's working alone. Aldrich wants solutions, not problems."

Max worked his jaw, annoyed, because he'd thought the same thing. Maybe Jack really should have been Venator instead of him. But he didn't seem as obsessed and frantic about KM as Max was. Whatever was going on with Jack, he was keeping it to himself.

Why had Aldrich asked Jack to talk privately anyway? The not knowing ate away at Max's insides. He wasn't used to being kept in the dark about anything. Anger spiked in his chest, and he lashed out.

"How did you *know* that the letter was from Kingsley Martin when I've never heard of the guy? Why do you remember him when I don't? Why do you think he's my best friend? What aren't you telling me?" He was shouting by the time he finished, but Jack didn't rise to his level.

He simply shook his head in disbelief and laughed. "You just won't quit, will you? Can't you trust me for once? You know the guy exists, that he's against us. Isn't that enough?"

"Because what if I think *you're* working with Kingsley Martin?"

There, Max admitted it. How else would Jack know this person, know this traitor?

Jack pressed his lips together, his hackles rising.

The elevator car shook for a moment, the lights flickering. Max wobbled off-balance, but Jack let out a calming breath and said quietly, "I'm not."

Max watched Jack for a moment, searching for truth laid bare. Jack had always been the honest one.

Jack continued. "If I was wrong—if it isn't Kingsley—can you imagine the hell you'd pay for saying it was? You'd be just as dead as Thomas. I gave you an out. You just have to follow through with it. Find out more about Kingsley Martin, what he's planning, and why. Prove to Duncan I was wrong, that there *is* something going on. It'll make you look good."

"It makes me look *weak*, bro."

"Is that all that matters to you?"

"It's all that needs to matter. You wouldn't understand."

"You're right, I don't understand," Jack said.

Max snarled. He didn't need to explain himself anymore. "You've changed."

"Maybe I'm growing up. You should try it sometime."

"I don't need you to tell me what to do."

"Well, someone has to do it."

Max's upper lip twitched. Heat rushed to his face, anger flaring in his gut. "I'm not a child," he said.

"You're right, you're not. You're just stupid. Tell me what the Silver Legacy is, Max." Max stiffened. He knew when Aldrich mentioned it earlier, it was inevitable that Jack would ask for details. "Is it what it sounds like?"

Max stayed silent, and realization settled over Jack's face. But Jack would never understand. Max wanted to be strong. He needed to be.

Max leveled his gaze and said, "The Silver Legacy is the only way. Aldrich is right. I'm sick and tired of waiting for heaven. I'm going to take it for us."

"Is that what you think will happen?"

"Lucifer is guiding us toward a bright, new future," Max said. "A future that will ensure we will never be confined to the darkness again. We'll be unstoppable. The Silver Legacy is my destiny."

"Like hell it is!" Jack slammed his palm against the emergency stop button on the panel, and the elevator came to a halt. There was that fire in his eyes that Max had been looking for. Jack wasn't so perfect after all. "You won't even entertain the idea that you're being used?"

Max rolled his eyes. "You always think you know best, don't you? I know what must be done."

Jack winced and raked his fingers through his hair.

"Oh, Jack. Why don't you understand all the possibilities in front of us?" Max asked. "I'm leading us toward greatness. And I'm the only one willing to make it."

"You can't be serious," Jack said.

Max lifted his chin defiantly. He *was* serious. "Like our current situation here on earth is any better."

"Don't say that. You can't mean it. You can't know what you're getting into. Don't go down this path."

Max reached past Jack and released the emergency stop button to start the elevator's descent again. He couldn't stay a fallen angel anymore, recycling his soul over and over into mortal bodies. He was so tired. The time was fast approaching. He would be the best, nigh invincible. Just like Azrael, the Angel of Death, should be.

To be the strongest, however, meant that he had to make some sacrifices. It was the price one paid for power.

"What happened to you?" Jack asked. His eyes shone with emotion.

"Something that should have happened a long time ago. I've been shown the way."

Jack clenched his teeth so hard, Max was almost convinced they would crack. "Have we really grown this far apart?" Jack asked.

"Maybe you should consider being more like me."

The elevator pinged as it reached the bottom floor. Finally, Max had struck a nerve.

"Think about it," he said, smirking. "Maybe all this time you've been holding yourself back."

The elevator doors opened, and Max walked through the lobby and out the revolving doors to the street. Their driver had been idling the engine for them, and he climbed inside. He glanced back at Jack, waiting for him to come.

Jack was still fuming inside the lobby, working his jaw muscles and tapping his heels aggressively. But finally, he exited the building and got in the car with Max. He didn't say anything as he slammed the door and the car took off down the street, heading for the Seaport, where they would personally oversee the clinic's final preparations before opening.

Together, they drove toward Lucifer's mission. Together, again. Together, as they were meant to be.

PART THREE
ANGELS AND DEMONS

THIS IS NOT SOME SILLY GAME. . . .
THIS IS LIFE AND DEATH.
ANGELS AND DEMONS.
—REVELATIONS

Twenty-Five

JACK

ack Force had the whole house to himself for once, which was exactly how he liked it. He loved his brother, but sometimes Max filled up so much space in every room he walked into. It was nice to be able to breathe. Ever since the day they saw Duncan kill Thomas, Max had been going above and beyond to make sure that Lucifer's vision was seen through to the end. In fact, Jack wasn't sure if Max had even returned home after leaving with a crew of wardens last night. When Jack got up for a run this morning, Max wasn't in his room or in his office, leaving Jack to work out all by himself. The good thing about that was he could catch up on his audiobooks during his miles-long run through the empty streets of Manhattan.

He didn't technically need to exercise. Both boys had super strength and speed as vampires, so Max always said going for a run was a pointless endeavor. But Jack liked the hypnotic rhythm of it. It was easier than meditation. His mind could relax, and he could simply exist in the moment. And seeing the sun rise over the East River was one of the highlights of his day.

He had a lot to think about these days. An ever-present weight bearing down on him, and no matter what he did, it only got heavier.

The Silver Legacy.

Just back from his run, flushed and energized, Jack found the house was as empty as he'd left it. He took a glass down from the cabinet in the kitchen, filled it up with cold water at the sink, and took a sip. He wandered to the living room, brightly lit by the morning sun, where the television murmured quietly, airing a news segment about clinic openings. He paused to watch.

The reporter stated, "Registration for appointments begins tomorrow, starting with the most vulnerable age groups."

Lucifer's plan was almost complete. Soon everything would change. Operation Argenti. The Silver Legacy. The whole world. Jack's chest tightened as he remembered his conversation with Aldrich, standing stoically next to the body of the dead warden on the floor, trying not to stare and imagine that it was Max lying there instead.

What Lucifer was asking of him . . . Jack knew he should do it. If he didn't, then Max would. His brother was so eager to impress. Jack wasn't sure he could bear to see Max go through such a thing. What he would become . . . No. Jack needed to take on this responsibility so Max wouldn't have to. He'd told Duncan he'd think about it. He had to protect his brother.

The glass in Jack's hand shattered into a million little pieces. Water spilled all over the wood floor, and his palm was covered in bright blue blood. Some pieces of the glass had sliced deep into his skin.

Because Jack was the Angel of Destruction, things had a

tendency to break in his presence. When he was little, his parents had gifted him and Max an indoor tree house that spanned the entirety of their shared bedroom for their sixth birthday. Jack had been so excited to play in it, because he'd just finished reading *Swiss Family Robinson*, but the moment he touched the tree house, the entire structure collapsed into a heap of lumber. His parents comforted the distraught boys by saying that it had probably been assembled incorrectly, but Jack knew the truth. He was cursed. Destruction was his destiny, his entire purpose in being. He would never be able to do anything else.

Over the years, he'd learned to control his curse somewhat. He'd noticed that the destruction happened when he was upset or angry, so he'd learned to temper his emotions. Sometimes it worked, sometimes it didn't, but it was harder now, especially since his nightmares had started getting worse. The dreams hardly made sense, like a hall of mirrors—a maze constructed of emotion—unfiltered, raw feelings—barely concrete scenes impossible to piece together. Jack felt like he'd been stumbling face-first into his reflection at every turn, and he didn't know which way was out. His dreams were trying to show him something, a face with bright blue eyes and soft lips. But his dreams were warped and too indistinct to grab hold of. And they always ended the same way: He'd be falling through a pitch-black void, hurtling toward a gigantic, unblinking bloodred eye, unable to do anything but brace for impact. Then he'd wake up, sitting upright, his stomach in his throat like he'd been falling for real.

He never told Max about the dreams. Max didn't need to know.

Jack wrapped his bloody hand in a kitchen towel, got on his knees, and cleaned up the mess. He was used to cleaning up messes.

A ring of the doorbell brought him to his feet, and he answered the door only to be surprised to find Schuyler Cervantes-Chase standing on the threshold. They'd only been going to school together for a few years, but he knew her face so well. She had her brown curls pulled up into a messy bun on top of her head. Her eyes were so big, and blue, and bright, and they melted when her gaze landed on him.

"Hi," she said breathily. Her fingers flexed like she had an urge to reach out but held herself back. She noticed the towel wrapped around Jack's hand.

Jack pressed his thumb firmly into his palm, so forcefully that it started to hurt. But he was afraid she would see the blue and know that he wasn't mortal.

"What are you doing here?" he asked in a hushed voice, and looked up and down Fifth Avenue, just in case anyone from the Coven was nearby.

"We need to talk," she said.

"It's really not a good time," he said. The longer she stayed, the greater the chance that Max would come back.

Her cheek twitched as if she was hurt. "I know I shouldn't have come here . . ." she said under her breath, as if to herself. After a second, she steadied her shoulders and looked him in the eye. "But I can't do nothing. I want you to remember that . . . you don't have to do this."

Jack's heart thumped. She couldn't possibly know . . . could she? "Do what?"

Schuyler twisted her lips thoughtfully. Whatever she wanted to say, she didn't look like she knew how to say it. "I'm not sure if you think you need to do it, or if you have no other choice, or if you're being tricked into it, but you don't have to do everything you're told."

"What do you mean?"

Schuyler's fingers twitched again. "I saw you."

"Saw me where?"

"At the Seaport clinic."

Jack's face went stiff. Was she one of the rebels Max had been hunting? Did she know Kingsley Martin? "I don't know what you're talking about."

Schuyler's eyes danced, but she didn't say anything. She simply looked at Jack as if imploring him to admit it. "I know you and I know who you can be," she said.

There was something about her. Something . . . familiar that he couldn't quite place. He'd known her, or known *of* her, for so long, but they'd never really spoken until recently. So where was this odd feeling coming from—like he *knew* her? He looked at her carefully, taking in the shape of her face and the sound of her voice, but his mind ran into a brick wall. For some reason, he saw a flash of his dreams in the maze of mirrors, but then the memory shattered like broken glass.

"You don't know me at all," he said. "If you did, you'd know to stay away from me. It's too dangerous."

"Jack, I—"

"Please, don't come back here."

"Do you remember anything else? About us?"

He paused. *Us?*

"I have to go."

"Do you even know who you're working for?"

Jack shut the door before she could say anything more. He went to the window and watched her from the shadows. She still stood on the threshold, even raised her hand to ring the bell once more, but she put her hands in her pockets, shoulders slumped in defeat. Jack's stomach twisted in knots as she descended the stairs, looked over her shoulder once, and disappeared down Fifth Avenue. He felt guilty for treating her that harshly, but it was for her own safety. It was dangerous for a human to be anywhere near him.

Did Schuyler know? How could she? She was mortal, right? She had to be. Jack knew every Blue Blood, having cycled with generations of them since the beginning. It couldn't be possible. Unless . . . He looked at the doorway to Max's office, a tingle of curiosity nagging at the back of his mind. He sighed and went in.

Sitting on Max's desk was the letter from KM. Kingsley Martin. Where the name came from, Jack didn't know. Explaining it to Max felt like he was trying to explain a dream, disconnected and full of nonsense. But he knew the name had to have come from somewhere.

Jack could have walked away. It would have been easier. He could have returned to the mess he'd made in the kitchen, gone upstairs, and finished reading his book, maybe taken a nap because he definitely needed it. But he didn't. He picked up the letter and read it over.

You're better than this.

He couldn't rest until he got some answers.

Twenty-Six

MAX

*E*arlier that morning, Max's phone had buzzed on his nightstand.

Still half asleep, he knocked over his bedside lamp as he clumsily fumbled for his phone in the beige haze of early morning. He had only come home a few hours earlier, having finally had some success in dealing with the vigilantes hindering Lucifer's plan. His team captured two suspicious individuals trying to break into the clinic in Chelsea early in the night, a sloppy mistake they were no doubt regretting now. They could be mortals, or they could be vampires, there was really only one way to find out. If they hadn't already, they would talk soon. Max's team had a way of loosening tongues. He expected the call was about that.

"Yes?" he said groggily, his tone of voice annoyed. He pinched the bridge of his nose in an attempt to rouse himself further.

It was City Hall. The secretary was curt and straightforward. "Mayor Duncan demands to see you. Immediately."

He had been looking forward to getting some rest, and his body ached to sleep for a decade. But he couldn't say *Please, let me sleep for just five more minutes* to Lucifer. "Understood. Jack and I can be there within the hour."

"No. The mayor specifically asked for you and you alone. You have twenty minutes," the secretary said, and then hung up.

Max tossed his phone into the depths of his down comforter. Duncan always asked for the two Force boys to report to him. Always. They were a matching set; buy one, get one free.

For the first time, Jack would not be at his side. Max's heart hammered in his chest.

He hauled himself out of bed and glared at the strip of pale daylight coming in through the slit in his curtains before he dressed in Duncan's preferred all-black ensemble. Even though his bespoke two-button jacket and flat-front dress pants fit him like a second skin, he felt like he'd been bent out of shape somehow during the night. The clothes didn't feel right, or rather *he* didn't feel right. His collar was too tight around his throat, no matter how many times he pulled on it.

He had been dreaming again.

Max looked at himself in the full-length mirror in his room. The sun had risen a little, casting deep shadows across his face. He looked exhausted and his hair was a mess, so he combed his fingers through it in a vain attempt to get it to cooperate. A section of hair kept flopping back in his face. He gave up trying to tame it. It would have to do.

If he were Jack, it wouldn't be this difficult.

He scowled, huffed loudly through his nose, and tugged on his lapel, trying to adjust the jacket as best he could, but still, it didn't feel right. What was wrong with him? He had to be perfect for Aldrich Duncan. Better than perfect—immaculate.

Yet no matter how hard he tried, he could never be Jack.

There was no more time to waste, so Max exited his room. He had to pass Jack's room on the way down, and he paused in front of the door. He wondered if he should tell his brother he was leaving.

But their argument about the Silver Legacy was a bitter reminder that there were still cards worth keeping close to his chest. He stared at Jack's closed door for a long moment before deciding against knocking, and left. Jack could keep his secrets; so would Max.

Duncan had called him alone for a reason. Jack didn't need to know.

It was strange not having Jack at his side as he took the elevator up. Jack's *affectus*—his aura—had always been something Max could feel that reminded him he was there, especially when meeting with Duncan. He took a deep, calming breath and fussed over his cuff links. He wasn't sure what to expect from the mayor today.

Duncan was impatient for his plans to come to fruition, and Max was ready to assure him that nothing else would go amiss. He was moving forward with the hunt for the fomenters of the rebellion. But he had no idea what else Duncan would want from him, especially without Jack there. Had there been another clinic attack? Not knowing made his insides twist sickeningly.

The piece of rubble Max kept in his pocket felt like a lead weight. He'd been carrying it around for days, obsessed with what it represented. He wished it had revealed its secrets before he faced Duncan again.

There was no chance to turn back now. The elevator doors opened, and Max's feet carried him into Duncan's office on mere momentum alone. Duncan was already waiting for him, sitting behind his grand desk and peering out the window at the rising sun. He turned when Max entered. His handsome face brightened when he smiled. The Prince of Heaven looked truly radiant, even more than he'd looked the day he fell.

"Max!" he said, still smiling.

"You wanted to see me alone, sir?" Max clasped his wrist behind his back and stood tall.

"Indeed." Duncan glanced down and organized the papers on his desk, then stood. He circled around to the front and leaned on the edge, like a teacher at Duchesne who wanted to be cool. "With Operation Argenti almost complete, I wanted to thank you for your hard work. My plan, thanks to you and your leadership, has been made real. Your dedication to our mission has not gone unnoticed."

"It has been an honor, truly."

Duncan's pale eyes looked over Max, taking him in with a careful consideration. "You know, you remind me so much of myself."

Heat rose up Max's neck, he was so flattered.

Duncan continued. "I too had great vision and drive, wanting only what I thought was best for me and my family. I'm so glad we can share this virtue. But not everyone understands us, isn't that right?"

"Yes, sir," Max said.

With a nod, Duncan added, "It's never easy being in a position of power. I was once where you are now, standing before my father, wanting to prove something of myself to him. Unlike him, though, I recognize talent and don't punish ambition. You are truly something special, Azrael. Which is why I wanted you to come here this morning. I believe you're ready to take on the next stage of my vision."

Max raised a curious eyebrow. "And what is that?"

"I want you to perform the Silver Legacy."

Max's heart fluttered. This was a dream come true. Those were the words he'd been so desperately wanting to hear. He had been chosen. He deserved this, he wanted it so badly, and he was being rewarded. "Thank you, sir. It would be an honor, sir."

"I'm so glad that you're eager to take up the cause."

"You sound as if you expected me to decline."

Duncan tipped his head. "I spoke with Jack about it, but I sensed that he didn't share the same ambitions that you have. He didn't have the look in his eyes that you have now. Do you know why that is?"

Max shouldn't have been surprised. So that was what Duncan had asked Jack to stay behind about. He should have known. Duncan had offered Jack the Silver Legacy first. Jealousy uncoiled from Max's chest, but he tempered it with a deep exhale. "Jack has always been aloof. His vision is shortsighted."

"You two truly are so different. I had to consider my options for a long time. But you've done such an extraordinary job with my mission, you've proven to me that you're more than capable of becoming my true heir."

Jack didn't know what he'd given up. He never tried to be

anything greater than himself, take what he could, or think beyond today. In that way, Max was stronger than Jack. He knew an opportunity when he saw it.

This was Max's destiny.

He was Maximilian Reginald Force III, the reincarnation of Azrael, the Angel of Death, the epitome of ultimate ambition, blood as blue as royalty, and he would not be denied his destiny as Lucifer's perfect scion.

"I'll do anything you need me to do," said Max. "Anything."

Duncan smiled warmly, showing his perfectly straight, white teeth. "You will make kingdoms tremble, Max. You're ready. You were always my favorite. I may not have been the best at showing it, but I want you to know it now. I've been so hard on you, pushing you for greatness, but only because I saw everything you could be. You are the epitome of Blue Blood excellence. And soon enough . . . you'll be something more than that. You are my shining prodigy, truly."

Max's knees shook with excitement. He could barely contain himself.

Duncan slapped his hands on his knees and stood. "But now! We must see that the clinics are opened and we can begin the harvest. Continue to make me proud, son. You're dismissed."

Son. He'd never called Max that before, even after Duncan had taken the brothers into his care, pulled them in close, and vowed to protect them from harm.

Max couldn't have been happier. He bowed his head, his lips curling wickedly, and turned to go.

Before he could leave, Duncan said, "Oh, and, Max . . ."

Max stopped and turned.

"Watch your brother carefully." Duncan's voice was smooth as ice. "Family has a way of disappointing. I do not want to see the same mistakes that I made be your downfall too."

Max tipped his head. "Yes, my lord."

He strode out of the office, his head held high, and walked to the elevator. He was victorious. He was better than Jack, better than everyone, the best!

The power he had so desperately wanted was finally his to take. He would be strong again, as beautiful as the rising sun. Humans would fall to their knees before him, crying out, begging for salvation. More beautiful than a forest fire, more awesome than a hurricane, more explosive than a supernova—a god! He, Azrael, was Lucifer's chosen.

He stepped inside the elevator, and the doors closed . . . and Max never stopped smiling.

Twenty-Seven

KINGSLEY

*K*ingsley Martin could keep secrets. Centuries of time as Venator had taught him how to mask his intentions as skillfully as any spy. He could become anyone and anything, be a whisper in the wind, as quiet as a rumor. So when he got a text from a blocked number with the ominously simple message *We need to talk. Trinity Church Cemetery. Tonight . . .* he knew this was a secret worth keeping.

He'd told his peers at the Repository that he was going out on patrol. They didn't need to know that he was meeting with the enemy.

Trinity Church Cemetery was a place Kingsley knew well. It was one of the most famous burial grounds in all of Manhattan, the final resting place of some of the most influential figures of history, many of whom Kingsley had personally known.

When he arrived at the cemetery at Broadway and Wall Street, his silver eyes flashed as he scanned the block for movement. Overseen by the dominating silhouette of Trinity Church, the graves were still and quiet, ghostly gray even in the low light, but so far Kingsley hadn't seen anyone, though he knew better than to think that he was alone. Fog had settled over the grass, and a hush lay thick with it. Kingsley's footsteps were nearly silent as he stepped onto the lawn.

He walked around the headstones, his hands raised to show he wasn't armed.

"I'm here," he said to the darkness. "I come in peace."

Of course, he wasn't totally unarmed. He had one of his blades tucked into the back of his belt, hidden beneath his cloak, just in case. He wasn't a total fool.

He waited a beat, and then another, thinking maybe he'd been stood up, but then a shape moved out from behind one of the headstones, and Kingsley smirked.

The Force boy looked out of place, like a rose growing out of a crack in a junkyard. With polished Chelsea boots, black slacks, and a long wool coat to damp down the chill of the night, he always had to dress like he was featured on the cover of some magazine. His emerald eyes lingered on Kingsley for a moment, taking him in, but he didn't say a word.

"You're not Max," Kingsley said.

"No, I'm not," Jack said.

"Funny. Definitely did not expect the other one to show up. I assume Max got my note?"

"Yes. It's why I'm here."

As a sign of goodwill, Kingsley deactivated his silver eyes, returning them to their normal dark color, and leaned against a headstone, his arms crossed over his chest. Jack didn't look like he was here for a fight either.

"What's the occasion?" Kingsley asked.

"I need some information."

Kingsley raised an eyebrow and smiled. "Bold of you to assume I'd give it."

"You came all this way, didn't you?"

"That's because I thought you were Max."

Jack's breath clouded in the cold air as he stood there silently.

Kingsley continued. "He doesn't remember me, does he? And he doesn't know that you're here." Jack's nonanswer was all Kingsley needed. "Makes sense . . . What does Lucifer's golden boy even want, anyway?"

"I'm here because I want . . ." Jack sighed. "Because I *need* answers."

"Depends on the question. Must be something big if you want to meet in the middle of the night in a cemetery."

"I know you, somehow, but at the same time I know we've never met before. How did you do it? Some kind of spell? Hypnotism? Telepathy?"

A prickle of hope lifted the corner of Kingsley's mouth. Was the famous Jack Force starting to remember the other world? "I'm flattered that you think I have anything to do with whatever you're going through. I'm good but not that good."

"Who are you, then? What are you?"

"Ah, where's the fun in telling?" Kingsley tipped his head to the side playfully.

"Fine. What can you tell me about Schuyler?"

That was not where Kingsley expected this conversation to go. He expertly kept his face passive. "Schuyler. You mean like the surname on a few of these headstones?"

"Schuyler Cervantes-Chase."

Kingsley had a sneaking suspicion that Schuyler had tried to see Jack again. Even though he had told her to stay away, she hadn't listened. Of course, he wouldn't have listened to himself either if it meant that he could get Mimi back. But he would never tell Schuyler that. It wouldn't set a good example. Kingsley might have been stubbornly enmortal, but a part of Schuyler was stubbornly human. No matter how many years a vampire like him lived, humans always surprised him with their tenacity.

"Never heard the name," Kingsley said. "Some mortal, probably."

"I know you're lying. She's special; I can feel it. And if she's special, you'd be the one to know about it. Who is she?"

"Nobody I'm acquainted with."

Jack clearly didn't believe him. "If she's not important, why do I keep seeing her in my dreams?"

Now, that was interesting. All this time Kingsley thought he and Schuyler were the only ones having the dreams. Kingsley's eyebrow rose; it was time. "You're starting to remember?"

But Jack shook his head. "Remember what?"

"Mark me down as intrigued. What do you know?"

Jack thought about it a moment, shifting his weight from one foot to another. "I'm not sure what I think about anything anymore. Who is she?"

Kingsley pointed his finger at Jack and winked. "I'm more interested in what's going on in that big, thick skull of yours."

"You're making fun of me."

"A little bit."

Jack's jaw clenched. He didn't look angry, more like he was battling himself for the right words.

"Please," Jack said. His eyes shone. "I'm begging you. Help me."

The *please* helped. It sounded so naked and vulnerable coming from him.

Kingsley regarded Jack for a long moment, calculating. Jack was not a strategist or a manipulator. Throughout his existence, he had always acted from his heart. That's what Kingsley liked most about him. But in this world, he was still Lucifer's puppet. Even if he might be remembering things from the other world, Jack wasn't on Kingsley's side. Kingsley needed to protect himself, protect Schuyler, and most of all, protect their mission until he could be sure where Jack stood on the battlefield of good and evil. He needed to act carefully, no matter how desperately he wanted his old friend back.

Kingsley strolled back and forth, waving his hands about casually as he talked. "What I'm more interested in knowing is why Lucifer's chief lieutenant has me, a—let's face it—traitor, alone and he hasn't taken his shot at killing me yet. What, the Angel of Destruction not in the mood to destroy?" Kingsley teased.

That struck a nerve. "My *name* is Jack."

"Yes, I know. We used to be friends."

Jack looked taken aback. "But where? How? Why don't I remember?"

Kingsley let out a low whistle. "Lucifer has both of you deep in his clutches. Some kind of spell to make you forget your past, I suppose, makes you easier to manipulate." He allowed himself to smirk. "You'd kill to know the truth, wouldn't you?"

"What would you have me do?"

"Nothing you can't already do yourself but haven't yet done. Go on, tell me what you already know."

Jack's gaze fell, and his eyes darted back and forth as he tried to recall. He looked pained as he did so. "When Max found your letter, I saw your initials and something just clicked. I don't know how I knew, I just did."

"Was that the first time something like this had happened?"

"No, before then, I'd been dreaming, nightmares mostly. But then one day, after the storm, I started dreaming . . . about her."

"This Schuyler person."

Jack nodded once, stiffly. "But it also wasn't Schuyler. Their eyes were the same, but . . . I felt like I knew her. Somehow."

"You did know her. Well, another version of you knew her. It was in another time, from another place. But then you . . ." Kingsley trailed off. He regarded Jack with caution. How much could he say without showing his hand? How much could he say while keeping Schuyler safe?

Jack sensed Kingsley's hesitancy. "What aren't you telling me?"

"You died, Jack."

Jack's eyelids fluttered.

"Do you remember dying?" Kingsley asked. "The Gates of Paradise? Fighting against Lucifer? The ultimate battle for our redemption?"

Stunned, Jack looked like he'd been hit over the head. "No."

"Maybe that's for the best."

"But none of that happened. It can't be possible. I'm . . . I'm alive," Jack said. "I'm right here."

Kingsley inclined his head. "Another earth. A Superimposition of realities. It's how you're dreaming of a person you don't know. Don't ask me how. The multiverse is operating in mysterious ways I'm not sure even I can understand."

"Multiverse," Jack repeated.

"Do you believe me?"

As Jack swallowed, his Adam's apple bobbed, and he said, "Yes."

He went quiet, the muscle in his jaw working constantly while Kingsley watched him. This Jack was barely different from the one Kingsley had known before. They even looked the same, despite the changes in his family. No wonder Schuyler was determined to reach out to him. Seeing his face would have felt like a constant reminder of the person she'd lost. Kingsley could relate more to that desperation than she would ever know.

"Tell me about this other world," Jack said. "It sounds like something out of a comic book."

Kingsley shrugged. "What's there to say? The end of the world didn't happen, so that was nice. Whiskey's much better there. Oh yeah, I almost forgot." His eyes sharpened. "You didn't work for Lucifer."

Jack looked shaken. "I don't have . . ." He clamped his mouth shut. Whatever he wanted to say, maybe he was too afraid to say it out loud. "I need to protect my brother."

"Keep telling yourself that, whatever you need to do in order to sleep at night."

A shadow of pain crossed Jack's face, and he looked at his shoes. After a long moment, Jack asked, "Who was I? To you?"

Kingsley softened and took a moment to answer, then said, "A brother by choice."

Jack's breath came out in a long shudder.

Kingsley moved in. "In another world, I knew a good man named Jack Force, and his beautiful twin sister, Mimi. And I loved her, warts and all. She was my bond mate. You were my friend. The Jack Force in that world would do anything for his friends, for his family, do what was right even if he knew it would cost him everything."

Emotion thickened Jack's voice. "And who was I to Schuyler?"

"Who do you think you were?" Kingsley asked.

Jack shook his head slightly. "I don't . . . I don't know what else I can be."

There was real pain behind Jack's eyes. Kingsley had lived long enough to see it plague great men and throw them into madness. "You don't have to do this forever, you know," Kingsley said softly. "You can change if you want to. Someone very special to me said that. I think the question you need to ask yourself is: Who do you want to be right now?"

"Was I happy in that other world?" Jack asked.

Kingsley didn't even hesitate. "Yes. You were. And that was worth fighting for."

Jack stared at Kingsley, a hard line forming between his eyebrows.

Kingsley kept going. "No one would come all the way here just to ask these questions if they didn't believe things could be better. Lucifer might be strong, but you're stronger. You also have something that he doesn't."

"And what's that?"

Kingsley rested his weight on his heels, watching Jack carefully. He saw the fire there, burning behind his eyes, the real power that so many worshipped. And in the same moment, he saw the boy who desperately asked for something different from a world that was already giving him everything.

"Maybe you need to figure that out for yourself," Kingsley said.

Jack's gaze dropped.

Kingsley turned and walked toward the cemetery's exit. He called back over his shoulder, "Even if you don't remember, know that you're never alone. You know where to find me."

TWENTY-EIGHT

MAX

ax spent all day and night going from one clinic to another all over the island, seeing to Duncan's operation with a renewed drive. He was to take on the Silver Legacy, and he wasn't going to disappoint now. He was going to show the whole world that they could never forget Max Force. Now that night had fallen, he headed home from the clinic in Battery Park City. The driver took him past Trinity Church Cemetery. In the darkness of the graveyard, Max spotted a familiar face. He'd had to do a double take to be sure . . . it was Jack.

"Stop the car," he said to the driver, who pulled up to the curb.

Max opened the door and stepped out, but paused when he saw that Jack wasn't alone. Another figure moved through the headstones. He had long black hair tied into a knot, a hawkish profile, and when he looked Max's way, his retro-reflective eyes glinted like silver coins.

Max thought it was a trick of the light at first, but his stomach dropped when he realized he knew that face. It was the man from the club, the one he had danced with, who put his hand over Max's heart and told him to remember. *He was a Silver Blood?* Max's whole body went cold.

But before he could act, the man dashed away and disappeared into the night.

"Jack!" Max called out, and Jack looked over.

At first he seemed surprised to see Max, but his expression soon shifted into neutrality. "What are you doing here?"

"I could ask the same thing of you," Max said. "Who was that?"

"I don't want to talk about it."

Jack neared the car and moved to get in, but Max stepped in front of him and slammed the door shut, blocking his path. Max kept looking in the direction the figure had disappeared, but he was long gone.

Jack's indifference wasn't going to be enough anymore. Lucifer had planted the idea that Jack wasn't totally trustworthy, and Max could see it plain as day now. His gut twisted painfully as old wounds reopened.

"Why are you sneaking around behind my back?" Max asked.

"It's not what you think."

"I thought I knew every Silver under Lucifer's command. How is there one just running around?"

"I don't know who it was—"

Max grabbed the front of Jack's shirt and shoved him into the stone wall bordering the cemetery. He slammed Jack's back so hard into the stone that pieces of mortar rained down on his shoulders.

"Enough of these lies," Max said, shoving his knuckles deep into Jack's rib cage. Jack groaned under the pressure, but he didn't push Max away. "Who was that?"

Jack didn't say; he kept his mouth shut. It infuriated Max even more.

Max seethed. "I met with Duncan today. He wants me to perform the Silver Legacy." Jack's eyes widened, but Max didn't care. "I know. Dream come true. But he also told me that you were hesitant. He said he wasn't sure that you were up to the task of fulfilling your duty to your bloodline, that you wavered, that maybe you had other motives."

Max should have been beyond overjoyed that he was chosen. It shouldn't have mattered that Lucifer had waited so long. But his jealousy of Jack had been rooted so deep, it might as well have been engraved in his bones.

Jack's hand gripped Max's firmly, and the twins stared each other down. "Let me go, Max," Jack said, his voice lined with warning.

"Tell me who that was. Or I'll do something I might later regret." Max's heart felt inky black as he spoke. He almost sounded like Aldrich Duncan, and a part of him wanted to scream in horror.

Jack strained against Max's grip and glared. Then he said, "Kingsley Martin."

Max's eyes widened.

He glanced at the darkness again, just in case Kingsley had returned, but no one was there. Jack took that as an opportunity to knock Max's hands away. He rubbed at the sore spot on his ribs and scowled.

So Kingsley Martin was a Silver Blood renegade. Of course; it all made sense. Kingsley had tried to cozy up to Max, one of Lucifer's closest allies, so he could get to Lucifer. Max bared his teeth. He had been such a fool. How could he have let the enemy get so close?

"You let him go—why?" Max asked. "We could have captured him."

Jack brushed the dust off his shoulders. "Because the timing wasn't right. If we're patient, we can ensure he's stopped once and for all."

Max regarded Jack carefully. "I thought you didn't care about Lucifer's plan."

"You thought wrong."

Max's mind raced, the wheels turning as plans came into place.

"This could be good. He'll lead us to more of them. You might be onto something, Jack. Let him go, and he'll take us back to the nest. We can set a trap, just like Lucifer did when he killed Gabrielle."

Jack's gaze fell. The topic of Gabrielle and Michael had always been a sore one for him. He was, after all, the one who failed to save her when Lucifer traveled through the planes of time, shattered the realms of fate, and struck her down. Max couldn't afford to feel guilty anymore. What was done was done. He had stamped out any feelings about the past; it was easier to move on. What was meant to be was meant to be. Gabrielle was dead. Michael was no more. Lucifer was in power, and Max would be too.

Max's eyes danced with delight. "Kingsley Martin has to be hiding somewhere, and when we find him . . . I'll kill anyone who stands in my way."

Jack's green eyes shone in the dim light of night. He watched Max with a somber expression that bordered on pity. Max scoffed.

"Let's go," Max said. He made for the car and opened the door, waiting for Jack to get in.

Jack didn't hesitate to climb inside. But before he fully sat down, Max leaned in.

"Aldrich also said family tends to disappoint. I'll be watching you. We're on the same side, understood?" It wasn't a question—it was an order.

Jack leveled his gaze with Max's. "Yes. I understand. I'm with you."

Twenty-Nine

MAX

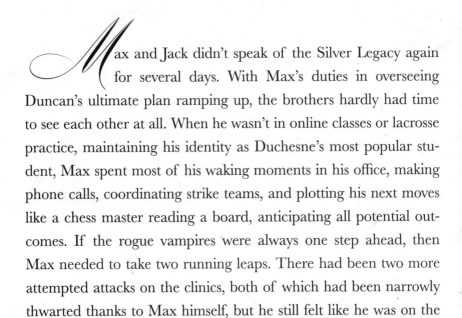

*M*ax and Jack didn't speak of the Silver Legacy again for several days. With Max's duties in overseeing Duncan's ultimate plan ramping up, the brothers hardly had time to see each other at all. When he wasn't in online classes or lacrosse practice, maintaining his identity as Duchesne's most popular student, Max spent most of his waking moments in his office, making phone calls, coordinating strike teams, and plotting his next moves like a chess master reading a board, anticipating all potential outcomes. If the rogue vampires were always one step ahead, then Max needed to take two running leaps. There had been two more attempted attacks on the clinics, both of which had been narrowly thwarted thanks to Max himself, but he still felt like he was on the defensive at all times. It was time for action.

Max was going to make Aldrich Duncan see his true worth.

Whoever this Kingsley Martin was, he was Max's sole focus. If Kingsley Martin fell, so would the others. As the saying went, cut the head off the snake and the body dies. Granted, to Max the expression seemed awfully narrow—cutting the head off any creature would kill it—but the biblical parallel seemed quite fitting. There probably weren't many rogue vampires left on Kingsley's side to make up much of a body anyway, not after Duncan had seen to their extermination.

But Max couldn't afford to underestimate their strength. After all, Kingsley had already managed to get close to him—twice. Too close. He needed to be adaptable and think like Kingsley, think like a traitor. But Kingsley was clever and had become a ghost. Max pestered Jack for more information about him, but Jack didn't seem to know any more than what he'd told Max that night in the cemetery at Trinity Church.

For days on end, Max dispatched dozens of Blue Blood reconnaissance teams to scour every inch of Manhattan, and still Kingsley was nowhere to be found. They overturned every potential hiding place—razed empty warehouses, demolished abandoned town homes, burned long-forgotten theaters—leaving nothing but smoke and ash in their wake.

And yet Kingsley and his followers were like cockroaches, hiding in the nooks and crannies of the city.

When Kingsley wasn't plaguing Max's every waking thought, he also invaded Max's dreams.

So when Kingsley—nothing more than a shadow—disappeared through a maze of winding tunnels, somehow getting farther away as he dashed around every corner, Max had woken up drenched in a flop sweat.

The pressure was getting to him, but he would never admit it.

He had come too far to fail.

Max was in his office, resting flat on his back on the rug with his eyes closed, when Jack found him early one morning.

"What are you doing?" Jack asked.

Max squinted in the morning sunlight. "What does it look like I'm doing? I'm thinking."

"Oh, that's what you call it." Jack was holding two mugs of coffee. He had clearly just woken up. He was still wearing his pajamas. He set one mug of coffee down on Max's desk next to his brother's laptop, still warm from being used all night. "I thought you might need this."

"Thanks."

"Late night?"

Max propped himself up on his elbows. "Would it surprise you if I said yes?"

Max hadn't showered, let alone changed clothes, since yesterday. Jack smiled into his mug as he took a sip. "It would not."

The lead Max thought he had regarding the two suspicious individuals they had captured trying to break into a clinic in Chelsea turned out to be a dead end. They really were just mortal Red Bloods after all, looking for a quick buck stealing drugs. Of course, they couldn't go free. His Silvers had a nice time cleaning up the evidence. However, that meant Max was back where he started, no closer to finding Kingsley Martin.

"What time is it?" Max asked.

"Does it matter?"

Max dropped back down onto the floor. "No."

Jack flipped his wrist and looked at his watch. "It's almost seven. A Friday, in case you were wondering. Classes start soon. What have you been doing?"

The concept of school was such a trivial one at this point. Max couldn't care any less about it. But he had to maintain the veneer of routine for his brother's sake if no one else's. "I'm trying to figure out how Kingsley has been sabotaging the clinics without leaving a trace." He held up the piece of rubble he'd found with the strange markings on it. He'd kept it all this time, rolling it between his fingers as if it might somehow help solve the mystery.

"I didn't know you were into rock collecting," said Jack sarcastically.

"Just give me a couple of minutes," Max said. He pinched the bridge of his nose tightly with his thumb and forefinger. It didn't help, but it didn't hurt either.

"Sure."

Jack turned to leave the study, but right before he was gone, Max asked, "If he was my best friend, why don't I remember Kingsley Martin?"

Jack waited a beat before answering. "I don't know. Forget I said it. I must have confused him with someone else."

"I'm tired of not knowing."

The strange markings on the shard and their origins still eluded him. He was no closer to finding Kingsley Martin than he was to flying to the moon. Being an immortal creature as he was, Max found not having all the answers awfully annoying.

"He really didn't say anything to you that night that would help us find him?"

"No. I told you. We barely spoke. When he realized who I was, he ran."

Max narrowed his eyes. He didn't believe his brother. Why had Kingsley approached Max twice at the club, keeping his Silver

Blood identity under wraps? And was Max expected to believe it was just a coincidence that he'd then met up with his brother in a cemetery? Something was not adding up, but he refused to tip his hand by asking questions.

"Come on." Jack stood over his brother and held out his hand. "Get up."

Max grasped his hand and got to his feet, but he stood too quickly and the blood rushed from his head, blinding him momentarily. He was leaning against the bookcase for a moment and blinking the light back into his eyes when his gaze landed on one of his father's old leather-bound history books. On the spine, beneath the title, was a shape, a crudely drawn symbol reproduced in gold leaf. The symbol itself wasn't what caught his eye, but the style. It was eerily familiar.

"What is it?" Jack asked. He had noticed the expression shifting on Max's face.

Max didn't answer. He pulled the book down from the shelf. It easily weighed seven pounds. The title in gold read *Text and Traditions of Sacred Polygraphia in Exequies.* Any other time, the book might have sounded like a bore, but now Max flipped through the tissue-paper-thin pages, scanning hundreds of years of history packed into giant walls of text like his life depended on it. But he didn't slow down to read any words. He was looking for something else.

"Isn't it a bit early in the day to do a little light reading?" Jack quipped, regarding the heft of the book in Max's arms.

"Shut up a minute."

Toward the middle of the book, Max paused at a chapter called "The Tomb of Honorius of Thebes." Right next to the title was the same gilded symbol as was on the book's spine. Printed on one whole page was a black-and-white photograph of a tomb uncovered in Thiva, Greece, in the 1920s. All across the stone walls of the tomb, drawn in kohl, were hundreds of different sigils, some used for protection, others for guidance and rebirth, as identified by the captions.

"Tell me those *don't* look familiar," Max said, pointing to the sigils.

Jack leaned in and his eyes widened. "They look just like the markings you found at the clinic. Same lines."

Framed in the center of the picture was a posh-looking archaeologist posing next to the body of the entombed Honorius, well preserved for being thousands of years old, the skeletal fingers still clutching a large tome to its chest.

Max read the caption aloud. "'A series of artifacts was taken from the tomb, including a pair of gold caskets, an embroidered shroud, and the Sworn Book of Honorius, thought to be the first-ever documentation of sigil magic used in the region. Artifacts were purchased by a private investor shortly after discovery.'"

Fire burned in Max's belly. He rushed to his desk, picked up the chunk of rock, and compared the shapes to the ones in the book. He was right—the debris left behind was a sigil. The book snapped shut with a heavy thunk, and Max's eyes fluttered closed.

"All this time I was so focused on the one piece, I didn't think about the whole puzzle," he said. "I thought it was part of a word. But it's not a letter at all."

"Mind filling me in here?" Jack asked.

Instead of complying with Jack, Max sat down at his desk,

opened his laptop, and started typing. His mind raced so quickly that his fingers could barely keep up. He didn't even notice when Jack, taking it as a sign that Max would not be joining him, slipped out of the office, leaving Max alone to work.

The whole day passed. Max barely looked up from the screen.

As if possessed, he didn't stop. He couldn't stop. He was so close, he could practically touch the answer.

Later that evening, Jack came back into the office to check on him. The sun had already set, but Max hadn't even bothered turning on the lights. Jack flipped the switch on the wall, and the office brightened. He found Max, still sitting at his desk, with a faraway look in his eyes.

"Are you going to keep sitting here in the dark, or are you coming to dinner?" Jack asked.

"I know everything." Max said it like he couldn't believe it.

Jack straightened. "You . . . You do?"

"The symbol. I've solved it. It's chaos magic."

Jack's shoulders relaxed some. He tipped his head curiously. "I still don't get it."

"Chaos is energy," Max said. "With chaos magic, intention is placed in the creation of sigils, like the ones in Honorius's tomb. Sigils can be something as simple as a protective circle drawn in the dirt or as complex as the layout of an entire city. Pagans used to draw sigils on their homes to protect against lesser demons, harness spirits, even attract luck. Sigils channel the energies of the universe with intention, and focus incredible amounts of power into a precise point. If the right one is used . . ."

"It can cause an explosion," Jack finished for him. He nodded, understanding. "So how come I've never heard about it?"

"Because I was born with all the brains. And all the good looks. Obviously."

"Yeah, right—you just listen to a lot of podcasts. Get to the point."

"The thing about chaos magic is it's not just one symbol that makes a strong spell work, but many symbols, employed in a specific order, in a specific pattern. And with something that complicated, you need a reference. You need a book. Honorius's book."

As he spoke, a smile stretched across his face. He had found exactly what he was looking for.

"Only two editions of the *Liber Juratus Honorii* are known to have ever existed: one the original, the other a copy. The copy was destroyed during the Second World War. The original text was then removed from a private collection in the 1940s and now resides here, in Manhattan. One guess where."

Jack didn't have to guess. He already knew, and his lips set in a thin line.

"I need the hellhounds." Max grinned hungrily. "We're going to set a trap."

I'm coming for you, Kingsley Martin.

THIRTY

MAX

Max smelled them before he saw them.

Brimstone. Sulfur. Ammonia.

In the basement below City Hall, Max pushed open the steel door and marched down the long, narrow hallway. His footsteps echoed down the gray walls as he walked purposefully, his shoulders thrown back and his head held high. He was Lucifer's most trusted Venator, his heir apparent, and he was going to act like it.

The only way to ensure victory was to use all the tools at his disposal. Kill Kingsley Martin, stop this damned rebellion, prove his worth to Duncan, and perform the Silver Legacy.

The smell was enough to make him gag, but he marched forward, even though the scent grew stronger and stronger the closer he got.

At the end of the hall was a door where a furnace room used to be. Beasts liked it hot and dark. Max unlocked the door. Inside were thirteen iron cages, and within them were great, hulking shapes, melting into the blackness. First, a pair of eyes opened, glowing like hot coals, then another pair, and another. Growls rumbled through the room, vibrating in Max's head.

He put a silver whistle to his lips and blew. The growling stopped.

Max smirked. It felt good to be in control.

One by one, he unlocked the cages. The creatures' glowing eyes followed him as he did.

He blew his whistle again, and the beasts emerged.

Lucifer's hellhounds were hungry.

THIRTY-ONE

SCHUYLER

Schuyler got the text message while she was eating dinner with her parents. It was from Kingsley.

Big trouble in Little China . . . town.

Her lips automatically twisted into a smirk. Kingsley had been getting into the Repository movie collection, apparently. But then it hit her—his text could only mean that there was something happening at the clinic in Chinatown and he needed her.

"What's wrong, Sassy Pants?" her dad asked upon seeing her expression darken.

"Is it Oliver?" Aurora asked.

"No, I forgot. I have a big essay due." It was scary how easily the lie came. She knew it was wrong to lie to her parents, but how else was she supposed to keep her secret while simultaneously keeping her family safe?

Aurora wiped her mouth with her napkin and said, "I can bring you dessert in your room if you'd like."

"No, it's okay. I shouldn't have any distractions. I need to focus."

"Okay, mi cielo," Aurora said with a smile. "I'm proud of you."

~ ~ ~

Schuyler was getting better and better at sneaking out. She had this whole vigilante-vampire-secret-identity thing down pat by this point. She found Kingsley on the fifth floor of an abandoned apartment building across the street from the Chinatown clinic.

He heard Schuyler approach and waved her over.

"We've had eyes on it all day, and there was major activity going on until they just left all of a sudden. It's been hours, and no one's gone in or out of the clinic."

"Isn't it going to be operational soon?" Schuyler asked, peering through a window. "I thought they were getting ready for the grand opening."

"That's why I don't like it," Kingsley said. "Something doesn't feel right."

"Can I see?" Schuyler asked, reaching for his binoculars. Kingsley handed them over.

The clinic did look empty now. No sign of activity, no movement. All the windows were dark, and the sign out front was turned off. Schuyler scanned up the building and stopped at a window on the second floor. There was the unmistakable shape of a figure, the slope of their shoulders and head just barely visible from her angle. Schuyler focused harder and saw rope wrapped around the person's upper body.

"There's someone tied up in there," she said in shock.

"What?"

She handed the binoculars back to Kingsley. "Third window from the left, second floor."

Kingsley let out a low breath. "You're right. But I don't see anyone else—no guards, no one. . . . Something's not right here."

"We can't just do nothing. That person needs our help."

"Think about it, Schuyler. We have to be careful about this. This could definitely be a trap."

"Haven't we waited long enough to act? People are getting hurt because all we've done is wait."

"Let's just talk through a—" But Schuyler had already run out of the room and down the stairs. She made her way stealthily through the night and across the street, taking cover around the corner of a building. She carefully checked her surroundings but didn't see anyone in the loading dock. Kingsley appeared silently at her side, his blades out.

"I guess we're doing this, then," he muttered.

Ignoring his reluctant tone, she gave him a single nod before they moved together. Following Kingsley's lead, she waited for him to break the lock on the door, and they slinked inside, quick and quiet as shadows. The clinic smelled like fresh paint and floor cleaner, and there were rows of medical equipment that was waiting to be used. Schuyler wasted little time moving through the first floor. She hoped they weren't too late. Had Lucifer already moved on to kidnapping humans? She paused on the second-floor landing, listening.

"Hear anything?" she whispered to Kingsley.

He shook his head and moved past her into the hall. The floor opened up to a large room, undecorated and unfinished, metal beams still exposed behind half-complete walls. Alone, in the middle of the space, was a single chair, where the person sat, their head covered with a burlap sack.

Kingsley moved around the periphery of the room, his blades out, but Schuyler approached cautiously.

"Hello?" she asked.

The figure remained motionless, either passed out or worse. . . .

Schuyler moved forward a little more. "I'm going to untie you."

When she got to the chair, something didn't seem right to her. She reached out with shaking hands and removed the sack from their head.

The head came clear off.

It wasn't a person. It was a dummy.

Kingsley cursed in the Sacred Language. "We have to go. Now."

Schuyler dropped the dummy's head, and it clattered to the floor. She spun around and rushed back the way they came. Kingsley had been right. She was so eager to help, she'd run right into a trap. They had to get out of this place.

"Are you going to set a sigil?" she asked as they hurried back downstairs.

"No time, let's move."

As they left the building, Schuyler could almost have sworn she smelled rotten eggs, but the odor dissipated in the wind. They took off down the street.

Kingsley and Schuyler didn't stop running until they reached the Repository. Kingsley rushed in, barely pausing to throw his cloak over the table, and uncorked his decanter of whiskey.

"What was that back there?" Schuyler asked.

"That, rookie, was a trap."

"But no one else was there. No one tried to stop us on our way out," Schuyler said. "What kind of trap is that?"

"It's a long game. Has to be. Who knows what they have planned?" Kingsley tipped the decanter into a garbage can and started putting stacks of documents inside it. He whipped around to the other vampires lingering on the perimeter of his makeshift classroom. "We need to evacuate, now. Gather all of our supplies and references, leave anything we can spare. Burn it if you can't carry it with you." He lit a match and set the garbage can on fire. The other vampires got to work without missing a beat.

Schuyler still didn't know what was happening. "Kingsley, if it was a trap, why didn't anyone come after us?"

"Because they're on their way," Kingsley said. "There's a warehouse on the other side of the island. We'll be safe there."

"Maybe we're overreacting. Maybe they set a bomb but it didn't go off. I smelled rotten eggs, so maybe they cut the gas line—"

Kingsley went very still. "What did you say?"

Schuyler didn't understand why his eyes got as round as they did. Her stomach dropped, but she answered truthfully. "That I smelled rotten eggs. Why?"

The floor beneath Schuyler's shoes vibrated, the sensation similar to that of a truck passing by on the street. At first, she didn't notice it, but it grew stronger with every second. Both she and Kingsley looked at the floor before it registered.

"Get down!" Kingsley yelled, and shoved Schuyler out of the way just as the stone floor exploded upward, shattering into pieces with a thunderous *BOOM!*

Schuyler fell flat on her spine but rolled up and over her

shoulders, landing on her feet, crouched and ready. She covered her face as the debris blew all around them, and then the dust settled.

A twenty-foot hole had opened up in the Repository floor. Desks lay in pieces, the chalkboard shattered, the stone floor now a dark, gaping hole from which growls and the scraping of claws on stone echoed. It sounded like a pack of wolves.

On the other side of the hole in the floor was Kingsley, unharmed and on his feet. The look on his face could only be described as murderous. His eyes had shifted, shimmering silver as his vampire powers activated. Debris had sliced his cheek open, and the cut oozed with the silver blood that ran through his veins. He unsheathed his twin blades and dropped low, poised to strike.

Rotten eggs. The smell was unmistakable. Though Schuyler realized now that it wasn't from a gas leak. It smelled . . . monstrous.

Growls rippled up from the cavern and grew louder. Shadows moved in the darkness, heavy sounds of paws hitting the floor. The room reeked of sulfur and acid.

Then darkness melted away as a sword, cast in pure white light, illuminated the space. The only sword that shone like that was the archangel Michael's sword, the Blade of Paradise.

But it wasn't Michael wielding it—it was a gorgeous blond boy with emerald eyes and a hungry smile.

It was Jack's twin, Max Force.

His smile split wider when he saw them.

"Knock, knock!" Max sang.

Aldrich Duncan's Venator had found them, and he had brought an army with him.

Thirty-Two

MAX

The explosion blotted out all sound.

The shock wave kicked up dust and swirled around Max, buffeting his golden hair, but his smile never wavered.

He had walked over the rubble and emerged in the Repository of History. How long had it been since he'd walked these halls? He tipped his head back and breathed in the familiar air, taking in the scents of chalk and decaying parchment.

He was going to miss this place, even after he'd personally razed it to the ground.

In his hand, he carried a fiery sword of light, the Blade of Paradise. The Golden Sword of Heaven. Anyone might be forgiven for mistaking him as a being who had been heaven-sent.

Thirteen hulking creatures that could only be described as wolflike—hellhounds in every sense of the word—circled Max patiently, waiting for his next orders, like good, obedient little dogs. He'd heard they used to be able to transform into human shape once, and were kin to angels, but there was nothing human or angel about them now. They were wretched, soulless creatures.

They reeked of brimstone. Their fur glistened in the low light, black as tar, rendering them almost invisible if not for the fire-hot glow of their eyes. Mortal men had looked into those eyes and gouged out their own so as not to ever gaze upon them again. Monstrous growls rippled through their throats, echoing through the hall, their knife-sharp claws scraping like sheet metal across the stone floor, and drool oozed out of their mouths, sizzling where it landed, like an egg on a hot pan. They were hungry.

Max wasn't surprised in the slightest that he had emerged in the Repository to find two figures close by, crouched low and ready to fight. One was the handsome stranger with black hair and silver eyes, which caught the light of Max's sword. A small streak of silver blood bloomed from a cut on the man's cheek, a result no doubt of the explosion. Max raised a curious eyebrow. "Kingsley Martin, I presume?"

"I see you got my note," Kingsley said.

"I admit, it was a struggle to find you. You're a hard one to pin down. I expected a little more, honestly. Imagined you would be . . ." Max gestured casually with his free hand. "More."

Kingsley's smile was cunning. "You know, the initials MF don't just stand for Max Force."

"Charming."

"Is that . . ." Kingsley gestured to Max's sword.

"A gift from Lucifer himself. I imagine this will be the first and last time you'll ever see Michael's sword."

"Kingsley," the girl cut in, her voice tense with fear.

Max turned his focus in her direction. She stared back, eyes wide and as big and round as a kitten's. He recognized her as the girl whom Jack had been talking to at the park a while ago. What was her name again? Tyler? Smiler? Who cared anyway? It didn't matter anymore, even though it was a curious coincidence. What was she doing here?

Kingsley, however, didn't take his eyes off Max. "It's all right, Schuyler," he said.

Max snapped his fingers, remembering. "That's it! Schuyler! Fancy seeing you here. Small world."

"Where's Jack?" she asked.

"Oh, he's coming. He's busy destroying the protective sigils you've laid around the perimeter so my Silver Bloods can enter without getting themselves blown up. He should be arriving with the cavalry any minute to block your escape. And kill you."

"Jack would never hurt me."

"He *will*. Lucifer's orders. He wants everyone in this place dead."

The girl didn't say anything more. She was practically foaming at the mouth. If looks could kill, Max would have been dead already.

"Get out of here, Schuyler, before it's too late," Kingsley said. "Save yourself."

"No! I'm not leaving without you. We're in this world together, remember?"

"I'm not going to tell you again. Go. Now."

"Kingsley!"

Finally, Kingsley ripped his eyes away from Max and looked at her. "You were right, Schuyler. If I can't allow a person to change . . . I won't allow myself that chance either. He won't hurt me. I know him."

Max's temper flared. There Kingsley went again, thinking he knew anything at all about Max. His fingers clasped tighter around the hilt of his glowing sword. "Wanna bet?"

He rushed at Kingsley so quickly that the wind burst in his wake, but he stopped just short of plunging the sword into Kingsley's chest, the tip a hair's width away. If he pushed just a little, it would pierce the skin.

Kingsley didn't even flinch. *Impressive.* He just stared at Max with a foolish determination.

"Schuyler," Kingsley said again, keeping his voice cool. "Go! Please."

Schuyler hesitated. She looked like she wanted to jump in. But what was this girl going to do? She was nothing, nobody. As Max expected, Schuyler turned and ran away into the depths of the Repository.

From all around, Max heard movement. The whip of a cloak, the whisper of a footstep on stone, the hush of a blade coming unsheathed. Kingsley's merry band of rogue vampires was closing in on him from all sides, even from above. They were trying to flank him.

Max put the silver whistle to his lips and blew a sharp note. The hellhounds froze at attention, their ears perked expectantly. Max smiled and paused, savoring the moment. "This one's mine. Kill the rest."

In an instant, the hellhounds pounced on the rogue vampires.

A hellhound tackled two vampires at the same time. Another dragged a vampire by the leg into the shadows. One scrambled up the bookcase, climbing like a monkey and toppling books as it went, then leaped onto the bridge above, pinning a vampire before he could release a shot from his crossbow.

Their victims' cries and shouts turned into gurgles as they drowned in their own blue blood. They didn't make another sound.

Kingsley's chest rose and fell rapidly as it all happened. He was made to stand there and listen to his brethren die, powerless to stop it. The tip of Max's sword snagged on one of Kingsley's shirt buttons. If he so much as twitched, he'd be dead. He had nowhere else to go.

Once the last vampire had died, the Repository fell as quiet as a mausoleum.

Kingsley snarled and clenched his daggers so tight that his knuckles turned white. He was alone. No one was going to save him.

"Still think I won't hurt you?" Max asked, tilting his head.

The hellhounds had finished their kills and returned to their commander's side. Dark blue blood like ink dripped from their jaws as they stared at Kingsley, still hungry.

Max wasn't sure he wanted to set the hounds on him just yet. It would be over too quickly. Kingsley Martin, the leader of the rebellion—the Silver Blood who had attempted to toy with Max's emotions—didn't deserve a quick death. Max smiled. He was going to enjoy this.

A large book hurtled out of the shadows and slammed into the side of Max's head. Colors burst behind his eyes, and he stumbled sideways, stunned, then whipped around.

And there stood Schuyler again. Like a fool, she had returned.

She gaped as if she too was surprised that she had thrown a

book at the Angel of Death's head. Blood the color of sapphires coated the tips of Max's fingers. He hadn't been injured in a battle in a long time.

"What are you doing!" Kingsley shouted. "Run!"

The girl disappeared once more into the maze of books.

Max's patience had run dry. Who did this mortal think she was? Annoyed, he wiped the side of his face with the back of his wrist and rounded on Kingsley. His emerald eyes glinted in his sword's light as he whistled to his dogs. Too bad he couldn't make Kingsley watch.

"Max . . ." Kingsley warned.

But Max just smiled. The dogs were waiting.

"Sic her."

"NO!" But it was too late.

The hellhounds were already chasing after Schuyler.

THIRTY-THREE

MAX

Kingsley readied his blades, dropping into a low, defensive position. His eyes flashed, same as the steel in his hands. Max admired his tenacity even in the face of certain doom.

Without the dogs, it was just Max and Kingsley, alone at last.

"Call them off, Max," Kingsley hissed through clenched teeth. "Don't hurt Schuyler. She has nothing to do with us. It's me you want."

Max tipped his head toward the vaulted ceiling and laughed. "So we're doing this?" He expertly swung his sword in a figure eight, as if warming up. The blade sang faintly like a chorus of angels.

"About time too."

They circled each other at a distance as they sized each other up. Kingsley was taller and more muscular, but Max was quicker. He wasn't sure what to expect from Kingsley. He'd never fought a Silver Blood before, a Silver Blood who had seemingly given up his ways. What secrets were hiding behind those eyes? Centuries of practice coiled in those muscles. How could a being such as himself deny his foe's power?

Kingsley's dual blades were short, meaning Max would have to get close for Kingsley to hurt him, but his footwork alone proved he would be a worthy opponent—Kingsley almost glided across the floor.

The last time Max had fought anyone was when he went up against Jack in the sparring ring at their home gym. He hadn't realized how much he wanted to do this. His veins buzzed with excitement.

Max smirked as he attacked first.

Kingsley blocked high with both blades, then parried, and Max backed off. He was only testing the waters.

"So, a Silver Blood," Max said, pointing to his own cheek in the same place where Kingsley's cheek bled.

"With a face as pretty as mine, something had to be wrong with me."

The corner of Max's mouth lifted, and he attacked again. He sprang forward, and Kingsley swerved while knocking Max's blade down. Max was just getting started.

He attacked again, swinging right, and Kingsley's double blades knocked him back.

Kingsley retreated and Max advanced, their footwork in tandem.

Max slashed, but Kingsley deflected each strike.

Their weapons sang every time they made contact, echoing through the Repository. Every attack was met with a response. They moved together like dancers at a ball.

Infuriatingly, Kingsley wasn't initiating attacks of his own. He blocked, parried, and retreated, but he never countered offensively.

"Come on," Max goaded. "Fight me!"

"That is not what I'm here for."

Max laughed again. "What's the point? That Schuyler girl is dead by now. Give up!" He could hear the hounds howling in the depths of the Repository.

Kingsley smacked another attack away and spun.

Max saw an opening. He cut forward, but Kingsley was faster than he thought.

Kingsley caught Max's sword between his two and pushed. Max stumbled backward and slammed into a bookcase. The impact caused pain to rocket up his spine.

Kingsley held him there firmly, but he didn't attempt a finishing blow.

"You always fall for my void dodge. You haven't changed as much as I thought," Kingsley said.

"What?"

"I know you. Very well," Kingsley said.

Max strained to break free, but Kingsley's weight pinned his arms to his chest. "You're insane."

Kingsley cracked a genuine grin. "We're soul mates, Max."

Max's heart fluttered, and it scared him. A sleeping creature stirred in his belly. "What are you even"—he rammed his knee into Kingsley's gut—"talking about?"

Kingsley recoiled, doubled over, and Max charged.

Kingsley recovered and blocked, but only just.

Max's sword whistled right by his throat and sliced downward, but Kingsley moved like water and shrank away, putting space between them once more.

"Soul mates," Kingsley repeated. "Bonded souls for eternity."

Max squeezed the hilt of his sword so tightly, it creaked. "There's no such thing."

"I can tell you don't believe that."

Max didn't have anything to say in response. Soul mates used to exist, finding one another again and again in every lifetime. But the bond made Blue Bloods weak, their love too suffocating. They were easy to find, hunted down, and slaughtered by humans terrified of the divine. Until Lucifer, in his wisdom, proved that love brought about disaster. He outlawed the archaic traditions for the Blue Bloods' own protection and severed any spiritual ties. It was for the best, he'd said. It was to save them all.

Bonds had to be cut out like a tumor. Max didn't ask why; it was Lucifer's will, after all. It was the way things were to be, and that was final.

Bonded soul mates had gone extinct.

But Kingsley's words reverberated in Max's head like a gong. He was radiant when he smiled. "I love you, Max. Always have. In every universe, in every iteration of our existence. No matter which life we live, we're together. I've seen it."

Max's blood began to boil. "You're desperate if you think these mind games will work on me." But his heart hammered loudly in his ears. Ever since that first night when Max had seen Kingsley at Block 122, some part of him had changed, even though he'd fought against it like an animal in a cage.

"I see it in your eyes, Max."

"Shut up," Max snapped. Kingsley was just trying to get in his head. "Stop talking."

"It's true."

Max's whole body began to shake. All he could do was scream. He was going to kill this Silver Blood animal and put an end to everything.

He stabbed for Kingsley's chest. Kingsley moved to block, but Max anticipated the move and feinted.

The sword edge sliced into Kingsley's side. He let out a yelp of pain and stumbled back, wincing.

Max wanted to feel something akin to victory, but it was hollow. Silver blood drenched Kingsley's black shirt, but Max hadn't cut him deep enough. It was just a flesh wound. Why had Max hesitated?

"I know Lucifer made you forget," Kingsley said. His face was tight with pain. "If you couldn't remember, then you'd be more pliable. He left a hole inside your soul. You felt empty, and you filled the emptiness with poison just to feel something again. Exactly what he wanted to create: the perfect weapon."

Max clenched his fist. "You're lying. You don't know what you're talking about." He moved, and Kingsley matched him step for step. When Max took a step to the right, Kingsley took a step to the left. They circled again, like planets in orbit.

Max charged, and Kingsley stepped out of the way and parried again. Even though he was injured, it didn't slow him down.

Fury spurred Max on. He yelled with every strike, storming blows on Kingsley, one right after the other, but Kingsley denied him each time. Experts in their art, they moved with precision. The crash of steel reverberated up Max's arms. He was strong, but so was Kingsley.

Kingsley was anticipating his opponent's every move. His smirk proved it.

They separated again while Max paused to catch his breath. He hated how easily Kingsley had gotten into his head, like Max was some novice. Rage narrowed his vision, making the room shrink as his blood boiled. He was better than this. He had trained for years, relearning centuries' worth of muscle memory passed down with each new cycle. He should have dominated Kingsley from the start. He had him right where he wanted him, and he hadn't taken his shot. Anger flushed his face.

Max lunged. The edge of his blade caught on Kingsley's hilt. Max twisted his wrist and knocked the weapon out of his hand. It clattered away into the dark.

Off-balance, Kingsley stumbled and warded off another strike with his other sword, then leaped forward.

For once, Kingsley started attacking. *Finally!*

Max met him with pleasure. He arced his sword but missed as Kingsley bowed and then sprang up and punched Max right in the jaw with his fist. Max's eardrums popped, and all he heard was the dull din of a bell ringing.

Max put his hand to his face instinctively, and Kingsley, quick as a blink, lunged at him. Their blades connected, grinding against each other.

They pressed forward, locked face-to-face. Max's hearing came roaring back like a rush of waves to the shore.

"I know this isn't you," Kingsley said. His breath was hot and heavy in Max's face. "You're better than this. We need you if we're going to stop Lucifer. You did it before. You can do it again, now, in this world."

"You're wrong!"

Max looped his foot around Kingsley's ankle and shoved him away. But Kingsley's balance was perfect. He skipped backward on featherlight feet.

He would never, in a million years, feel love for anyone like Kingsley. A blood traitor. Love was a concept he refused to accept. It could only lead to weakness. And Max felt nothing at all for Kingsley except contempt.

"Believe me or not, it doesn't change anything," Kingsley said.

"My Silvers will be here soon. You'll suffer at their hands."

"Even if I did, we'll find each other in the next life. And we'll do this all over again until we're together once more."

Max charged. "The Angel of Death doesn't need love. That's what makes me strong."

Kingsley flipped back and narrowly missed Max's hit. The sword sang through the air as Kingsley landed in a crouch and leaped forward, changing direction so quickly, Max barely had time to react. All he saw was the flash of Kingsley's eyes.

Max's vision had tunneled. He had lost his edge.

Kingsley had the advantage.

He was so fast, Max felt a split second of fear. He almost couldn't keep up, blocking each thrust with not a second to spare. Each hit was harder than the last, and panic rose in Max's chest.

With all his focus on Kingsley, he found himself on treacherous terrain. He stumbled backward and slipped on a broken table leg.

Kingsley lashed out and grabbed Max by the front of his shirt before he fell. There came a split second's pause as Max, hovering mid-fall, looked up at Kingsley, who dared to smile.

Max snarled, grabbing him around the neck and pulling him closer. Off-kilter, they tumbled together to the floor with a thud and became a tangle of limbs as each of them grappled for dominance. Both of them had lost hold of their swords. Max connected his fist to Kingsley's side, but Kingsley wound his thighs around Max's and squeezed.

Max bucked his hips to throw him off, but Kingsley had other plans. He pinned Max to the floor and kept him there, leaning over him so that his face was just inches from Max's own. His arms were pinned to his sides, completely helpless. Kingsley held him down, his forearm stretched across Max's chest.

It took a second to register what had happened. Max had lost. How?

The pair breathed heavily for a moment, staring into each other's eyes. The silver and red of Kingsley's eyes shone as he peered down upon Max, not with an expression of victory, but with benevolence. He looked at Max then like no one had ever looked at him before in his life or any of the thousands before it.

Max's heart lodged in his throat.

"You're not going to call your goons," Kingsley whispered.

THIRTY-FOUR

SCHUYLER

*H*ounds barking.

Claws scraping.

The hellhounds were coming. And Schuyler was running for her life.

She couldn't believe she had been so impetuous as to throw a book at Max Force's head. The Angel of Death himself! But she had done it to protect Kingsley. She couldn't let him sacrifice himself, not after she'd finally found someone she could confide in.

And now, all because she hadn't known when to quit, she was being hunted.

The hounds scrambled through the aisles of the Repository after Schuyler, their heavy panting getting louder with each bound.

She pumped her legs as hard as she could, willing herself to go faster. But she was losing ground. Even with her extraordinary speed, the hounds were nipping at her heels. She jumped and juked, zigging and zagging into other aisles, like a rabbit in a field. The hounds skidded on the slick stones and crashed into bookcases, but they didn't slow down.

If she couldn't outrun them, she could try to outmaneuver them.

Terror tasted white-hot. Schuyler knocked over lamps and chairs behind her, dropping obstacles, but the hellhounds didn't waver from pursuing their target. They growled, the sound like sawing into sheet metal, and a whoosh of air spurred her on as fangs just barely missed her ankle. She jumped as a hound lunged, then leaped back over its head. It was bigger than she was, had too much momentum, and wasn't fast enough to catch her.

She ran down another row of books and dared not to look back. The hounds were coming. She heard them, she felt them. Her hair whipped out behind her as she sprinted.

Schuyler backed up and changed direction again.

She wasn't sure where she was running to. She'd lost track of the exit. For all she knew, she was running toward a dead end.

How she wished for Michael's sword right then. Her hands were empty.

The hounds cut her off at every turn. Around every corner, a hound bounded toward her, and she was running out of options. She took a running leap. Clinging to a bookcase, she climbed up the shelves, scrambling up them like she was climbing a ladder. Books toppled down onto the hounds' heads as they chased, but they climbed too.

Schuyler's fingers slipped, and she almost lost her hold, but she kept going. She had to. She couldn't afford to stop.

At the top of the bookcase, she kept running, leaping between the gaps of the aisles, taking two more strides and leaping once more. The hounds followed close behind, bounding from one platform to the other. The bookcases had turned into stepping-stones, but she couldn't look down. It was easily a two-story drop straight to the bottom. One wrong move and she'd be dead.

Towers of bookcases stretched higher toward the vaulted ceiling, surrounding her on all sides. Everything looked the same. She had no idea which way was the right way. So she just ran.

Hounds howled and screamed. Schuyler leaped, landed, took two steps, and leaped over a gap, hurtling herself through the air. Hounds crawled up the taller bookcases, snarling as she flew past. A hound snapped at her coat.

Before she could jump again, a massive hound landed on the platform in front of her. She pinwheeled her arms to stop herself, but she was going too fast. She had no choice but to jump, slamming belly-first into the top shelf across the aisle, then falling.

Schuyler cried out, hitting every shelf on the way down. Books and loose paper went flying. And then something yanked her sideways, snatching her from the air.

A hellhound had leaped and caught her coat sleeve in its massive jaws, carrying her upward once more. It had come dangerously close to clamping down on her arm. The acid from its mouth sizzled like grease on a hot plate.

She kicked, and her coat ripped. She fell once more and landed hard on her back. Air punched out of her lungs in a wheeze, but she had only fallen a few feet. Dazed, she stared up at the dark shapes, her vision going double for a moment, and then a hellhound pounced.

Schuyler rolled and stood. She threw her scarf at the hellhound's face, covering its eyes. It snapped at the air blindly. That bought her a second. But in front of her, a row of books exploded as another hellhound crashed straight through and stood among the broken books, splintered wood, and dust. Its glowing eyes landed on her. The massive bookcase groaned and wobbled like a tower ready to fall. The foundation was weak.

Schuyler thought fast and jumped high. She used all her weight to slam into the bookcase, her momentum enough to push it over.

"No!" she cried as gravity took hold, pulling her faster and faster.

She rode the bookcase down, holding on for dear life, and nearly lost her grip when it knocked into the bookcase behind it, starting a chain reaction. Like dominoes falling, one by one, the bookcases in the Repository came tumbling down. The noise was earsplitting, like thunder right next to her head.

A handful of unlucky hellhounds got caught off guard and were squashed as literally tons of vampire knowledge collapsed on top of them. Momentum carried Schuyler to her feet, and she ran across the fallen shelves like they were ramps. But still, hellhounds were coming.

The last of the bookshelves fell. That was when Schuyler saw it: the door. She was almost there. She was going to make it!

But she skidded to a stop because a figure stepped into view.

Blocking the exit from the Repository was Jack Force. "Jack!" Schuyler gasped, still panting.

He looked surprised to see her at first, but then he recovered. His dazzling emerald eyes narrowed. His gaze was deadly. Kingsley had been right. This was not her Jack, not anymore.

With a jolt, Schuyler remembered that he had come here with his brother.

He was working for Lucifer.

He was here to block her way out.

And he was going to kill her.

She had run away from one Force only to barrel right into another one. No place left to go. She was trapped.

Jack's sword appeared in his hand. His angelic weapon, a gleaming blade glinting with a silver light like moonlight over still waters. It was Gabrielle's sword that he held, just as Max now held Michael's.

Schuyler clenched her fists. Every muscle in her body told her to fight.

Her blood ran cold at the thought of what she was about to do. But if Jack gave her no other choice—if she had to kill him—then she would.

He was trying to do the same to her.

The hellhounds were right behind her. Gaping maws, foaming saliva, and piercing claws. And Jack was standing in her way.

Before she could react, Jack reached back, bringing his sword high, and then let it loose. His sword went end over end, wobbling through the air, right for Schuyler. She saw her own wide blue eyes reflected in the blade. At the last moment, she closed her eyes and waited for impact.

There came a thud and a loud squelch, the yelp of pain, and something heavy landed by her feet.

Beside her, a hellhound lay dead on the floor. Jack's sword had pierced through its mouth and emerged from the back of its skull. Its dull eyes had rolled to the back of its head as its green blood flowed along the cracks on the stone floor.

Her gaze shot to Jack. Something in his face had changed, a look that Schuyler couldn't understand. He looked like he had just sealed his own fate.

More hounds were coming.

Jack rushed forward and yanked the sword from the hellhound's head. His mouth was set in a straight, grim line. When he looked at her, his eyes were deadly serious.

She stared at him, wild and shocked.

He grabbed her hand and pulled her behind him. His touch sent a jolt right through her. He put himself between her and the hellhounds that were furiously closing in.

The second he let go of her hand, it felt empty with his absence.

"Go!" he told her.

He hefted his sword and lunged at the demonic dogs as Schuyler ran.

THIRTY-FIVE

MAX

ax's soul was at war.

A part of him wanted to rip Kingsley's throat out with his teeth and taste his silver blood for himself, wanted to feel it run hot down the skin of his neck, his chest. He imagined it would be like the nectar of the gods. He wanted to find out so badly, it was driving him mad. His whole being ached with the need for power. Kingsley's throat was right there—the artery pulsing a fast, rhythmic tempo—tempting him. All he had to do was take it.

But another part of Max fought that desire, kicking and screaming, because it knew that Kingsley was right.

They were bond mates, bound souls destined to find each other throughout time.

Many cultures and religions on earth had a soul-mate mythology. The ancient Greeks had the reunion of twin flames, the Japanese the red thread of fate, the Celts had the Anam Cara. And the angels from heaven were no different.

Why he couldn't remember Kingsley, Max still didn't know, but he felt the bond as sure as he could feel sunlight on his bare skin or the air changing before a storm quickly approaching. It was a bond that had been carved into their souls and answered to nothing but fate.

The edges of Lucifer's power were starting to peel away from Max's heart.

The moment he and Kingsley had locked eyes at the club, Max had known it. He tried to deny it, but he was powerless to stop it. His angelic spirit stirred. Even the Angel of Death couldn't outrun his destiny.

It was excruciating. His mortal body felt like it was possessed by two different beings. It hurt more than Max thought possible. He was afraid he was going to be torn apart from the inside out. One side of him was trying to get free, but the Max who had been shaped, molded, whipped by Lucifer was terrifying and brutal. That Max wanted blood.

The two forces scraped and clawed at each other in a battle that was never going to end. Max wasn't sure he could take it anymore.

He hated Kingsley, but he felt drawn to him.

He wanted to kill Kingsley, and he wanted to kiss him.

He tried to move, but Kingsley didn't let up.

"Look at me," Kingsley said, sensing the battle raging inside. "Remember me."

Max shook his head, but Kingsley soldiered on. "I know your favorite color is purple. I know you like to sit on your windowsill in your bedroom and watch the moon. I know you hate licorice with all your heart. You sing when you think no one is home. And you have this really cute habit of pinching the bridge of your nose with your fingers when you're thinking. I love you, Max. I'm not giving up on you."

Everything Kingsley had said was the truth. Kingsley knew him . . . impossibly.

A shadow lifted from Max's eyes, and his body relaxed. He inhaled deeply, as if he had been holding his head underwater for too long. Kingsley smelled like burned sugar, and coffee, and whiskey. The lock on Max's heart turned.

"Kingsley . . ." he began, but he couldn't finish. It was the first time he had said his name without it tasting like bile on his tongue.

Kingsley softened. His eyes flitted to Max's lips, and then they locked eyes again. Their gazes were open and wanting. Max didn't feel like he deserved to be looked at that way.

Slowly, Kingsley lowered his face toward Max's and paused, halfway, waiting—leaving Max in agonizing suspense. His breath brushed eagerly against Max's cheek, but Max wasn't afraid.

The part of him that wanted blood screamed at him to take it, to finish this. Instead, he lifted his head, met Kingsley's lips, and kissed him.

It was tender at first, careful and shy. Then it grew stronger and deeper. Max opened his heart and took Kingsley in, in a way he never had with anyone else.

Max closed his eyes and let himself go.

Kingsley's lips were warm and soft yet strong and certain. His stubble scraped against the tip of Max's nose, gritty as sandpaper, but Max didn't care. Kingsley tasted like whiskey—terrible, terrible whiskey—and smelled like chalk and sweat. Visions came to him in the gloom, flashes of Kingsley's feelings in colors and impressions, filling Max with warmth like drinking hot, spiced wine on a winter night.

Max's insides began to thaw.

Kingsley lifted himself off Max, but they stayed connected as if they didn't want to waste any more time. Max sat up, free to move, and his hand gravitated toward Kingsley's cheek, tenderly resting there. His thumb brushed against the silver blood on his face, cool now in the open air.

As if shocked by electricity, he broke away from Kingsley and looked at his hand. The silver was tacky as it dried against his skin.

Kingsley was hurt.

It had been Max's doing.

This was his fault.

Blood. Silver Blood.

He rubbed his fingers and thumb together, and the world snapped back into focus around him. A door shut somewhere in Max's soul.

"Max?" Kingsley asked, with a smirk.

Like the flip of a switch, a shadow returned and took over Max's features. Lucifer's Venator was back. He glared at Kingsley from under his hooded brows. That smirk on Kingsley's face enraged the part of Max that still needed control, needed power and blood.

Lucifer's spell hadn't been broken. So much for true love's kiss.

From afar came the sound of hurried footsteps. The Silver Blood Venators had arrived.

"Seize him!" Max shouted.

The Venators appeared from the depths of the Repository and rushed forward. Kingsley didn't fight them as they hauled him to his feet and shoved his arms behind his back. His jaw was set as he stared determinedly. Even captured, he looked defiant. And still, he dared to smirk. "I still mean what I said, Max. Every word."

"Get him out of here," Max barked.

The Venators dragged Kingsley away.

Slowly, Max got to his feet and picked up Michael's fallen sword and Kingsley's daggers.

He hadn't realized before how cold he was now that Kingsley wasn't there to hold him.

PART FOUR
ABBADON OF THE DARK

I WILL STRENGTHEN YOU AND HELP YOU;
I WILL UPHOLD YOU WITH MY
RIGHTEOUS RIGHT HAND.
—ISAIAH 41:10

THIRTY-SIX

SCHUYLER

*I*t hadn't even registered on Schuyler's mind that she had run all the way across town, sprinting as quickly as her aching legs would carry her. She made it back to SoHo, back to Wooster Street, climbed up her fire escape, and only fully realized what she was doing when she started sliding her bedroom window open. It was as if she were operating on autopilot. Reality didn't seem to be functioning the way it normally did.

She paused a moment, crouching on the fire escape, her mind rewinding like an old videotape, replaying everything.

Jack had saved her.

He didn't have to. He could have let those hellhounds finish the job. But he had saved her and let her go. Why?

Max had said that he had orders to kill anyone who was in the Repository. Jack had to have been given the same orders. So what did it mean that he hadn't killed her? Was Jack remembering?

An alley cat knocked over a trash can, snapping Schuyler out of her daze.

She ducked into her room and yanked off her coat and scarf. One sleeve had been totally shredded. Hellhound slobber had burned a hole right through the other sleeve. She could put her whole finger through the wool, coming out the other side. It could easily have been her skin that was burned.

She peeled off her Jack Purcells. They were covered in dirt and pieces of green hellhound brain, and they reeked like rotten eggs. She left them outside on the fire escape. She was too tired to deal with them now. She stripped down to her underwear and left her clothes in a heap on top of her already-full laundry basket.

Her arms were covered in scratches and bruises from the explosion and her escape. She turned her forearms this way and that, inspecting them in the low light pouring in through the window. She was lucky that this was the worst of her injuries. If her parents saw them, they would know she had broken curfew and snuck out. She wasn't going to be wearing tank tops anytime soon.

If she told them the truth about everything—about her being a Blue Blood, about the Repository, Kingsley, the Superimposition, the hellhounds—they would lock her up forever.

She couldn't tell them. She had to protect them.

Max Force was dangerous. If he tracked her down, what if he came after her parents? She couldn't stand the thought of watching them get dragged away by those monsters.

With a heavy sigh, Schuyler collapsed onto her bed and stared up at her horror-movie-poster-covered ceiling, but she wasn't really looking at it. She was thinking about Kingsley. Was he even still alive?

No. The look on Max's face when she threw a book at him had been murderous. Kingsley was dead. She knew it in her heart. He'd sacrificed himself so she could escape. The one lifeline she had to another world had been snatched away from her.

It was all her fault. She'd been so stupid. She led the enemy right to them. Kingsley had done everything for her, and what did she do to repay him? Get him killed.

Guilt churned in her gut like a boiling pot of sludge.

She pulled her pillow in close and hugged it. If Jack hadn't shown up when he did, she probably wouldn't be home right now. Her parents would probably wake up in the morning, make their coffee, eat their breakfast, and wonder, *Where is Schuyler?* Then they would find her bed empty, and they'd call around to all the police stations and hospitals, and they would never know what happened to their baby girl. She would be hellhound chow. And Lucifer would win.

Schuyler pressed her face into the pillow, muting and darkening the whole world. When she closed her eyes, she saw Jack. The glint of his sword in his hand. The wobbling sound of it hurtling through the air. The slime of a hellhound's brains on her shoes.

What was Jack's plan? Why let her go? Why work for Lucifer and still save her? She didn't understand. She wanted to, but she couldn't ask him. He was frustratingly just out of reach.

Kingsley had been right. The Jack in the other world was dead. This Jack was beyond her understanding. She didn't know him; she never could.

There came a *tap-tap-tap* on her window.

Schuyler looked up from her book. She'd been on her bed, studying all morning and trying not to check her phone every couple of seconds for a call from Kingsley telling her that he had successfully defeated Max and was hiding out somewhere safe. Even her cozy teddy hoodie couldn't make her feel any better.

Instead, at her window was Oliver, crouched on her fire escape, waving at her.

She slid the window open for him as quietly as possible. "Ollie!"

"I have found the princess in her tower," Oliver whispered. "Does this make me a knight? Prince Charming?"

Schuyler looked over her shoulder, but she didn't hear her parents outside the closed door. "Shush! What are you doing here? If my parents hear . . ."

"I'll be quiet as a mouse. I promise. I've brought you presents."

Schuyler stepped aside as Oliver slipped through her window, then ducked halfway back outside to grab another small cooler, similar to the one tucked under her bed. He opened it up for her, grinning wide. "Special delivery," he said. Sure enough, there were twenty more blood packets. On the labels, she recognized Duncan's clinics' symbol that had been front and center on every clinic in town. "I've been thinking, I could kick-start this company, make millions delivering blood to vampires all over the country. I could call it Blood Eats!"

Schuyler shook her head. She wanted to laugh, but she couldn't; it would have been easier to cry. "Oliver, listen to me. I need you to stay as far away from the clinics as possible. They're not safe."

"What's the big deal? Blimey—what happened to your arms?"

He had noticed the bruises and scratches on Schuyler's arms. She pulled her sleeves down toward her wrists.

"Never mind that. Things have changed. How much do you know about the virus? About what's really going on?"

"What are you talking about?"

A thud came from outside Schuyler's door, and both she and Oliver fell silent, waiting and listening. Stephen's voice carried through the thin walls, calling out to Aurora, asking about some vinyl records, and his voice grew fainter as he moved away.

Schuyler kept her voice to a whisper, even though she wanted to scream. "Remember that day when I was acting . . . weird? Came to you in the rain? And I fainted?"

"Hard to forget. What's your point?"

"You *very helpfully* reminded me that the virus is killing everyone, that nobody is safe. You said that the Venators and the Regis are working on it."

"Right," Oliver said expectantly. "Aldrich Duncan. And . . . ?"

"Aldrich Duncan is evil. He's behind the whole pandemic. The disease is us, Blue Bloods, draining people of all their blood."

Oliver coughed out a laugh. "Look, I might be a 'puny Red Blood' and not in the know about all this vampire stuff, but that sounds crazy."

"It's not crazy if Lucifer is the one pulling all the strings."

Oliver's brow furrowed. "Lucifer? Who told you all of this?"

A thought struck Schuyler. Oliver must have known about the first attack on the Repository, right? How it had been totally wiped out and, like Kingsley had said, the Red Blood Conduits eliminated? How had Oliver gotten away unscathed? Why was he still operating as if nothing was wrong? Didn't he have other Conduit contacts?

The hairs on the back of Schuyler's neck stood on end.

She turned away from Oliver for a moment, tracing her knuckle against her lower lip thoughtfully. Should she tell him about Kingsley? About the Superimposition?

For the first time in her life, Schuyler wondered: *Can I trust Oliver? Can I trust my best friend?*

"Sky? What's wrong?" Oliver's voice was sweet but imploring.

She sensed him come up behind her, brushing his fingers on her elbow. She spun to look into his eyes. The morning light hit his irises at just the right angle, and the brown in his eyes lit up like honey. His straight brows were knitted with worry, and his lower lip pushed out in a small pout. He looked so handsome, especially when he was concerned about her.

Regret panged through Schuyler's heart. How could she have thought that he was untrustworthy? Paranoia was leeching common sense from her brain. If she wasn't careful, she would end up pushing her best friend away when she needed him most. This was the same Oliver she had spent so many years with in this very bedroom, watching old black-and-white monster flicks late at night, throwing popcorn kernels at each other to keep from falling asleep, yelling increasingly funny insults as a distraction to win a round of *Mario Kart*, lying on the rug and listening to classic rock music and staring up at the ceiling, their heads nestled side by side like matching pieces of a jigsaw puzzle. When they were together, Schuyler was happy. This was the same boy who had been there for her when the blue veins started streaking down her arms at the beginning of her transformation, the boy who hadn't run when her fangs had come in, or shied away from the incredible strength that would make any normal person fear for their life. Oliver wasn't normal, in the best ways possible. That made him extraordinary.

She could trust him. This was Oliver! Best friends were like bond mates. No matter what dimension, they were forever.

"Do you need . . . something fresh?" he asked, and he swallowed.

"No," she said. "I can't ask that of you."

"Okay," he breathed. "I just want to help."

Schuyler stepped forward and wrapped her arms around his torso. When he lifted his arms, she caught a whiff of his deodorant, smelling like vanilla and lavender. He pulled her in closer, wrapping her up tightly. Warmth radiated off his body. She hadn't realized how desperately she wanted to be held by someone who knew her, truly knew her. She buried her face into his collarbone, clutching him so hard, she could feel his spine through his hoodie.

He was so tall, he put his chin on the top of her head, and they stood like that for a while, slightly swaying to music unheard except for the synchronized rhythm of their hearts.

"I can't lose you too, Ollie," she said against the front of his shirt. "I'm going to protect you, no matter what."

"Hey now, I remember saying just a minute ago that I was the knight in shining armor," Oliver said. She could actually hear him smiling. "Not that I'm complaining, but what's brought this on? Obviously something's wrong. Talk to me."

Schuyler led him to her bed, and they sat down together, knees touching. Oliver rearranged one of her pillows and leaned back, his head resting on the wall, his hand cupping the base of his skull. He was as at home in her room as she was in his; he was almost like a permanent installation.

"Do you know Kingsley Martin?" she asked.

The corners of Oliver's mouth turned downward in contemplation, and he looked to the ceiling. "Posh-sounding name, so you'd think I'd remember it, but no. Doesn't sound familiar."

Schuyler took a deep breath. She needed to tell him everything. The only way she could possibly hope to save him was to have her team at her side. Anxiety swirled like a hurricane inside her belly, but she knew if anyone was going to believe her, it would be him.

So Schuyler started from the beginning. She told him about waking up in the middle of the road, disorientated from the Superimposition, and how she remembered another life in another world. She talked about Kingsley, about who he was, and how he remembered too, and what had happened last night as he fought off Lucifer's best Venator, Max Force. She explained Lucifer's plan to kill all the humans in New York City and how people like Oliver weren't safe anymore.

As she spoke, Oliver sat up, processing the information with slack-jawed wonder. She could see the cogs turning behind his eyes as he finally understood why she had been acting so strangely, making a fool of herself at school, asking weird questions.

"Kingsley was one of the last obstacles in Lucifer's way, and I'm not sure if he's alive or dead," Schuyler said. She'd been able to hold it together for so long, but her voice cracked now, and she inhaled sharply. "My best hope is that they're keeping him somewhere locked up to get what information they can from him, but if that's true, I don't have much time."

"The scratches on your arms . . ." Ollie said. He moved to hold her arm but stopped himself. He didn't want to hurt her. She tugged on her sleeves self-consciously. He shouldn't have to worry about her; she wasn't the mortal one who was walking around every day practically with a piece of paper taped to his back saying FREE LUNCH.

"I'd rather be attacked by hellhounds than have them attack you," she said.

"Schuyler . . ." He said it almost disapprovingly. "Are you hurt anywhere else?"

"Nothing I can't handle. Tonight I'm going to try and find Kingsley. Maybe I can pick up some clues at the Repository and try to follow a trail to where they're keeping him."

Oliver's brows angled down. "Like hell you are!"

His voice had gone up a level, and Schuyler patted the air, shushing him and glancing at the door. She expected her parents to come flying in any second.

"It's my sacred duty as your Conduit to help you," Oliver said, pointing to himself and then to her. "Thousands of years of tradition mean I'm not just going to stand by and watch as you go it alone. Why didn't you come to me for help earlier?"

"I wasn't sure I could explain it. You know how crazy it all sounds. . . ."

"You get used to that when it comes to Blue Bloods."

"That's why I need to protect you. I can't help but think this is all my fault."

Oliver licked his lips, determination setting his jaw. "I can do this. Let me help. I'm human. They won't think of me as a threat. I'll blend in with the rest of the city."

"Ollie—"

"You're in no state to go running around after bloody *hellhounds* of all things. You are going to sit here, drink this blood I brought you, and I'm going to find Kingsley Martin."

There came a knock on Schuyler's bedroom door. Her head snapped in that direction as her mom's voice came from the other side, "Schuyler, sweetie! I need you to run some errands!"

"O-okay!" Schuyler stammered, heart hammering.

She looked back at Oliver, but he had already slipped out the window, his dark hair disappearing below the ledge.

He had made his decision.

Thirty-Seven

SCHUYLER

*J*ust because Schuyler was a half vampire and trying to save the city from impending doom didn't mean that her regular life as a teenage girl was about to stop. Being part of the family meant being tasked with picking up some groceries from the Whole Foods on Houston Street. It was a chore that she didn't mind doing, especially if it meant that her parents could stay inside, where it was safe.

Eggs, chili powder, garlic powder, milk, butter, cheese . . . Schuyler read over the handwritten list Stephen had given her as she walked down the sunny sidewalk.

She was grateful for something to do while Oliver went and did his best Conduit research. Even if it was something as mundane as picking up a half gallon of milk, she felt like she was at least contributing to her family's well-being in some way.

The blood Oliver had dropped off that morning helped heal her injuries, but she was still sick with worry about what to do next. All of the Blue Bloods—including Bowman—were dead. They'd died distrusting her, and she failed them. How could she possibly go up against Lucifer—who was clearly running the Coven with an entire army of supporters—all alone? How could she even hope to stand a chance?

The grocery stores were less packed than before the pandemic. When people ventured out of doors to get their supplies, they didn't linger too long, constantly looking over their shoulders as if expecting the worst. Schuyler understood their fear. She didn't mind wearing a mask. At least it made her more anonymous. She kept her head down, but she watched people on the street warily, wondering if they were secret vampires waiting to jump her and tear her to shreds.

Last night, Max hadn't seemed like he'd known who she was. Could it be that no one else in the Coven knew about her? She couldn't hedge her bets on that. She still needed to keep quiet and lie low until she could find Kingsley and plan their next move.

Oh, how she wished Oliver would call her soon with good news.

She entered the store and waved hello to a cashier ringing up an elderly woman at checkout. Grocery shopping was one of the least bothersome chores she was tasked with. It wasn't tedious like folding laundry or downright gross like cleaning the bathroom. She moved through her list, systematically picking up the fresh produce and dairy products and moving into the aisles.

Schuyler turned around the corner and nearly crashed right into a boy.

"Excuse me," she said, and looked up to see a pair of emerald eyes looking at her from behind a black mask. They were round with surprise. Blond hair peeked out from beneath a Mets baseball cap.

Her heart jammed in her throat, and she slipped down another aisle. Was that who she thought it was? She poked her head out from around the corner to watch as the boy disappeared down another aisle. She didn't get a look at his face.

Had Max Force found her? Was he stalking her? Or was that . . . *Jack*?

Whoever it was, Schuyler needed to get out of there. She didn't want to waste any more time trapped in a building if the boy she'd seen really was Max Force. But she also didn't want to stick around and find out if she was wrong. She needed to play it cool in case her paranoia was really making her lose it.

She hurriedly got the rest of the items on her list and went to the checkout. The boy in the Mets cap was in the lane in front of hers, ringing up a Gatorade and a protein bar. If he had recognized Schuyler, he didn't show it. The slope of his shoulders was casual, and Schuyler kept waiting for him to turn his head so she could get a better view of the side of his face. The cashier waited patiently for her to pay for her groceries, but Schuyler was too busy staring to rush.

The cashier cleared her throat, and Schuyler snapped to attention. The boy was moving out of the grocery store now and disappeared through the automatic doors.

A seed of doubt had taken root in her belly. The pressure was getting to her. Everything was piling on top of her shoulders, one thing after the other; eventually she would break.

She rushed outside with her bags of groceries and looked up and down the street. No sign of the boy in the Mets cap.

"Schuyler?" A voice from behind made her whip around. There

he was, waiting for her in a recessed doorway of a building. It really was Jack. He removed his mask, looking at her with a pained expression.

"What are you doing here?" He didn't live anywhere near here; what reason would he have for shopping for food outside his side of town? Schuyler didn't know if she should run or fight. He didn't come any closer. "What happened to Kingsley?"

Instead of answering her question, he asked, "Do you have time to talk?"

THIRTY-EIGHT

SCHUYLER

Jack led the way down the street, Schuyler keeping a few paces behind him. She watched him warily, expecting his true colors to show themselves at any second. Why she followed him, she still wasn't sure. He could be leading her into a trap. All she could think about was Kingsley, and if he were here right now, he'd be telling her to get away as fast as she could. But the only way to help Kingsley was to follow Jack. Kingsley would have to understand that.

They stopped at a small park, a tiny plot of land that was just big enough for a single bench, a set of swings, and a spring-mounted rocking horse. In another world, Schuyler had imagined that she and Jack would visit one of these parks together, watching their own children play. That, of course, was little more than a dream now.

Jack took a seat on one side of the bench and waited.

Except for them, the park was empty. Schuyler scanned the hedges for any sign of movement, vampires lurking in the shadows. There really wasn't anyplace for someone to hide, but she couldn't be too careful.

"Are you stalking me?" she asked.

Jack shook his head. "Happy accident. Come on, sit. I don't bite," he said.

"Yeah, right."

"I was trying to make a joke."

"Leave the jokes to clowns."

"Clowns aren't funny."

"Neither are you."

Jack's mouth slipped into a smile. But he tucked his lips in, catching himself, and cleared his throat. He waited patiently for her to sit.

He was dressed casually in Adidas joggers with stripes down the legs and a long-sleeved henley shirt. With the baseball cap and his mask, he didn't look dangerous. He looked . . . normal. If she didn't know any better, she might have thought he was trying to hide his identity. What reasons could the deadly Jack Force have to hide his face from the world?

Admittedly, Schuyler hadn't come all this way just to turn back now. She sat on the other side of the bench, perching halfway off the edge, ready to spring away if she needed to. Jack didn't comment on her jumpiness. He must have known that she felt like she was wading into shark-infested waters and couldn't see the bottom.

He leaned forward and rested his elbows on his thighs. His knees bounced as he looked out on the park. A swing moved back and forth in the slight autumn breeze. Schuyler adjusted her scarf around her neck. The air was cool, but the sun was bright and warm.

"What have you done to Kingsley?" she asked.

"I haven't done anything to him. He's alive."

Schuyler's eyes widened. "Where?"

Jack shook his head. "City Hall basement, but they took him someplace else this morning. I don't know where." He was telling the truth. It was plain on his face, right down to the tightness around his eyes.

Guilt crashed down on top of Schuyler, and she slumped onto the bench. The basement at City Hall! He was Lucifer's prisoner. Kingsley was slipping farther away from her. If she didn't act fast, he would be dead.

"I'm sorry," Jack said.

Her eyes snapped to him. Something hot bubbled up inside her chest. She wanted to feel anger, or spite, or hatred, but instead she felt confusion. Why was he apologizing? He was one of Lucifer's best weapons. It was like a nuclear bomb apologizing for decimating an entire city.

"When I spoke to Kingsley, he mentioned something about a phenomenon called a Superimposition?"

Schuyler fiddled with the zipper on her coat. "Yeah. Quantum levels of complicated, in my opinion."

"He also said that you both have memories of another world. Is that true?"

Schuyler glanced at him. The muscle in his jaw worked so hard, he looked like he was chewing gum. She nodded. There was no point in lying to him. "It's all true."

Jack took in a deep breath, his shoulders rising to his ears. He removed his cap, ran his fingers through his hair, and replaced the cap lower down on his brow. It was apparent that he was agitated. She didn't need to have memories of him from another world to see that much.

Whatever it was that he wanted to hear, she hoped her words had helped.

They sat together on the bench, separated by two arm lengths, a vast canyon spanning the space between them. Schuyler looked upward, watching the clouds pass across the bright blue sky; Jack looked down at his sneakers.

"Why did you save me last night?" Schuyler finally asked, breaking the pregnant pause.

Jack held his breath. He looked at her, his eyes scanning back and forth on hers. "I . . ." he began but didn't finish. Whatever he was looking for in her eyes, she wasn't sure he found it. He looked back down at his shoes, a blush turning his ears pink. "I don't know," he finally admitted.

Schuyler's heart constricted. It was not the three-word sentence she was hoping for.

"Thanks for doing it anyway," she said.

Jack dipped his chin, a conciliatory nod.

Schuyler chewed on her lip and stood up. Her grocery bags rustled in her hands. "I should be going," she said.

"Wait." Jack reached out a hand to stop her. "You asked me once if I remembered you. Should I? What are we to each other?"

Schuyler's heart broke then. The pieces of it turned to dust.

He didn't remember her after all. She already knew that. She had prepared herself for it. Hearing him say it, though, confirmed her worst fears. She had lost Jack at the Battle for Heaven in more ways than one.

If he didn't remember her—didn't love her—in this world, she couldn't make him. He was not her Jack anymore, even if her heart wished it were true. That world was gone, that Jack was gone, and she would never get him back.

But she was brave. She was the daughter of Aurora Cervantes and Stephen Chase. She was strong. *Facio valiturus fortis.*

Schuyler straightened her shoulders and looked down at Jack, mustering up what needed to be said. "We're friends," she said. "That's all."

With that, she turned and walked home.

THIRTY-NINE

SCHUYLER

Before Schuyler went inside the building, she called Oliver. He picked up before the first ring even finished.

"He's still alive!" Schuyler said.

"*Shhh!* Hold on." She could hear the sound of the phone rubbing up against something, and footsteps. After a moment, Oliver continued in a stage whisper, "You nearly blew my cover. I'm near the Repository, and it is absolutely crawling with Silver Bloods."

Schuyler could barely contain herself. "I just saw Jack. He told me that Kingsley is still alive!"

"Did he say where they were keeping him?"

"City Hall at first, but they moved him. He wasn't sure where they've taken him now."

After a moment, Oliver asked, "And you're sure you can trust him? He *is* working for Lucifer, after all."

Schuyler tapped the toe of her sneaker into the concrete sidewalk and chewed on the inside of her cheek. It was a question that she herself was too afraid to ask. After all, Duncan's side had already set a trap for Kingsley and her once; what was to stop them from doing it again? It was what got Kingsley captured in the first place. But Jack had saved her at the Repository when he could easily have killed her. There had to be a reason. "Hope is all we have left," she said.

Oliver sighed into the phone. "Okay, it's a lead at least."

"I can meet you at the Repository."

"No, you sit tight. This place is a hotbed of activity. The last thing I want is for you to draw attention to yourself. I'll be your eyes and ears and then I'll call you when I know more."

Sitting and waiting was the absolute last thing she wanted to do, but Oliver wasn't the type to budge. "Oliver, please be careful."

"You too." And then he hung up.

Schuyler came in through the front door and dropped the groceries on the dining room table. Aurora had been sitting at her music corner and furrowed her brow when she saw Schuyler. "Everything go okay at the store?" she asked.

Schuyler nodded stiffly and then shut herself in her bedroom. Waiting was the worst feeling.

Aurora must have sensed that something was eating at her, because while Schuyler was putting away her coat in her closet, she heard a subtle knock, and a sliver of her mom's face appeared in the crack of the open door. She waved Schuyler over to the bed, and they lay down together.

Aurora wedged herself between the cold wall and Schuyler and propped her head up on her fist. Having her mother at her back soothed Schuyler in ways she hadn't realized she needed.

As Aurora gently ran her fingers through her hair, Schuyler remembered another world when that kind of thing was all she wished for, a mother who was awake, and noticed her, and comforted her. Something cold and stiff and sharp had carved a hollow hole in the middle of her chest. Talking with Jack had taken a piece out of her heart, and Schuyler needed time for it to fill back up. Aurora's fingers brushing through Schuyler's curls lulled Schuyler into a half-lidded doze. She was so tired—emotionally, physically, psychologically, spiritually. All she wanted to do was close her eyes and rest.

She had always been emotional, a person who had big feelings and a bigger heart. When she was in kindergarten, she had attacked three boys who were poking a frog with a stick and laughing, cornering it on the playground so it couldn't run away. She had screamed and cried over that tiny frog, felt its fear and desperation to get away. She gave one of the boys a big black eye and another a split lip, and the third one ran away before she could chase him down. The principal had told her parents that she did more damage to the boys than they did to the frog. She didn't regret it, though. The frog had escaped.

In a way, she envied people who could walk away from something that had become too difficult to deal with, who knew when to throw in the towel because the opposition was so unbeatable. But she was too stubborn, and walking away wouldn't be the right thing to do.

"I can't help but wonder, is it something to do with Oliver?" Aurora asked.

"No. What makes you say that?"

Aurora shook her head slightly and again furrowed her brow. "I don't know. Something about him feels off lately. I'm sure I'm just imagining things."

"Oliver is the one person keeping my whole world from crumbling around me right now, actually."

"Do you want to talk about it?" Aurora asked. *It* being the overwhelming, all-encompassing weight of the world on her shoulders, in Schuyler's case.

Schuyler pinched the corners of her mouth. She didn't say anything back. Where to even begin? She couldn't tell the truth.

Aurora kept running her fingers through Schuyler's hair. Then she started to hum. It wasn't a song about anything in particular—Schuyler had the sense that Aurora was making it up as she went—but she understood what it meant: that Aurora was here, and that everything was going to be okay, that Schuyler was safe. She closed her eyes and breathed. A knot unwound behind her sternum as her mother's voice washed over her like sunlight.

She wanted to remember this moment. How the desk lamp glowed defiantly against the waning afternoon light, how the confidence resonated in her mother's voice. The spicy smell of Aurora's perfume, the soft pillow beneath her head, the warmth of Schuyler's body pressed against her mother's. She would look back on this memory sometime in the future and be grateful she'd lived it.

She couldn't help but wonder what Jack was doing right now. Was he still sitting on that park bench? Were his eyes turned upward, watching the clouds pass across the pink sky? Did he think of her? Did he know she thought of him?

"How did you know Dad loved you back when you first met?" Schuyler asked, turning her head.

Aurora paused a moment, her fingers stuck in Schuyler's hair, and then continued, a small, knowing smile lifting her lips. "Well, if there's one thing we know about your father, it's that he's not subtle."

"What did he do?"

"Different people have different types of love languages, whether it be through words, taking time off to spend together, physical touch, or gift giving. Your father used all of those to show his feelings and more. But his actions stood out to me the most. Whenever he could help, he did. He was always ready to jump in and give back, even when he didn't have to. In fact, probably any person in their right mind wouldn't have. But your dad was different."

Aurora smiled a little wider. Schuyler could see the memory unspooling behind her mom's dark brown eyes.

She turned her head to face the ceiling once more.

Was Jack's love language in his actions? He shouldn't have saved her, but he did. He could have obeyed his orders and let her die. Did he do it because he loved her after all? Even he didn't seem to know the answer to that question.

She worried that she had closed a door on him at the park, a sign never to speak to her again, and that she had shut him out too quickly. Could there still be a chance for him? She'd said they were just friends, but as long as he worked alongside Max and Lucifer, could she ever really believe he could love her in the end?

Schuyler's phone buzzed on her nightstand. It was a text from Oliver. She propped herself up, her stomach suddenly filled with butterflies, and she read his messages as they came in quick succession:

I found him.

I know how we can get him out.

Meet me at the Mercer Hotel.

"Everything all right, mi cielo?" Aurora asked. She couldn't see the screen on Schuyler's phone.

"Uh, yeah," Schuyler said, closing her eyes hard. She barely heard her mother. Her ears had filled up with white noise.

Oliver had done it.

She took a breath. She came up with a lie on the spot. "I have to get started on a group project right now for school."

"Okay, sweetheart," Aurora said. She kissed the back of Schuyler's head and scooted off the bed. "You'll let me know if you need anything else? Your father's almost done making dinner."

"I'll be fine," Schuyler said. "I promise."

Aurora watched her daughter for a moment, as if looking right through her, like trying to see shapes through a fog. Schuyler smiled, even though it hurt.

Aurora didn't say anything else, though. She just tipped her head and left, closing the door behind her.

Schuyler hated lying, but it was necessary this time.

She was truly her father's daughter: If she could help someone, she would, even if it was wiser not to.

She was going to save Kingsley.

FORTY

SCHUYLER

$\mathscr{T}$he Mercer Hotel was fortunately less than half a mile's walk from her loft, so she made it in practically no time at all to the corner of Mercer and Prince Streets. The hotel was a redbrick building with six floors devoted to making guests feel at home in rooms designed to embrace the modern SoHo feel of the neighborhood. Despite the pandemic, its doors were open, welcoming guests, who were few and far between. To think that Kingsley was somewhere in there, behind the hotel's unassuming façade and soft lights, chilled Schuyler to the bone. What horrors lay behind every door?

Oliver had given her a room number to visit first, 303, but she didn't go through the lobby. If vampires under Lucifer's command were lurking around, she wanted to stay out of sight as much as possible, so she went around back to the service entrance and broke open a door leading to a laundry room. White sheets stacked in towers led Schuyler through a maze until she found a dimly lit stairwell. Her senses were tuned in to any sound. She heard a custodian filling a bucket in a janitorial closet, listening to the radio, while a bellhop whistled as he walked down a nearby hallway. Schuyler stayed out of sight the whole time, expertly moving from shadow to shadow.

Kingsley's training had rubbed off on her in so many ways. Even though she was scared, she didn't let fear control her. She used it to make herself move quickly through the hotel all the way up to the third floor. As she walked down the hall, she glanced at all the closed doors, wondering if Kingsley was locked behind one of them. She didn't want to think about what state he was in, what terrible things had been planned for him, and these thoughts quickened her pace all the way to room 303. Oliver should be waiting for her there, ready with a plan. Whatever it was, she was prepared for a fight.

She rapped lightly on the door, and Oliver flung it open as if he had been waiting for her right there. He looked nervous but relieved that she had made it to the room. She couldn't blame him. He was like a lamb who had walked right into a lion's den. With a tip of his head, silently beckoning her inside, he shut the door behind her.

The room was decorated much like she expected from a bougie hotel, with a lone king-sized bed, a desk, and a television that was dark and unused. Oliver's coat was draped over the desk chair, and he had kicked off his Chuck Taylor shoes at the door.

"Ollie, you are brilliant!", she said, flushed with nerves. "Where is he? Which room? How did you find him?"

Oliver put a hand to the back of his neck and rubbed it. "Yeah, um," he said, cringing. "About that."

Schuyler's heart sank like a bowling ball dropped in the middle of the ocean. "Don't tell me he's . . ." She couldn't finish.

"No, it's not that. He's not here."

"What?"

"I don't know where he is. I never did. I just wanted to get you alone, and away, so we could do what needs to be done. You must take me as your Familiar and feed on my blood. Then you can be strong enough to face Mayor Duncan—Lucifer."

Schuyler took a step backward. She couldn't quite believe what she was hearing. "Why would you lie to me? Why would you say you knew where to find Kingsley?"

He brushed past her and walked to the window. "It was the only way I knew I could get you somewhere private so we could do this without your parents finding out your secret. Someplace safe and quiet and alone."

"Oliver, that's . . ." Schuyler was reeling from his rationale. "I don't understand. I told you, I don't need you as my Familiar. I can't feed on you."

"Why not? Every single vampire has fed this way before."

"Yes, but . . . in the other world, I performed the *Caerimonia* with you, and I could never repay you for it."

"You don't need to repay me. That's not what it's supposed to be. I'm *giving* myself to you."

Oliver crossed the room and took her hands into his. His touch was smooth and warm, and it sent a shock wave of heat across her cheeks when he brushed his thumbs over her knuckles. No matter what world she was in, Oliver had always been there for her.

Those eyes spoke volumes. Everything he wanted to say out loud but couldn't hung suspended in his gaze. Drinking directly from him would unlock a spiritual connection between them that was more intimate than anything she had ever experienced in this world before.

"In order for you to reach your full potential, you need fresh blood, straight from my veins. I can do this. I want to do this. Schuyler, I . . ." He didn't finish what he wanted to say, but she understood.

Her insides churned with desire. She wanted to, she needed to. Her vampire instincts yearned for fulfillment, tightening every muscle in her body, and her head swam with nothing else but thoughts of him. She could even hear his blood pulsing, the rush like the ocean tide going in and out, inviting her closer. Her vision sharpened and her mouth watered as her gaze drifted downward to the hollow slope of his neck.

"Okay," she breathed. "Thank you."

Willingly putting his life into her hands—a human trusting a vampire not to kill him—was one of the most selfless acts she could imagine. He trusted her so completely that her heart melted. He cared about her so much, and she cared about him. She didn't need to drink from him to know that. But she had to be careful. She wasn't like other vampires.

Schuyler gently pushed on his chest, and he backed up and sat down on the edge of the bed. He looked at her with those puppy-dog eyes, expectant and pining, waiting for her to act first. That flop of his dark hair, his shy smile, his hopeful and expectant brown eyes . . . He had always been so handsome. To perform the *Caerimonia Osculor* with him would take their relationship to the next level.

"If you want me to stop, at any time," she said, "tell me. I don't want to hurt you."

He raised her hand to his lips and kissed it, like a prince in a fairy tale. "I'm ready."

Oliver pulled his T-shirt down and stretched his neck for her. She took a long moment, simply looking at him, then moved in.

She dragged her lips across the skin, breathing him in, then pierced his neck with her fangs. He let out a small gasp, and his blood flowed. Schuyler held on to his hand firmly as she drank, and he fell with her backward onto the bed.

And, like the turn of a key in a lock, his soul was bound to hers forever.

FORTY-ONE

SCHUYLER

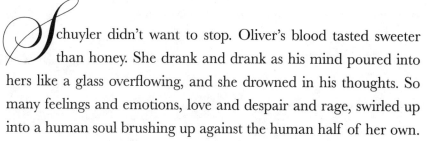

*S*chuyler didn't want to stop. Oliver's blood tasted sweeter than honey. She drank and drank as his mind poured into hers like a glass overflowing, and she drowned in his thoughts. So many feelings and emotions, love and despair and rage, swirled up into a human soul brushing up against the human half of her own.

Oliver's back arched. "I'm okay," he gasped.

Already she could feel herself getting stronger, her muscles bursting with energy and her heartbeat racing with life, at the cost of Oliver's life draining away.

His thoughts were made up of images, and the sound of his voice, and bursts of color, and feelings she couldn't even describe, but one thing was for certain: He was in love with her. He'd always been in love with her.

Schuyler. Love. Schuyler. Forever.

Just like in the other world, she'd known it, but feeling it in his blood all over again made it all the more real. It was so real, she could almost touch the physical form of his feelings, cupped in her hands like a fragile thing.

Schuyler pulled herself away and put her hand to her lips, savoring the last of Oliver's blood as the flavor faded and her fangs retracted. She couldn't handle any more, not of his blood but of his heart.

Oliver's head tipped to the side, his eyes closing as he fell fast asleep. It was normal for a Familiar to sleep, especially after the first *Caerimonia Osculor*, but even so, she checked his pulse, just to be sure she hadn't gone too far. Everything was normal; the holes in his neck were even starting to close. He was okay.

She climbed off him, put a pillow under his head, then pulled a blanket over his body. She watched his chest rise and fall softly with each breath as guilt churned inside her. It was like she had over-indulged in chocolate cake, and she felt sick.

This had been a mistake. Everything was all wrong.

Oliver stirred awake, faster than she'd anticipated, and he sat up. He put his hand to his neck and checked his fingers for blood but didn't find any.

"That was . . . amazing," he said. His eyes sparkled when he looked at her. "Better than amazing."

Schuyler couldn't stay still. She felt ready to take on the world, take on Lucifer himself, with Oliver's blood coursing through her like nitrous oxide.

"How do you feel?" he asked.

"We shouldn't have done this."

"It didn't work?"

"No, it's . . . I should have known how this would affect us. I know how you feel about me, how strong it is."

Oliver's eyes filled with emotion. "I've been meaning to tell you about it for years, and I never felt ready before, but I realized this morning that I can't let you fight a literal army without you knowing that I love you, Schuyler. Ever since we first met."

She hated what she would have to say. She knew how it would hurt. "I don't," she said, and took a step back.

Oliver's expression fell. "What?"

"I don't feel the same way about you, Oliver. I'm so sorry, but I don't."

"Don't say that." Oliver's voice broke.

"You're my *best friend*, Ollie. Can't we just be that?"

"I thought we could be more."

"Not right now." She gestured to the hotel room. "Not with everything going on. The timing isn't right."

"I've given everything for you—my *whole life* is dedicated to you. Especially now. Is it not enough?"

"It's more than enough!" Schuyler said. "And right now you're giving too much. Please. You're not thinking this through. We are running out of time. We still have to find Kingsley."

Sorrowfully, Oliver's brows cinched. He wasn't going to let this go. "I don't care about Kingsley! I care about *you*. You're everything to me. Why can't you love me back?"

"I love Jack." She said it without intending to. It tumbled out like a wrecking ball ramming full tilt through a brick wall.

Oliver's face twisted in fury. He got to his feet. "Jack? Jack *Force*? You don't even know him!"

It was true. This day was not going the way she had wanted it to. First Kingsley getting captured, and then talking with Jack in the park, and now feeding off her best friend's blood only to break his heart. It felt like the world had tilted, and Schuyler didn't know where else to go.

"I love Jack. And I always will," she said. "Even if he can't love me back, my heart won't let me forget. It's not fair to you."

"Fair? You want to talk about fair?" Oliver spun away from her, his shoulders tight. Schuyler watched him, a balloon of anxiety swelling in her chest. It was getting harder to breathe. She never wanted any of this to happen. Why couldn't they just go back to the way things were? Being regular kids, making up games at the Met, and quoting their favorite movies as the only means of conversation, and passing each other funny notes in class?

Maybe there was still a chance they could go back to being normal. Schuyler wanted that so badly. But apparently Oliver wanted otherwise.

Oliver went to the window again, his hands on his hips. His shoulders moved up and down, each breath rocking his whole body, his face tight in the glass reflection. She'd never seen him so angry. No, not angry. *Entitled.*

It occurred to her that he had expected this night to go very differently.

Eventually, after an excruciatingly long minute, Oliver said, "Fine." He turned around, his face set, picked up his coat, and pulled on his shoes.

"Ollie, don't be upset, please. I don't want this to change us."

"Too late."

"Oliver!"

He wrenched open the door and turned to Schuyler. "You can't choose him. You won't," he said, agonized. "I know you love me."

Oliver slammed the door behind him as he left.

FORTY-TWO

SCHUYLER

*I*n the span of twenty-four hours, Schuyler had lost her soul mate, her surrogate brother, and her best friend.

She walked back home in a complete daze and collapsed onto her bed without getting undressed. She tried calling Oliver on the phone, but it went straight to voice mail, and she considered sending him a text, but she knew he wouldn't answer.

They were done.

Oliver's last words still sent a chill down her spine, making her hands clench and her teeth grind.

I know you love me. . . .

How could he say something like that? It wasn't fair! She didn't owe her love to anyone. Her love was hers, and hers alone, to give to whomever she wanted. What an astounding display of manipulation tactics.

She yanked her pillow over her face and screamed into it, muffling the sound, but it didn't make her feel any better.

Had that been all Oliver ever wanted—years of friendship to win her heart? Had he only been there for her just so he could be more than that someday? Did he think he deserved a reward for being her only friend, the only one she could lean on, the only one she could confide in? She wanted to shake him, to knock some sense into him.

Boys were so stupid.

Tap . . . Tap tap.

Oliver, come back to apologize? Schuyler pulled the pillow away from her face and saw a pair of green eyes peering at her from her bedroom window, looking meek and modest, a figure crouched on her fire escape.

Jack.

She sat up, staring at him openmouthed.

He was dressed exactly as he'd been when she'd seen him earlier, with his Mets baseball cap pulled low over his brow, a corner of his mouth lifted in a lopsided smile. Silently, Schuyler stood up but paused at the window. They looked at each other for the breadth of a moment.

A single pane of glass was all that separated her from Lucifer's best weapon.

He must have seen her come home. Had he followed her? Was he there to kill her? Was he finally here to follow through with Duncan's plan? She sucked on her lips, peering into his eyes, but Jack's didn't hold any sign of malice. Those green eyes, shining like real emeralds in the soft light from her room, were uncorrupted.

A girl who had seen as many horror movies as Schuyler had knew better than to invite a vampire into her bedroom. She would only be asking for trouble, especially if the vampire was part of an evil plot to drain every single mortal in New York City.

But it was still Jack. The same Jack who had saved her at the

Repository last night, who'd had so many chances to kill her but hadn't done so yet. He was a mystery that she wanted to solve.

Her heart had always been too big.

She slid the window open and stepped back for Jack to climb inside.

Looking at her mess of a room, she really wished she had anticipated having a visitor. She would have picked her dirty clothes off the floor and thrown away the empty bags of potato chips on her desk.

Jack's eyes scanned her room too, taking in all her posters and her monochromatic clothes hanging in her closet, her Barbies perched next to her graphic novels and other books on her shelf, her stuffed animals on her bed. Color rose in his cheeks.

"What are you doing here?" she whispered. Even if her parents weren't within earshot, she wasn't sure she could have spoken any louder.

"I'm sorry. I didn't know how else to talk to you," he said.

"A phone call would have worked."

"I had to see you."

Schuyler's skin felt ten degrees warmer. "Why? What else is there?"

Jack took off his baseball cap and rolled the brim in his palm, nervously spinning it. "Earlier today, you said that we were just friends. But I don't think that was true."

"No?"

"No." He straightened his broad shoulders and then sighed, collapsing into himself. It was as if he'd cut a line that had been pulling him upward, severing a rope wrapped around his neck. "I know we're so much more than that."

Schuyler's heart hitched. "So you remember?"

He shook his head, his jaw clenched. "No."

She didn't hide the disappointment on her face. "Then why did you come?"

Jack ran his hand down his face. It took him a moment to gather his thoughts, but his gaze held hers intently.

"I met with Kingsley in secret a while back, and I asked about you. But he told me you were human. He was trying to protect you. But I knew . . . I *felt* that you were special. It took me too long to realize it. Only at the Repository did I know for sure. You're a vampire."

It was time for Schuyler to lay all her cards on the table. She took a deep breath. "Yes. Though not like you. *Dimidium Cognatus.* I'm half human." She pulled up her sleeves to show him the blue veins on her wrists.

Jack's eyes danced in the low light. "That's . . . How is that possible? There's never been one before."

"I don't know." She took a step back. "Are you going to kill me now?"

"No. I . . . It makes sense now."

"What does?"

"Why I dream about you."

Butterflies swarmed in her belly.

He continued. "Rather, I dreamed about a version of you, but you all the same." His expression fell open. The color deepened in his cheeks. "You smelled like spring and your touch was so sweet. It was like waking up from a nightmare and knowing that I was safe." He ran his fingers through his hair. "And you've never left my dreams. They stirred something up inside me that I can't ignore, that I don't *want* to ignore."

"Do you dream about the other world?" Schuyler asked softly.

"Maybe. Listen. Tell me the truth. Kingsley said that I died?"

She swallowed with difficulty. "Yes."

Jack nodded gravely. "I asked him who I was, who I should have been, and he said that I needed to ask myself better questions. That I had something Lucifer didn't have."

"And?"

"And I've done nothing but think, and walk, and think some more. I haven't slept. I feel like I'm going crazy. And when I saw you today, I realized . . . The truth has been in front of my eyes all along. You. You're what makes me different."

Schuyler couldn't speak.

"It's the only thing Lucifer doesn't have—someone who loves him. And you love me, don't you?"

Schuyler's eyes fell to the floor. She could tell him no, follow through with the lie she'd told that afternoon. But she couldn't do it anymore. She looked into his eyes.

"Yes," she said proudly. "I love you."

"Maybe you shouldn't."

"What? Why?"

"It's my fault that my brother found Kingsley. I remembered his name after seeing a note he'd left for Max. Once I said it out loud, it was only a matter of time before Max tracked him down."

"How did you remember him?"

"I can't explain it. It was like déjà vu. I wish I could take it back, wish I could have kept my mouth shut. But it was like a spark in the night, and I instinctively grabbed at it because I'd been lost for so long. Now because of me, Kingsley's in trouble. They're planning something terrible for him." He looked like he wanted to throw up.

"And you swear you don't know where he is now?"

He shook his head. The knot in his jaw throbbed like it was about to burst, he was clenching his teeth so hard. "Last I spoke to him, he was alive. He spat on me, told me to go to hell, but I couldn't tell him what I was planning. I needed to keep him in the basement of City Hall so I could safely get him out, but I needed more time. Then Lucifer took him somewhere else before I could get to him. I wasn't fast enough. I'd killed two Silver Bloods guarding his cell but found it empty. I didn't know . . . I wanted to—"

"You . . . wanted to save him?" Schuyler's eyes swam with unshed tears.

Jack nodded.

Schuyler put her fingers to her lips, thinking. She was running out of options to save Kingsley. Oliver's lead had turned out to be a dead end, and now Jack didn't know where Kingsley was either. Schuyler needed to act, but she didn't know where to start.

"What will happen to you if they find out that you tried to help Kingsley?"

Jack shrugged a shoulder. Clearly he'd thought about this possibility, but it didn't worry him. "I guess they'll hunt me down as a traitor." He said it so nonchalantly, it shocked her.

"What about your brother? Where does he stand?"

"Max is . . ." Jack's brow furrowed. "Max doesn't know I saved you. And he definitely doesn't know I tried to break Kingsley out. He can never know."

"Why did you start working with Lucifer in the first place?"

Jack flinched, like simply saying the name Lucifer twisted a knife in his gut. "When Max and I were eight years old, our parents died in a plane crash over the Atlantic. My dad was Regis at the time, and Aldrich Duncan was next in line to lead the Coven. He took us under his care, adopted us, raised us like his own. I know it's not an excuse, but we didn't have anywhere else to go. We hadn't come into our powers yet; we needed help. Max, he—he was so angry, and so hurt, and he needed someone to guide him. It was only after some time that we realized what Duncan was planning. By then it was too late. The Coven had shifted its perspective. The other Blue Bloods wanted to follow Lucifer's plan, and we were to be his shining examples of exceptionalism. Max wanted control, and I needed to protect him. I don't know what I'll do if I fail to protect him from himself."

"Jack . . ." Schuyler's heart broke for him.

"Look, I'm not asking for forgiveness. And I'm not expecting you to believe me. It sounds farfetched, I know. I only needed to tell you the truth."

"Thank you," she said. "It helps."

Jack looked grateful, but he chewed on the inside of his cheek. Even though he was one of the most powerful vampires she had ever known, he was also just a boy. For all his confidence and popularity in school, at the end of the day he was just like her, looking for answers.

"You want to say something more?" she asked.

He nodded with determination. "I want to be different. I want to change. I want to make things right. I want to be with you."

Schuyler hadn't expected that. Her eyes widened.

"While my mind might not remember, my heart does," he said.

Schuyler's whole body quaked. She clutched her hands together, wringing them for lack of anything else to do, and held her breath. She had been waiting for this moment for so long.

"Oh, Schuyler . . ." His voice melted. "I—"

Before he even finished talking, he took a step toward her, and she took a step toward him, the two of them drawn together as if by gravity. They collided into each other like war-torn lovers reunited. He lifted her off the floor, holding on to the back of her head with one hand and clutching her body against his with the other. Schuyler's arms wrapped around his neck, and a stifled whimper escaped her lips. She had missed him so much, she wanted to touch him everywhere at once. Her legs wrapped around his slender hips, and they held each other.

Schuyler gently pressed her palms to the sides of his face and rested her forehead against his. Hot, happy tears streamed down her face, and she couldn't stop smiling. Jack too smiled, from ear to ear, and he looked so relieved, like he hadn't truly smiled in years.

Her Jack.

He'd come back.

Back to the Light.

They kissed deeply.

They'd found each other again.

PART FIVE
NOBODY IS THE VILLAIN
OF THEIR OWN STORY

HATERS ONLY HATE
THE PEOPLE THEY CAN'T HAVE
OR THE PEOPLE THEY CAN'T BE.
—ANONYMOUS

FORTY-THREE

MAX

$\mathcal{M}$ax hated sunsets.

They brought back too many bad memories. A funeral at dusk, twin caskets, the pungent too-sweet smell of flowers wreathed atop the coffins, and the empty, hollow understanding that his parents would never come home again. Of all the things to remember from that day, it wasn't Jack sitting listlessly at his side, or the firm squeeze of Duncan's hand on his shoulder, or the itch of drying tears on his cheeks. It was the slash of red sunlight streaking across the polished oak coffin lids.

Looking out over Manhattan at the setting sun from Aldrich Duncan's office, Max felt like it couldn't set fast enough.

Tonight, he would begin the ritual of the Silver Legacy.

Tonight, Max would kill Kingsley.

Max had been summoned to City Hall earlier that afternoon and had seen for himself what was in store. Duncan spared no expense in planning Max's debut as the most prized symbol of a new age of Blue Blood domination. A red carpet had been draped from the front doors and down the stairs, which were flanked by thousands of bouquets of bloodred roses, a grand entrance for hundreds of people sitting in white chairs facing a podium, waiting to see Lucifer's heir. In a few hours, the pavilion would be packed with vampires ready to celebrate the coronation of a new king.

At midnight, Max would complete the Sacred Kiss, drink every last drop of Kingsley's silver blood, absorb all of his memories, his fears, his hopes and dreams, his power. In doing so, he would become something new, more powerful than Silver. No one had ever drained a Silver Blood before—it was heinous to even think of it—but it was Max's destiny to show the world just how incredible it was.

Whatever he would become, Max would be a god.

Duncan had extracted everything he needed from Kingsley, personally torturing him for any last trace of his little rebellion. He had taken Kingsley to the Blue Blood clinic closest to City Hall in Lower Manhattan. There, Silver Blood scientists in lab coats ran tests, performed scans, and carved the flesh off his bones for analysis. They needed sample data to compare to Max's body after he transformed. They needed to record every data point. Max would be just the beginning of the end of the world. If his powers doubled, or even tripled, he would be the first in a new line of vampires that history had never seen.

Max hadn't been there to see any of the tests performed on Kingsley. He didn't know the specifics and had made up an excuse to stay away. He needed to prepare mentally—to meditate and ready himself—so he only imagined Duncan standing above Kingsley, his eyes bright with venom, telling him it would all be over soon.

Kingsley was all alone. Kingsley was the last soldier on an empty battlefield. No more Blue Blood rebels on his side, no more

Schuyler girl. Kingsley might have cried as he lay strapped to the table; he might not have.

Duncan was right, though. It would all be over soon.

Once Duncan had been satisfied that Kingsley's last remaining use would be through the draining of his blood, Kingsley had been returned to his cell in the basement. Max pictured him lying on the floor, too exhausted to move, waiting for the inevitable. He knew what was coming.

Hours passed. No one disturbed Max while he waited in Duncan's office. He barely moved, long after the sun went down and what few city lights were left came on.

Duncan's voice floated in from the hallway, speaking to his secretary. ". . . is prepared. My brother, Leviathan, will be here to witness the debut. He is not to be left waiting in the lobby. Make sure his chair is front and center. Oh, and be sure to track down the two guards we had stationed in the dungeon. They weren't at their posts when we arrived. If those oafs have gone on an unauthorized hunt, I will flay the skin off their faces myself."

The secretary made a noise of understanding. Aldrich Duncan entered his office and paused, regarding Max with a fond smile. He approached and took a place beside Max to look out over the city.

Duncan's voice was proud and strong when he asked, "Are you ready to receive the Silver Legacy?"

"Yes, my lord," Max said.

"The sacrifice is waiting for you. He is weak but prepared. Once you have disposed of Kingsley Martin, you will meet us on the front steps, reborn again, baptized in blood. The adoring masses await."

"Yes, my lord."

Duncan looked down at his prodigy, pride shining in his eyes.

"We have waited a long time for this day," Duncan said. "I'm honored to be the one to bestow it upon you."

Max bowed his head.

Duncan took Max by the shoulders and turned him.

"The next time I see you, you'll be more beautiful than the brightest star in the universe." Duncan squeezed his shoulders, much like a father might squeeze his son's, then he walked away. Before leaving, he paused at the door and asked, "Oh, by the way, where's Jack?"

"I don't know. I haven't seen him in days."

"It would be a shame if he missed your Ascension. He should be here to witness it."

"Yes, my lord."

"Everyone is waiting. We love you, Max."

When Duncan left, two Silver Bloods, thick as running backs, appeared at the door and waited to escort Max downstairs. It was time.

Mechanically, Max flipped the cuffs of his sleeves up his arms, ready to get to work. He removed his black tie, folded it neatly, and laid his watch—his father's watch—on the desk next to it. He wanted to look his absolute best, but he couldn't allow any distractions. This was to be done quickly and cleanly.

The Silvers escorted him in the elevator all the way to the basement level. He didn't say anything to them as he led the way down the dimly lit and narrow hallway, getting ever closer to the farthest door, the door at the end.

When he stopped in front of it, he took a deep, steadying breath.

"Leave us," Max said to his escorts. Their silver eyes rimmed in red glanced at each other, then at Max again. "Who knows what chaos my true form may cause. Once I've turned, I may be as dangerous as a bomb. Leave now."

The Silver Bloods didn't need to be told a second time. They left, hurrying down the hall, and Max opened the door to Kingsley's cell.

FORTY-FOUR

SCHUYLER

*S*chuyler felt at home in Jack's arms, but she pulled away from their kiss, cupping the sides of his face gently and lifting his head to meet her gaze.

"I would love to do this all night," she whispered, "but we have other matters to attend to first."

"Right," Jack said, blushing a little as he let her back down to the floor. He checked the watch on his wrist. "It's almost time anyway."

"Time for what?"

Not able to meet her gaze, Jack looked away.

"Don't start holding back on telling me things now. What do you know?"

Jack steeled himself and said, "Duncan mentioned the next stage of his ultimate plan. He called it the Silver Legacy."

A chill raked down Schuyler's spine. Her mind's eye conjured silver pupils, bloodred eyes, rage, and greed. "Is it as bad as I think it is?"

Jack's lips pressed into a thin line. "Yes. At first, when Lucifer took over as Regis, it had been a secret that some members of the Coven all over the world were turning Silver. They broke the code and started draining humans for sport, hence what the humans thought was a plague. He built a team of elite Silvers to become his bodyguards, Venators who would obey his every command. But he needed someone to control them, who would be their superior. A new kind of vampire."

Schuyler's stomach twisted painfully. It frightened her how easily Lucifer could get people to do anything for him. He had such a grasp on hearts and minds, he could do anything.

Jack continued. "Duncan wanted one of his prodigies to take up the mantle. He wanted one of the Twin Angels of the Apocalypse. Me. He wanted me to take on the Silver Legacy."

Schuyler gaped. "What was he asking you to do?"

Jack looked like he wanted to throw up as his eyes glistened in the soft bedroom light. "He wanted me to drain a Silver Blood."

Schuyler held her breath. "What would that do to you?"

"I don't know. Make me something . . . more than Silver. Whatever it is, no one's ever seen it before. But the transformation would set the spirit of Abbadon truly free."

Schuyler remembered her dream from a few nights ago. New York City in flames and a demon of destruction. Abbadon. The Silver Legacy. Schuyler's hands shook. Gabrielle, the archangel of messengers, had been sending her dreams this whole time, trying to warn her.

"But you turned him down," said Schuyler.

Jack nodded. "I told him I would think about it. It was the only way I could buy some time, try to figure out how to stop all this. But he started doubting my allegiance, and then he went to Max. Max was eager to impress. And I think he's going to kill Kingsley to prove it. Kingsley was Duncan's biggest threat; it would make sense that he would be the sacrifice."

Schuyler's heart pounded. They were racing against the clock. "When is all this happening?"

"At dawn; they're gathering all of the Blue Bloods from around the world at City Hall for Max's reveal as Duncan's heir. Kingsley will be there, I know it. If we go now, we might be able to save him before it's too late."

"It'll be hard to find him, let alone break him out. He'll be under heavy security if he's so important."

"That's why we can do this together. You and me. We can put a stop to all this."

She trusted him, down to her core. The desperation in his eyes broke her heart into little pieces. She grasped his hands tightly.

Jack held her gaze steadily. "If we save Kingsley, we might even be able to save Max too."

Schuyler didn't like Max, but he was Jack's brother and he deserved a chance at redemption. They had only a few hours. It wasn't too late—if they were fast, and lucky, they had a slim window of opportunity. But they needed a plan. "How do you think we can do this?" she asked.

"I know City Hall like I know my own house by this point. If we can move quickly, we might be able to blend in with Duncan's people and find Kingsley. A Venator team discovered they've brought Kingsley back to the basement, until it's time."

"Then what?"

From the back pocket of his jeans, Jack pulled out a silver whistle.

It was the same whistle Max had used when he was controlling the hellhounds. His smile was small but clever. "Cause a distraction."

Schuyler gaped. "How did you get that?"

"Turns out looking like Max sometimes isn't a bad thing."

"You are brilliant," Schuyler said, beaming.

"Here." Jack handed her the whistle. "I think it's best if you have it. You'll be safer if I . . ."

Schuyler took the whistle and held it tightly. She knew what Jack was trying to say. "You're not dying again. Not while I have anything to say about it."

Jack blushed but smiled. "Come on. We should go."

He moved to the window and waited for her, his hand outstretched.

Schuyler glanced at her closed bedroom door, looking beyond it to her parents, who she imagined were curled up on the couch watching TV together, her mother's feet kicked up on her father's lap as they laughed, watching *The Late Show*'s monologue.

She knew she was running straight into trouble, knew that she might never return to this bedroom, that she might never return to her parents' smiling faces. But she had to go.

She grabbed her coat and her scarf and took Jack's hand. Together, they vanished into the night.

City Hall was the only building lit up for blocks. A red velvet carpet had been rolled out down the stone steps in front of the main entrance, and a podium had already been erected, awash in golden laurels. Hundreds of white roses in wreaths lined the area where a hundred more chairs sat facing the podium. Workers must have been going all night to set it up. Today was going to be a very busy day for Aldrich Duncan, indeed. His clinics would be open to the public, and his newest prodigy, Max Force, would take the stage as his latest, greatest weapon. Schuyler fought the urge to run over to the podium and kick it over. Instead, she and Jack skirted the perimeter of the block, quietly dipped into a loading ramp, and entered the basement loading docks.

Jack barely left her side, looking around warily in case of any surprises. "They don't know who you are, so stay close."

"I'm sure once they do, they'll never forget me," Schuyler said.

Jack looked at her with a small, amused smile. "Come on. We can start from the bottom and make our way up."

If that wasn't a fitting description, Schuyler didn't know what was. With Jack finally at her side, after so many things had gone wrong, she couldn't help but feel like the only way she could go from here was upward.

Jack pulled his baseball cap lower on his head and Schuyler pulled up her scarf as they entered the first stairwell. A set of stairs went up, and another set went down.

"Which way?" she asked, barely keeping her voice above a whisper.

Jack tipped his head to the lower stairs and moved in front of her. "I'd rather someone see me first before they see you," he said. She didn't argue with that logic; she was the trespasser, after all.

The hellhound whistle was cold in her hand as they descended. The air was thick and damp the farther they went, the stairway feeling more and more like a proper medieval dungeon. She could almost smell the dread. To think that something like this had been hidden underneath City Hall this whole time set Schuyler's teeth on edge.

The stairs opened on the very bottom floor to a long hallway that seemed to stretch on into darkness. Jack paused, listening, and so did Schuyler. She couldn't hear anything or anyone except for the hum of a generator somewhere close by. Rows of doors lined the hallway, and she was tempted to open each and every one to see if Kingsley was there, but the smell of sulfur made her gag. Hell-hounds. They were close.

"Someone's coming," Jack whispered. Schuyler heard it too—hurried footsteps coming their way.

Schuyler leaped into a nearby alcove, her back pressed up against a custodian's door, and Jack shielded her with his body, his chest pressed up against hers as they listened to the footsteps getting closer.

He looked at her with wide, round eyes and tightened his jaw.

She nodded once, an unspoken understanding passing between them. They were going to have to fight. Jack glanced at her lips as if wanting to kiss her one last time, but he didn't.

He made a gesture with his hand, and Gabrielle's silver sword appeared in his fist. Schuyler, weaponless, clutched the hellhound whistle. It was better than nothing. Instinctively, she held her breath as the footsteps drew near.

Together, Jack and Schuyler jumped out to do battle.

FORTY-FIVE

KINGSLEY

Kingsley Martin was well acquainted with death.

When he became a Silver during the fall of Rome, he'd laid waste to thousands of souls. Decimated entire armies, became a scourge of humanity, murdered his own kin.

It had taken him a long time to become the person he was now.

He had been a young Blue Blood when Lucifer—going by the name Caligula at the time—convinced him to turn Silver. He was so weak, desperate to be strong and powerful. Lucifer barely had to plant the idea in his head. Kingsley remembered every single person he had killed. They lived with him, even now, lingering on the periphery of his vision, silently judging him like a ghostly jury for the rest of his days. They were a part of him.

He couldn't ever hope to erase his past; he didn't want to. He never tried to deny the terrible things he'd done. The only way he could reckon with his past was to do better in the present.

Being immortal meant that he'd witnessed the best and worst of humanity. He'd seen empires fall and rise throughout time, but after so many centuries, events started to blur together. He'd dined with and seduced Leonardo da Vinci, failed to save his beloved princess

Drusilla in Pompeii when Mount Vesuvius erupted, gotten drunk with Cao Zhi while on his travels through the Three Kingdoms, danced with the beautiful men and women of Constantinople before the Fourth Crusade, held the hands of victims of the Black Death when no one else could, sailed with pirates to the farthest reaches of the world, stood shoulder to shoulder alongside mortal Frenchmen in the trenches at Verdun.

But Kingsley's soul was tired. He'd lived a thousand lifetimes, lost lovers and gained new ones, watching people he cared about turn to dust and fade from time's memory. Perhaps dying was the next best thing to do.

Funny, really, how he was destined to love the Angel of Death at the end of all things.

And still, Max Force was always his one true love. It surprised him.

No matter what name he went by or what face he wore, Max Force was a fixed point in Kingsley's universe. Love and death were two spools of the same thread weaving through all of human history. It was an incredible and powerful thing.

To ensure that Blue Bloods remained under his control, Lucifer had eliminated any competition. When he severed all Blue Blood bonds, it seemed he'd never considered that love was stronger than he had been all along.

When Kingsley was captured at the Repository, the Silver Bloods had taken him to the basement below City Hall. It had been specifically designed to imprison Blue Bloods and had seen much use over the years. Since Duncan's successful rise to power in the Coven, though, it hadn't been used in some time.

There were no more Blue Bloods left to detain. Except one, if Schuyler was even still alive.

The dungeon, once a boiler room, was damp and cold, with gray-painted concrete walls that dripped with condensation onto empty rows of shackles nailed to the bricks. Divided in half by a thick row of iron bars, similar to a Red Blood jail cell, the dungeon smelled like iron, of blood and metal both. The sweetly acrid scent of its history lingered, no matter how much the dungeon had been cleaned. Jack had been there for some reason, watching Kingsley as the wardens locked the cell with a skeleton key. For a moment, Kingsley actually thought maybe he could get through to Jack after their talk in the cemetery. He'd been a fool. Kingsley spat on him for good measure, told him to go to hell. He would meet him there. But Duncan wanted Kingsley left alive. He ordered that Kingsley be confined within reach to extract as much information out of him as possible, however the Silver Bloods saw fit to extract it. Although all the vampires at the Repository had been eliminated, Lucifer wanted to be sure that any other plans for insurrection were identified and crushed into oblivion. No one else was to stand in his way.

They couldn't kill Kingsley, but the Silver Bloods did not treat one of their own with kindness. They beat him bloody, smashed his bones, tore his flesh. But as Kingsley was a vampire, his wounds would heal—slowly, without drinking blood—but heal all the same. They could break his body forever if they wanted to, and Kingsley still wouldn't die. Like the mythical Prometheus, Kingsley's immortality was the ultimate punishment.

Once he could barely stand, they took him to a clinic and performed tests, taking samples and readying his body for what would come next. Kingsley didn't need to know everything to understand what was going on. He knew they were using him to kick-start the Silver Legacy, heard them talking about it with reverence as if it was a great gift upon the world. Kingsley's death would be the start of a brand-new era.

Back in the basement of City Hall, Kingsley had a lot to think about. Time passed by without his knowing if it was night or day, making it feel as if he was stuck in a premature stage of purgatory. Waiting, waiting, waiting.

He thought of Schuyler and wondered if she was still alive, praying to whoever might still be listening to a damned soul like his that she had managed to escape and that she was safe. For her sake, he hoped that she was far away from here. Coming to save him would be a mistake. It was too late for him. She needed to kill Lucifer without him.

Light from the hallway flooded into the room as the dungeon opened and a figure walked in. They had come for him at last, earlier than he thought, but who was he to demand more time when he'd already had so much of it?

Kingsley was ready.

He barely had enough energy to lift his head when Max came into view. It took everything in Kingsley to rise to a seated position. His shirt had been lost somewhere along the way, and the cold, damp chill of the bare cement had stiffened his back. There was no denying that the Force who stood there in his cell, sleeves rolled up, eyes narrow, was Max—the one whose soul Kingsley was destined to love.

They had taken so much blood from Kingsley that he barely had enough to stay alive. It didn't matter how much blood he had left, though. It was the simple act of draining him completely, removing every bit of his life, that would initiate the transformation.

Kingsley was almost jealous. He wished he could live to see how beautiful Max would be after his transformation.

Max unlocked and opened the door to Kingsley's cell. It creaked on heavy hinges, grinding like nails on a chalkboard. If Kingsley weren't so weak, he would have laughed. It was a cruel joke that the last sound he would ever hear was the sound he most hated in the entire world.

"Take it, take my blood," Kingsley said. His words came out slurred, like he was drunk. He hadn't had enough time to heal, and he sounded like a human who was too weak to hold his liquor. Kingsley tipped his head to the side, exposing his neck. "Take it all."

Max loomed over Kingsley. His shadow blocked out the light. Kingsley only saw Max's emerald eyes, pinpricks of fire-hot desire.

Kingsley did not fear the death of his immortal soul. The only thing he feared was having everything he'd done be for nothing.

He went on. "I give you everything of me. You can have it, including my life. I love you."

Max knelt down in front of him, evidently not caring that Kingsley's pants were covered in dried silver blood and grime. His beautiful face was the last thing Kingsley wanted to see in this world. He imagined after this he would never see anything else. There would be no pearly Gates of Paradise, no eternal bliss, no afterlife for him. His soul would simply cease to exist. Only pain, and then nothing.

Max's fangs came out.

Kingsley silently thanked the heavens. It had been a good run.

Max placed one hand on the side of Kingsley's head and the other on his shoulder. He leaned in, and Kingsley closed his eyes.

He had expected it to hurt, had expected to feel a sensation like a sweeping drop, as if he'd gone over the first loop of a roller coaster while his blood got sucked from his body. Instead, it felt . . . *good*.

Kingsley's eyes fluttered open.

With growing realization, Kingsley understood—Max wasn't biting him. He was kissing him.

When he pulled away, the tip of Max's sharp nose dragged over Kingsley's skin, his hands gently holding Kingsley upright as if he were worried that he might fall. He whispered, his lips brushing against Kingsley's neck, tickling him. "You still smell the same. Like home."

Max reached into his pocket and produced the key to Kingsley's cell. He wedged it into Kingsley's palm and closed his fingers around Kingsley's, making him hold it.

FORTY-SIX

MAX

*M*ax had never felt so alive.

He was breaking every single oath he had sworn to fulfill Lucifer's mission.

He was disobeying every order, every promise he'd made, condemning himself to a life on the run, all because his heart told him to.

He helped Kingsley to his feet, but Kingsley was so exhausted, he could barely stand. Max would have to carry him. They needed to hurry, or else someone might come looking. Max's private car was waiting for them a block away, and carrying Kingsley that far would be almost impossible. He was as unwieldy as a sack of potatoes.

Max threw Kingsley's arm over his shoulder and helped him stand upright. Kingsley leaned on him; he could at least stand. Getting him to walk would be another thing.

"Come on, I know you can do it," Max said, practically dragging Kingsley across the floor toward the dungeon door.

Kingsley stumbled over his own feet, but a sudden second wave of energy got him going. His eyes widened as he realized what was happening. Max smiled despite the weight of Kingsley straining against him.

"I thought you were going to kill me," Kingsley said, his head lolling to the side.

"It's still an option if you want me to," Max said. He flung open the door, and he and Kingsley shuffled down the hall as one. Kingsley tried to keep up, and Max pushed them onward. "If you don't move, I will make you move. Come on, are you a Silver Blood or not, Kingsley?"

Max's heart pounded; sweat dripped down the side of his face. He was racing against the clock. He had planned the route, to sneak out the back and avoid the crowd waiting for them at the entrance. His plan hinged on one factor, and that factor was heavier than Max had thought.

They rounded another corner, down the longest stretch of the hall. Max was so busy dealing with Kingsley that he didn't see the shadow move out of the corner of his eye until it was too late.

Two figures sprang out from a small alcove, and Max's heart leaped with fear.

Then he recognized who they were.

"Jack?" Max asked, shocked. Standing next to his brother, her fists raised, was Schuyler Cervantes-Chase, alive after all.

"Kingsley!" she cried.

Kingsley's face melted with relief as he smiled.

"What are you doing?" Jack asked Max. He must have known that this was not a part of Lucifer's plan.

"Um." Max glanced at Kingsley, then back at Jack. There could only be one reason why Jack had come here with the Schuyler girl, and he had a sneaking suspicion that he and Jack weren't so different after all. "Jailbreak."

"We were coming to rescue you!" Schuyler said to Kingsley.

"I'm *sssso* popular!" Kingsley slurred. "I'm blushing."

Max hefted Kingsley up higher on his shoulder. "Wish we could take advantage of this happy reunion, but we've got to go."

"So you're not starting the Silver Legacy?" Schuyler asked. How she knew about that, Max didn't have time to ask. He looked at her down his nose, his chin lifted.

"Silver is *so* not my color."

The corners of Schuyler's mouth lifted.

"How can we help?" Jack asked.

Max's eye caught on the flash of metal in Schuyler's hand. "I've got a car waiting for us outside, but we could definitely use a clear path to get there." He met Schuyler's eyes. "Two whistles to get their attention, and another to give instruction. Got it?"

She clutched the whistle tighter. "Kingsley, are you going to be okay?"

"Never better, rookie," Kingsley said with a smirk. "I'm in good hands."

"I'll stay with her," Jack said. "We'll meet you on the other side of this."

Max's curiosity about this girl got the better of him. First she had escaped from the Repository; now she was here with Jack like she was ready to take on the world? Who *was* she? *What* was she? There was no time to ask; they had wasted enough time as it was.

Max and Jack shared a long look. Max wanted to say so many things: that he was sorry, that he had gotten caught up in Duncan's plan, that he had turned his back on the only family he had left, but he couldn't manage to form the words. Jack seemed to sense this, and he held out his hand for Max to shake. Max grasped it firmly. It was an awkward, formal apology, but Max would tell him for real later. Before either of them could say anything else, Jack and Schuyler took off toward the hellhound cages.

Max watched them go for a moment before he noticed Kingsley looking at him. "What?"

"You're cute when you're nice."

Max rolled his eyes and scoffed. They continued their march down the hall, coming all the way to the alcove and stairs that Jack and Schuyler had just sprung out from.

"Door?" Kingsley asked, but Max dragged him away from the main stairwell.

"Nope. Bad guys that way."

Max avoided the stairwell and took him around a corner, down a darker hallway lined with pipes. The hallway ended at a brick wall.

"It's a dead end," Kingsley said.

"Oh, please. If there's one thing you taught me—when you can't find a door, you make one."

Max glanced at Kingsley with a raised eyebrow. Need he explain more?

Understanding blossomed on Kingsley's face, and he smirked. He put his hand to his mouth and grunted in discomfort as he bit into the space between his index finger and thumb. Silver blood dripped down his palm and his wrist.

He smeared his fingers in the blood, then put his hand to the wall and drew a large sigil of chaos magic.

When it was complete, the lines of the sigil glowed brighter than the sun. Max shielded his eyes, and the wall disintegrated, crumbling into dust. When the light faded, a rudimentary opening stood before them. Max climbed through first and then braced himself to carry Kingsley's weight. They stumbled together, holding hands, through another hallway, the basement of an adjacent building.

Howls echoed down the hallway. Schuyler had released the hellhounds. Max's spine tingled with excitement. They were going to cause such a distraction that Kingsley and Max would easily get to freedom. They were going to win. Something behind his heart unwound, releasing all the tension and anxiety that had been building for so long. It felt strangely like hope.

Max had memorized the route. They were almost there.

Max kicked open the door to the stairwell, and by then Kingsley had sensed that they were almost to the end. He was able to climb the stairs mostly on his own. Max held on to him tightly, steadying him.

They were going to get out of this together.

They burst into the open air in a back alley. But the car wasn't waiting for them.

A storm of Silver Blood Venators blocked the way, their eyes flashing like coins, their weapons drawn. At the head of the pack was a woman whom Max had seen all over the news. May Woldock, the mayoral candidate running against Duncan.

She smiled at them, though her smile was too wide, and her features melted as the *mutatio* illusion wore away.

In her place was a man, tall and broad shouldered, with dark hair and eyes black as pitch to match. He looked to be in his late forties, with cheekbones so sharp, they rivaled the knifelike edge of his eyes. He was dressed in a dark purple crushed-velvet suit.

In a bored drawl, the man said, "I told my angelic brother again and again that it was foolish to trust a boy to do a devil's job."

"Leviathan," Max said through clenched teeth. Lucifer's angelic brother, in the flesh.

Kingsley stiffened at Max's side, but he didn't waver.

Leviathan sneered. "Wearing May Woldock's face was becoming such a pain in the neck. Alas, what we do for family . . . It was so easy knowing you'd betray him, Azrael," he said. "Who would have thought a Red Blood Conduit would have been more trustworthy than Lucifer's prodigy . . . ?"

Another figure stepped out from behind Leviathan. Max held on to Kingsley's wrist tighter. He'd rarely paid attention to anyone at school who wasn't in his circle of friends, a very tight and exclusive circle that rarely included humans, but he knew that face. He'd seen it at Duchesne for years.

"What was your name again, mortal?" Leviathan asked.

"Oliver Golding-Chang."

Oliver had been at the park with that Schuyler girl when she'd come to see Jack. The two of them were friends—or so she thought. But Max never would have imagined that Lucifer had a Red Blood spy working for him. He'd been so focused on his mission, he had been completely oblivious.

Leviathan smiled. "I believe Lucifer will be very pleased indeed. I should think your request for immortality will be more than a just reward."

Oliver glared at Max and Kingsley, and then a small, victorious smile spread on his lips.

FORTY-SEVEN

SCHUYLER

he time for secrecy was over.

Schuyler blew the whistle twice, just like Max had
told her to, and the seven remaining hellhounds, those who had
survived the bloodshed at the Repository, didn't question her command. They burst from their cages, snarling and ready at attention.
"Good dogs," she said. Schuyler's head rushed with adrenaline, but
she didn't hesitate. She blew the whistle again, and their ears perked
up, waiting for her orders.

"Kill the Silver Bloods," she said.

The hounds howled, the sound vibrating in Schuyler's chest,
and they led the charge, barreling through the basement of City
Hall, clambering over one another to taste first blood, and Jack and
Schuyler ran after them.

It felt good to finally be running toward rather than away.

The hellhounds stopped halfway down the hall and leaped, bur-
rowed up through the ceiling, and burst out onto the floor of the
main lobby of City Hall. Glass shattered, and Blue Bloods scattered
and screamed in the confusion and chaos. Schuyler and Jack followed, blinking in the dust and destruction.

Like tanks, the hellhounds barreled through the wall, exploding cement and brick, surprising Silver Blood Venators who had been setting up for the ceremony. While Schuyler blew the whistle, commanding the hellhounds, Jack took care of any Silver Bloods moving in to attack, cutting them down with Gabrielle's sword like the skilled fighter he was. He'd lost his Mets cap somewhere along the way, but that meant his enemies could clearly see the fight in his eyes. Jack and Schuyler barely had to speak, they worked so closely in tandem. Schuyler blew the whistle and sent a hellhound to flank a Silver Blood as Jack fought from the front.

But while Schuyler was distracted by a pair of hulking Silvers coming through the front door, another one snuck up behind Jack and bit into his neck. He yelled out in pain.

Schuyler's eyes widened in fear, and her stomach dropped.

But Jack threw the Venator over his shoulder. The Silver Blood fell onto the marble floor so hard, it cracked under his back, and Jack stood upright again.

"I'm okay! Stay focused!" he said to Schuyler, pressing his hand tightly to his neck and wincing. The bite would heal quickly. He was right, though, Schuyler couldn't lose focus; they had a lot more work to do. She ordered the hellhounds to charge through the latest arrivals, sending the Silver Bloods crashing back through the front doors and sprawling on the carpeted steps.

She commanded a hellhound to charge, and it crashed right through the podium as it chased a Silver Blood Venator who was calling for backup on a walkie-talkie. More of Duncan's loyalists came flooding into the area, down the escalators inside and up the stairs out. Good. The more vampires who were here, the fewer there

BLUE BLOODS: AFTER LIFE

would be to catch Max and Kingsley. But there was only so much Schuyler could do at one time. They were up against an army, and the hellhounds were doing a good job of keeping that enemy back, but they would not stand forever.

One of the hellhounds took a sword to the neck, and its head rolled down the stairs. The Silver Blood who had killed it turned his gaze toward Schuyler, but Jack leaped in and kicked him square in the chest. The Silver Blood fell backward down the stairs, tumbling to a stop at the bottom.

Another hellhound leaped and tackled a pair of Silver Bloods coming in, tearing out their throats with a swift flourish and a howl, but it was cut short when another Venator came up and snapped its neck with his bare hands.

Every direction Schuyler looked, she saw more Silver Bloods surrounding her.

"There's too many of them," Jack said, his back pressed up against Schuyler's. His sword was at the ready, but the last of the hellhounds hit the ground with a sickening thump, dead at the feet of yet another Silver, whose eyes were trained squarely upon her. Schuyler's whistle had become useless.

Schuyler racked her brain, stamping down the fear that was building inside her chest.

"Give me the sword," she said.

Jack didn't even question her; he just handed over Gabrielle's sword. The weight of it in her hand was exactly as she remembered, the shine of its bright white flame so familiar and at home in her grasp. But she wasn't going to be using it to smite anyone today.

She put the tip of the sword against the marble floor. The Silvers started rushing in.

"Schuyler . . ." Jack warned.

The Silvers were almost upon them.

But Schuyler was done, her intent clear. The sigil she'd drawn with the blade in the dust beneath their feet began to glow like the rising sun before it erupted into a huge cloud of fire and smoke. Kingsley's patented, portable bomb.

Kingsley would be so proud, Schuyler thought as she grabbed Jack's hand and pulled him into the smoke with her, the two of them disappearing like ghosts in fog.

They'd done what they could for Max and Kingsley. It was time to go.

When she and Jack got a few blocks away, something made Schuyler stop and turn around. Smoke—evidence of the destruction she and Jack had wrought—was already curling up to the sky. People would be able to see it all over the city. But that wasn't what made her turn. She felt eyes boring into the back of her skull.

Her gaze was drawn up to the very top floor of City Hall. There, the office was lit up, one of the only remaining lights that were on in the whole building, and she distinctly saw a silhouette of someone standing, still as a statue, their arms casually resting behind their back. Calm. Calculating.

Aldrich Duncan.

And even though she couldn't see his eyes, she knew he was looking right at her. Her skin crawled and her head thumped as if trying to get her attention, warning her to stay away.

She had won this battle, but it was not a war she could win in one day. She knew that, and Aldrich Duncan knew that. Whatever he was doing, now he knew that there would always be someone there to stop him. Schuyler set her jaw tight, glaring at him, and then she turned and kept moving forward.

FORTY-EIGHT

MAX

$\mathcal{M}$ ax summoned Michael's sword to his fist with a twitch of his fingers. The golden Blade of Paradise appeared in his hand. The human boy Oliver must have sensed what was coming and turned and ran. Max pulled Kingsley's arm down from around his shoulders and stepped toward Leviathan, who actually laughed.

"You really think Michael's sword will have any effect on something like me?"

"Why not try?!" Max brought the sword down, aiming for Leviathan's neck, but Leviathan simply flicked two fingers and Max went flying across the alley. He crashed in a heap on top of a dumpster and rolled off.

"Weak. You haven't even fully come into your powers yet," Leviathan said, his lip curled in a sneer.

Max felt like he'd been hit by a city bus. He groaned and managed to rise on all fours to see Kingsley fighting in his stead.

Despite being injured, Kingsley had disarmed one of the nearest Silver Bloods and sliced him across the chest with his own blade, but Leviathan had turned his attention to him now.

With another flick of his fingers, Leviathan beckoned Kingsley to him. As if drawn by invisible strings, Kingsley was yanked across the pavement, his weapon clattering helplessly to the ground, drawn right into Leviathan's outstretched hand.

Leviathan gripped Kingsley by the throat. Kingsley's bare toes scraped against the pavement as he kicked and flailed to get free. But he was too weak; he'd lost too much blood. Kingsley's face turned gray.

"Gemellus," Leviathan cooed, looking at Kingsley, calling him by his ancient name. "My, my—how time flies. We'd wondered where you'd run off to."

Kingsley was unable to speak. He tried, but the only sound that came out was a grunt.

"What was that?" Leviathan asked, pulling Kingsley closer to his ear. But of course, Kingsley couldn't speak.

Leviathan turned to the crowd of Silver Bloods. "So this is what Max Force would die for?"

A chorus of laughter echoed around the alley.

Wincing, Max rose to his feet, but a group of Silver Bloods descended upon him, holding him back. A sword pressed on Max's Adam's apple. His whole body ran cold. He couldn't do anything. He was forced to watch, his blood pounding in his ears, and he wanted to scream.

Leviathan looked at Max, a smile splitting his handsome face. And with a final squeeze, Kingsley's eyes rolled up to the back of his head, and Leviathan dropped him to the ground like a rag doll.

Max's entire body went cold. He stood, frozen.

Get up.

Kingsley lay still on the pavement, unmoving.

Get up, Kingsley. Get up! You stubborn, beautiful, impossible, foolish, brave idiot. You are MINE! Now get UP!

Max's blood roared like a hurricane in his head as he panted, breathlessly, waiting for Kingsley to do anything. But Kingsley was still.

Tears blurred Max's vision. His whole body went numb.

The one who had helped Max dream again.

Max's one true love.

Dead.

"No!" Max cried in anguish, and broke free of the Silvers' grasp. He leaped for Leviathan, sword raised, eyes burning with rage.

Leviathan didn't even react. "Pity. Wish I didn't have orders to keep you alive."

Max's head whipped to the side as the invisible strike came from somewhere to his right, and his body slammed into the hard ground. More Silver Bloods piled on top of him, but no matter how hard he struggled, they were too strong. He reached out for Kingsley's body, but his hands were forced behind his back, and his face smashed into the pavement. He tasted blood, and still he screamed.

"Kingsley! *KINGSLEY!*"

"Shut him up!"

Stars burst in Max's vision, obscuring Kingsley's body from view, as something hard hit him on the back of the head. Excruciating, blinding pain. The edges of his vision darkened.

Kingsley . . . Kingsley . . .

Max felt the world falling away from him as he started to pass out. "No. No!" Everything went dark as a hood was pulled over his head, and then Max's world went darker still.

FORTY-NINE

SCHUYLER

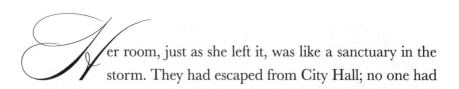

er room, just as she left it, was like a sanctuary in the storm. They had escaped from City Hall; no one had followed. All was quiet and safe.

Jack and Schuyler agreed that it was too dangerous for him to go to his house, so they went to her apartment instead. Together they climbed the fire escape, and he helped her in through the window, and even when she made it inside and put her feet on her bedroom floor once more, they didn't let go of each other. They panted heavily, adrenaline still coursing through their veins, as they looked at each other for a long moment. The dawn was starting to rise, and Jack's eyes were pinpricks of light in the gray haze of early morning. To see those eyes again, to remember how far the two of them had come together, made Schuyler's heart leap.

"That was incredible. You are incredible," Jack breathed. She could feel his pulse racing beneath her fingertips. He had done something extraordinarily brave with her, made himself an enemy of Lucifer, not because he remembered what he and Schuyler had been to each other in another world, but maybe because of what they could be in this one.

Jack turned his head to face the window. "But I should go," he said. "They'll be hunting for me."

Schuyler shook her head. "It's not safe."

"If I don't, I'll be leading them straight to you."

Schuyler squeezed his hand and whispered, "Jack . . ." His gaze softened when he looked at her. She saw his thoughts working behind those emerald eyes. He made a choice, though, and he chose her.

Jack swooped in and kissed her, breathing deeply, pressing his body against hers. It was the type of kiss that stirred Schuyler's insides, warming her from within, and she was sure she would explode. He held the side of her face as they connected, grounding her to the world as if he too was afraid she would float away. Or maybe he would. His hand felt so strong, she leaned into his touch. Heaven would be to relive this moment again and again.

"Please. Stay with me. Here," Schuyler whispered between kisses.

Jack sighed with want. He lifted her into his arms, their lips locked, and then he carried her to the bed. They were real, they were alive, they were together.

Schuyler ensnared her fingers in Jack's hair. He smelled like citrus and sweat, and his teeth scraped along her lower lip and she wanted more. Their noses bumped together as they took a moment to breathe. She felt secure beneath him, his arms bracing either side of her body, and the corners of his eyes wrinkled when he smiled. Schuyler's lips had gone numb, but she still tingled with pleasure. She couldn't stop smiling, and it was beginning to hurt in only the best ways. Another kiss, another chance.

They found solace in each other's arms, safe at last. They were home.

Schuyler awoke in her bed, already smiling. If last night had been a dream, then it had been a good one. But it wasn't a dream. She and Jack were finally together. The universe truly worked in mysterious and wonderful ways.

They must have fallen asleep, but only for a few hours. Despite the excitement in her heart, her body was sore and exhausted. She desperately needed the rest.

She rolled over. Jack's place at her side was empty; the spot, cold.

"Jack?" she whispered to her room, hazy with yellow morning light. Unless he had gone out to the loft, probably giving her parents the shock of their lives, he wasn't here. A boy spending the night? She'd be grounded until she was dead from old age.

For a moment, she thought maybe she really had dreamed Jack's return, but a note had been left for her on her nightstand. It was in Jack's neat handwriting.

Schuyler,

I'm too dangerous to be around.

Max still hasn't called. I'm worried about him.

If Aldrich Duncan finds out who you are, he will hunt you down.

I can't risk your life. I can't put you in any more danger. I have to leave to keep you safe.

Please. Don't try to find me.

My heart is yours,

Jack

Schuyler looked at the window, her stomach on the floor. He'd left?

"Schuyler!" her father's voice called from the living room. "You've got a visitor!"

Schuyler put the note down and scrambled out of bed. She flung open the door and hurried out, praying to whoever was listening that it was Jack, changing his mind and coming home. How could he have just left after they had only just reunited?

Schuyler's heart lodged in her throat when she saw who the visitor was.

"Here she is! I'll leave you to it. Good to see you, Ollie," Stephen said, giving a little salute to Oliver, who was framed in the doorway, looking flushed and disheveled. He appeared as if he had run all the way to her apartment.

"You as well, Mr. Chase," Oliver said.

"Please, how many times— Call me Stephen. We're practically family."

"Right. Stephen."

Stephen patted Schuyler's head lovingly and said, "Breakfast in ten, kiddo," before disappearing into the kitchen. Aurora was already setting the table, watching the two of them curiously.

"Ollie!" Schuyler said, rounding on him once the coast was clear. "What are you—"

"I came as quick as I could." He pulled her into the hallway and almost shut the door, leaving it open just a crack. "It's Kingsley."

"Yes, I found him. He and Max Force escaped from Duncan last night."

His expression was grim. "Schuyler—Sky, I'm so sorry."

Schuyler's chest seized up. "What is it?"

"Kingsley is dead."

Her blood turned to liquid nitrogen. "Wh-what?"

"I was there, Schuyler. I saw it."

She collapsed against the wall. It was a miracle she was still standing.

She couldn't believe it. It couldn't be true.

While she'd been sleeping peacefully in the arms of her one true love, Kingsley had needed her.

"Are you sure? How?"

Oliver stared at his shoes, his face pulled tight with pain. "This . . . strong, impossibly strong vampire killed him," he went on.

It was her fault that he was dead. Tears of guilt burned the backs of her eyes. "Max Force?"

"No, it wasn't him. Someone named Leviathan."

"*What?* Why were you there? Leviathan is—"

"I know, but I felt so stupid about what happened with us at the Mercer, I needed to make it up to you. I went back to the Repository to see what else I could find, and I spotted a whole procession of fancy-looking cars headed downtown. I knew a Blue Blood event was going on, so I followed them to City Hall. Workers were setting up for what looked like a kind of coronation. I hid in the alley, trying to figure out a way into the building. I had a gut feeling that Kingsley was in there and that he was involved somehow. Before I could do anything, I saw Max carrying a guy he called Kingsley out, and then these hellhounds started tearing up the place—I couldn't stay long. I had to get out of there."

She was having a hard time wrapping her brain around all the information. It was all coming at her too fast. She shook her head, trying to clear it.

"Kingsley . . . I shouldn't have let him go."

"You knew?"

"I was there too. So was Jack. We ran into Max and Kingsley, and we were the ones who let out the hellhounds. What about Max? What happened to him?"

"They captured him after killing Kingsley. But that's all I know. It was chaos. I came straight here when it was safe." His eyes were so wide and frightened, and his hands shook. "What do we do?"

Schuyler grasped his fingers. They were cold and clammy. She held him tight. "It's going to be okay. We'll figure something out. We're together. That's what matters."

She led him into the apartment, glanced around for any prying eyes, and then closed the door.

FIFTY

OLIVER

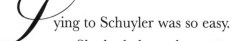

*L*ying to Schuyler was so easy.

She had always been too trusting.

From the first day that they met, Oliver had known how to take advantage of her heart. When they were in elementary school, he had shared his lunch, knowing that she wouldn't have any because he had taken it out of her backpack and thrown it away when she wasn't looking. He had offered half of his sandwich with a kind smile, and he had her right where he wanted her.

He never forgot his mission, never slipped up or fooled even himself about what he was supposed to do. For years, he made her think he was her friend. He learned her interests and studied her likes and dislikes, molding himself into the perfect best friend. He hated campy horror movies, and pizza with mushrooms, and talking about boring things like which college they wanted to attend together or what they wanted to do when they grew up, but he was the best at pretending.

He was practically a shapeshifter. He needed to be everything she didn't know she needed. And she desperately needed a friend.

He eliminated all other possibilities, making sure that no one else could share her. Boys and girls at school would try to talk to her, and Oliver made sure they knew she wasn't interested. He needed her alone. She would be more easily manipulated if she couldn't turn to anyone else.

Poor little Schuyler.

It was sad, really, watching her grow up thinking that she only had Oliver as her friend because other kids just didn't understand her. It was true—no one *would* understand her, not when Oliver knew her secrets from the start, planned his every move down to the minute.

He had known about her Blue Blood lineage but pretended to be surprised when she told him her secret. She needed a sidekick, and he was ready to fill that role.

There was a secret room in his penthouse dedicated to keeping track of her. It was tucked away behind one of the paintings in the art gallery, with a dedicated server and tack board for all the information he had needed over the years to ensure that his plan would be followed to completion.

Schuyler almost surprised him when she told him about her experience with the multiverse. How she had known about Lucifer at all was still a curve ball to his plans that Oliver had been trying to figure out. A Superimposition of worlds? Memories of another reality? It was not something that he had ever anticipated, and he had planned for anything and everything. Almost.

He wanted immortality. The way his parents, Conduits in their own right, talked about Blue Bloods like they were something to be revered at first made Oliver revere them too, like fairy-tale heroes. But as he grew older, he thought it wasn't fair. Why couldn't he be immortal too? What made Blue Bloods so special? What made them so deserving of power?

As far as Oliver was concerned, he was just as deserving of that power as they were. He would get it by any means necessary. He wanted to live forever.

And Schuyler had been his ticket in.

Lucifer had gotten to him just after his eighth birthday, coming to him in his dreams and promising everything, so long as he did him a little favor.

He taught Oliver all he needed to know, shaped him into the perfect undercover agent. He was Lucifer's secret weapon.

Jack and Max Force had failed. And with Kingsley Martin eliminated, there were only a few loose ends left. It was time for a mortal like him to take his rightful place among the gods.

And Schuyler just let him right into her life.

Oliver was so convincing in his deception, he might have even fooled himself. But the truth was, he did love her, and once he had succeeded in convincing her to make him her Familiar, he knew every one of her secrets. The better to protect her. And that was what he was doing. Protecting her. He would protect her for the rest of their immortal lives.

She sat Oliver down on the plush blue couch, assuring him that everything was going to be okay, and then she spoke in a soft voice to her parents.

"Can he stay with us for a few days?" Schuyler asked.

"Of course, sweetie. As long as he needs," Aurora said, watching Oliver carefully. He could have sworn she narrowed her eyes at him, but what would she know? His cover was perfect. Who would ever suspect little, weak, human Oliver to be a secret agent working for the devil?

Certainly not Schuyler.

She joined him on the couch, curling up at his side, silent tears streaming down her face while her parents made them both breakfast. Schuyler was so, so alone.

"It's okay," Oliver said, rubbing Schuyler's back, smiling. "I'm here. I'll always be here."

To be continued . . .

ACKNOWLEDGMENTS

Eternal love and thanks to my Hyperion dream team: my amazing editor, Kieran Viola, who found the best parts of this book and made them shine; Brittany Rubiano, for the perfect title; PR great Seale (Edy) Ballenger; Marci Senders and Joann Hill for the most beautiful books ever; Holly Nagel and Elke Villa, marvelous marketing mavens; and girl boss Tonya Agurto! Thank you, thank you for fifteen years of Blue Bloods and counting!

Nothing happens in my life without the help of Richard Abate and Martha Stevens of 3Arts. Thank you to Ellen Goldsmith-Vein, DJ Goldberg, and Jeremy Bell for everything TV and film. Thanks to all my friends and family for putting up with a crabby writer. Thank you to my #beloveds. Thank you to my Blue Bloods beta readers. Everything in my life is for Mike and Mattie Johnston.